christmas in paris

christmas in paris

ANITA HUGHES

St. Martin's Griffin · New York

CHRISTMAS IN PARIS. Copyright © 2016 by Anita Hughes. All rights reserved. Printed in the United States of America. For information, address St. Martin's Press, 175 Fifth Avenue, New York, N.Y. 10010.

www.stmartins.com

The Library of Congress Cataloging-in-Publication Data is available upon request.

ISBN 978-1-250-10550-9 (trade paperback)
ISBN 978-1-250-10551-6 (e-book)

Our books may be purchased in bulk for promotional, educational, or business use. Please contact your local bookseller or the Macmillan Corporate and Premium Sales Department at 1-800-221-7945, extension 5442, or by e-mail at MacmillanSpecialMarkets@macmillan.com.

First Edition: October 2016

10 9 8 7 6 5 4 3 2 1

To my mother

christmas in paris

chapter one

❧

Isabel took a deep breath and thought Paris at Christmas was like one of the elaborate dollhouses she played with as a child. Everywhere she looked there was something wonderful: The holiday markets lining the Champs-Élysées with their snow villages and stalls of mulled cider. The carousel next to the Tuileries Gardens that spun around like a golden snowflake. And the Christmas tree that rose so high above the Place de la Concorde, Isabel had to crane her neck as if she was watching an airplane.

She rested her elbows on the creamy stone balcony and suddenly pictured her parents' estate on the Main Line in Philadelphia. During the holidays, the living room was always decorated with a live fir tree that touched the ceiling. Christmas cards lined the marble fireplace and Bing Crosby filtered over the speakers. Even when Isabel was at Bryn Mawr, and the only music she listened to was classic rock and Beyoncé, she still loved coming home and hearing "White Christmas."

She rubbed her hands and suddenly noticed the indentation in her ring finger. She flashed on Neil's diamond-and-sapphire

ring, and for the first time since she had arrived at the Hôtel de Crillon and the manager personally escorted her to her suite and showed her the heated marble floors and selection of caviars and soft cheeses, her mouth trembled.

She wrapped her arms around her chest and reminded herself she wasn't going to cry. Why was her heart beating like a race car driver's as he approached an impossible curve when she was the one who had called off the wedding?

A young couple in glittering evening wear entered the revolving doors, and Isabel thought of the months she spent planning the reception. The carpets in her parents' grand salon had been rolled up and the cherry floor was scattered with round tables and gold filigree chairs. There was going to be a sixteen-piece orchestra and a carving station and a twelve-tier vanilla buttercream cake from Sylvia Weinstock in New York.

When she and Neil got engaged last fall, everyone assumed they would have a June wedding. Her mother led Isabel onto the porch and pointed to the green lawn and white gazebo. They would put a dance floor over the swimming pool and serve cocktails on the tennis court. The aisle would be lined with tulips, and the caterers would use her baby carrots in the summer salad.

But Isabel had always dreamed of a winter wedding with great bouquets of white and red roses. She imagined a satin Vera Wang dress and beige silk gloves that were soft as butter. A silver Bentley would wait in the driveway, and guests would arrive wearing wool overcoats and brightly colored cashmere wraps.

If they got married during the summer, she would be drenched in sweat the minute they took the photos. The groomsmen would complain they couldn't possibly wear their white dinner jackets in the hundred-degree heat, and the leather upholstery in the Bentley would be so hot, she couldn't bear it.

She inhaled the cold night air and remembered finding her mother in the kitchen three days before the wedding. Never mind the caterers had taken over the kitchen for days, shelling pecans and slicing green beans and asparagus. Adele loved whisking cream and decorating the pies with sugary frosting.

"EVERYONE IS SO health conscious these days." Adele wiped her hands on her apron. "You have to use whole cream in the eggnog and butter and rum in the bread pudding, or you may as well celebrate the holidays in the steam room of the Red Door Spa. I fed you and your father baked yams and creamed spinach every year, and neither of you gained an ounce."

"Your baked yams were delicious, but Dad took our plates of creamed spinach and hid them in the pantry." Isabel smiled, gazing at the stack of polished silverware. "Didn't you wonder why he was so eager to do the dishes?"

"Your father and I have stayed married for thirty years for one reason." Adele tasted the whipped cream. "Unless something is going to cause mortal harm or financial ruin, it doesn't need to be mentioned.

"Couples argue over who takes out the garbage or why no one brought in the newspaper when they could as easily do it themselves." She sprinkled brown sugar into the bowl. "But I'm not going to stand here three days before your wedding and offer you marriage advice like a character in a 1950s sitcom. I'd much rather hear how the cake tasting went and if you stopped at Zabar's and picked up chestnut puree."

Isabel fiddled with the linen napkins and took a deep breath. "Neil thought the buttercream was too dry, so we canceled it."

"You canceled the cake three days before the wedding?" Adele exclaimed. "I suppose the caterer will rustle up something. We

have baskets of strawberries and cartons of eggs and fresh cinnamon sticks."

Isabel's large brown eyes flickered and she perched on a leather stool.

"We canceled the wedding."

"What did you say?" Adele gasped.

"We can't agree about anything. Neil wanted our signature drink to be Bellinis, but I suggested Manhattans," Isabel explained. "I thought we could serve sorbets between courses, and he said, why would anyone want to eat syrupy ice when they could be enjoying Cornish hens?"

"Couples planning a wedding are like preschoolers playing in a sandbox," Adele mused. "They squabble over who gets the toy truck and plastic bucket, but at the end of the day they share chocolate chip cookies and forget the whole thing." She patted her hair. "In four days you'll be reclining in the business-class cabin of an Air France plane and won't think about anything except sipping café au lait and nibbling crème brûlée."

"A month ago Neil announced he planned to quit Bell and Logan," Isabel began. "His grandparents are retiring to Jupiter Island and asked if we wanted to take over the farm. He said the best part of his childhood was mucking out the stables and he doesn't want to wait until he's sixty with high blood pressure from taking clients out for martinis when he could own Whispering Arches now." Isabel's eyes were huge. "I do love the farm, but we're too old to spend our days catching butterflies and too young to sit on a porch at night and listen to the frogs," she continued. "I'd have to rent an apartment in the city. We'd only see each other on weekends, and I'd be so tired from working on the train we'd spend the first night back at each other's throats."

"Why didn't you tell me?" Adele asked.

"I thought we were perfect for each other," Isabel sighed.

"We both have exciting careers in finance and love playing squash and eating lobster rolls at Luke's Lobster in Rittenhouse Square." She stopped and her eyes were dim. "I really thought this time I got it right."

"Don't even think about Rory." Adele shuddered. "You were just out of business school and didn't know what you wanted. Now you are a mature woman, but you can't marry someone unless the thought of being apart makes your heart pound.

"Couples think they can conduct a marriage by Skype or emails. But the only times John and I have been apart for more than a week are when he got stranded in London during an airline strike and when I ended up in the hospital with tonsillitis." She smiled. "And even then he convinced the nurse I could only get better if I was spoon-fed pecan ice cream and he slept on the linoleum chair in the waiting room."

"I thought that was the way I felt about Neil," Isabel wavered. "But lately, instead of imagining candlelit dinners or curling up on the sofa together to watch Netflix, I can't wait to take a hot bath and read *Time*.

"What if I never find the right man to marry?" She gazed at the kitchen's beamed ceiling and oak floors. "I'll never have a mudroom crammed with rubber boots or a playroom overflowing with Dick and Jane books or a Christmas tree decorated with glitter snowflakes."

"You're twenty-eight and this isn't the nineteenth century." Adele squeezed her hand. "But you have to be in love or it isn't worth it at all. It's hard to face a laundry basket filled with dirty socks and smelly T-shirts every morning unless you adore the person who wears them."

"Neil does his own laundry." Isabel grinned.

"You know what I mean. You don't get married so you can send a joint Christmas card," Adele replied. "If the wedding is

canceled, we'll go to St. Bart's. I'll have the caterers clear away the spinach crepes and tuberoses, and when we return it will be as if nothing happened."

"The holidays have to include roasting chestnuts and children caroling on the lawn," Isabel insisted. "When have we ever missed opening our presents in the grand salon or sipping buttered rum in the library? Don't worry about me, I'll be fine."

"Are you sure?" Adele asked.

"Perfectly sure." Isabel sat up straight. "I am the one who called off the wedding."

NOW ISABEL GAZED at the twinkling lights of the Eiffel Tower and the dim outline of the Luxembourg Gardens and wondered if she had been hasty.

She heard carolers singing and remembered creeping upstairs to her childhood bedroom a week ago. She glanced at her old trigonometry books and lacrosse trophies and thought she should have driven back to their condo. But she didn't feel like seeing Neil's L.L. Bean sweaters in the closet or his Burberry overcoat hanging in the entry. And she didn't want to discuss who would keep the Pottery Barn sofa or the Krups espresso machine her parents gave them last Christmas.

Her phone buzzed and she picked it up.

"It's me," Neil's voice came down the line. "I wasn't sure if you'd still be up."

"I was going to drive home, but it looks like it might snow." Isabel suddenly felt her heart beat faster.

"I'm staying at my parents', but I had an idea . . ." Neil paused.

"You did?" Isabel sat up.

"Do you remember when I proposed and you said you've

been dreaming of a honeymoon in Paris since you were fourteen?" Neil continued. "You saw *Gigi* starring Leslie Caron and Louis Jourdan in your French class and wanted to ride in a horse and buggy in the Bois de Boulogne and stroll along the Seine."

"At Christmas the barges are decorated with colored lights and it's like watching a thousand fireflies," Isabel mused.

"You should use the plane ticket and stay in the suite at the Hôtel de Crillon," Neil suggested. "It's too late to cancel and it would be a pity for an eight-hundred-foot suite with a private butler and view of the Champs-Élysées to go to waste."

"You want me to go Paris by myself?" Isabel felt the room tilt as if she had drunk a glass of champagne too quickly.

"We have tickets to *Swan Lake* at Opéra de Paris, and you can see the Christmas displays at the Galeries Lafayette." Neil paused. "When you come back it will be the new year and all this will be behind us."

Isabel thought of her mother's suggestion to go to St. Bart's and wondered why everyone thought a change of scenery would make the last ten months disappear.

But Paris! Isabel had spent a semester studying at the Sorbonne and loved everything about the vintage boutiques on the Left Bank and Le Bon Marché with its windows filled with impossibly chic dresses and pumps.

At the end of the semester she came home and mooned around her parents' house, wishing she could run down to a patisserie and buy an almond croissant and a copy of *Le Monde*. But she got accepted to Wharton business school and then landed a job at JPMorgan Chase. She couldn't take more than a long Thanksgiving weekend or an extra day off at Christmas if she wanted to be a senior analyst by the age of thirty.

But now her boss didn't expect her back until January and she didn't want to drink crème de cassis and nibble canapés at

the Ritz or watch the New Year's Eve fireworks over Sugar-house Casino alone.

"That's a wonderful idea." Isabel gripped the phone. "I'll go."

"Your Coach suitcase is in the hall closet and the ballet tickets are with our passports." Neil paused. "One more thing."

"What is it?" Isabel closed her eyes and thought Neil would say of course he wasn't going to quit Bell and Logan and they wouldn't live on the farm; they both had too much invested in their careers. Peach sorbet sounded delicious, and they could ask the pastry chef to use more cream in the filling.

"Send me a postcard," Neil said. "I've always wanted to see the Arc de Triomphe decorated for the holidays."

ISABEL GAZED AT the bright lights of the Champs-Élysées and thought it didn't matter how she had arrived in Paris; she was glad she was here. She was going to ice-skate at the Hôtel de Ville and sip vichyssoise in the dining room at the George V. She'd buy a crepe evening dress at Givenchy and a bottle of French perfume from one of those dazzling salesgirls at Le Printemps.

The fog settled on her shoulders and suddenly she longed to climb into bed. She pictured the master bedroom with its canopied bed and blue velvet wallpaper and original Degas above the fireplace. The bathroom had a pedestal tub and gold lacquered dressing table and pink-and-gray marble floors.

She turned the handle on the French doors and grimaced. She peered through the glass and saw her phone tossed on the cream damask love seat. She had locked herself out and there was no way to call for help.

"Well, that's a fine way to start the vacation," she said aloud. "Freeze to death on the balcony of the Hôtel de Crillon."

She considered shouting, but she was too high up and the valets in their gold uniforms and pointed red hats wouldn't hear her. She noticed the light on in the neighboring suite and wondered if anyone would come outside. But it was almost midnight and the guests were probably asleep under embroidered silk sheets.

Why hadn't she checked the door handle before she stepped outside? And why wasn't there a key in the lock? Surely other visitors rushed out to admire the sights of Paris.

She wrapped her arms around her chest and wished she had worn a cashmere sweater and a pair of boots. But she had deliberately chosen the outfit she purchased for their honeymoon: a red Nina Ricci dress and a pair of ivory pumps.

Suddenly she had an idea. She took off a pump and cradled it in her palm. She aimed at the adjoining suite and tossed it on the balcony. She waited, but there was no movement behind the silk drapes. She took off the other shoe and threw it squarely at the French doors.

The lights flickered and a man appeared on the balcony. He was in his early thirties with dark hair and narrow cheekbones. He wore a long blue robe and felt slippers.

"If you're having a party, please take it inside." He rubbed his eyes. "I was fast asleep and dreaming about girls in grass skirts serving me frosty drinks on a desert island."

"I'm not having a party and I can't go inside. I stepped out to admire the lights in the Place de la Concorde and locked myself out. I threw my shoe on your balcony to see if someone would help me." Isabel rubbed her hands.

"You threw your Ferragamos on purpose?" He picked up one of the shoes.

"I would hate to ruin them, but I can't wear them if I have frostbite on my toes." She tucked her hair behind her ears. "How did you know they are Ferragamos?"

"My fiancée has the same shoe in three colors." He turned the shoe over. "She bought me a pair of Ferragamos for my birthday, but I refuse to wear loafers that cost more than a month's rent."

"I hope I didn't wake her," Isabel replied.

The man stuffed his hands in his pockets and his brow furrowed.

"That would be difficult. Two days ago she ran off to Melbourne with an Australian cricket player."

"That sounds terrible, but could we discuss this inside?" Isabel shivered. "My eyelashes are frozen and I can't feel my fingertips."

"I'm afraid I have a healthy fear of heights." He peered down at the yellow taxis lining the boulevard. "But I'll call housekeeping and they'll let you in."

ISABEL SAT ON the brocade sofa and tried to stop her hands from shaking. Housekeeping had opened the door, and the man insisted on visiting her suite and heating up two brandy snifters.

"Thank you, I do feel better, I didn't realize how cold it was, I was so excited to finally be in Paris." She sipped the gold liquor. "Do you always dream about girls in grass skirts?"

"I was drawing a picture before I went to bed," the man explained. "I'm a children's book illustrator. I always dream about what I sketch right before I fall asleep. That's why I never draw trolls or witches except in broad daylight."

"That sounds sensible." Isabel nodded. "Sometimes I keep a journal, but I never write anything sad at night. It's like the old saying 'Never go to bed angry.' Even if I'm sleeping alone, I want to feel warm and happy when I climb under the covers."

He perched on a velvet love seat and gazed at the crystal

chandeliers and blue silk drapes and Regency desk. The suite had gold inlaid double doors and thick white carpet and a dining room table set with silver candelabras. There was a marble sideboard with a silver coffeepot and porcelain demitasses.

"I thought all the suites on the fifth floor were honeymoon suites." He glanced at Isabel's single Coach suitcase and the pile of paperback books on an end table.

"I was supposed to be here on my honeymoon," Isabel explained. "But four days ago the wedding was canceled."

"There seems to be an epidemic." He scooped up a handful of pistachios. "Did your fiancé run off with a female soccer player?"

"Nothing like that . . ." Isabel hesitated. "Neil thought the vanilla buttercream filling was too dry."

"A delicious wedding cake is the first thing guests remember about the reception," he agreed. "But surely you could have compromised: serve each slice with a spoonful of chocolate ice cream?"

"There were other things." Isabel fiddled with her gold necklace. "He wanted to take over his grandparents' farm, when we'd both spent years building our careers."

"That's more like it." He shrugged. "I would hate to think he passed up a suite at the Hôtel de Crillon because of the lack of whole cream."

"It was my idea to call off the wedding, we seemed to fight about everything." Isabel sighed. "My parents have lived at the same address for thirty years. I always thought I'd get married and have two curly-haired children and a golden retriever. We'd live in a big house on the Main Line with a vegetable garden and a swimming pool.

"I'd hire a nanny, because I love my career. But on the weekends, we'd attend Phillies games and visit the natural history museum and Independence Hall."

"Have you already picked out your children's names and filled out their college applications?" He raised his eyebrows. "I've read Americans sign their children up for kindergarten while they're in the womb."

"I'm a financial analyst, I'm paid to think ahead," she said. "I'm very good at what I do, I just can't seem to get marriage right."

"I thought Celine and I were perfect for each other. We both love skiing and eating dark chocolate." He rubbed his forehead. "But she took one look at Patrick in his white cricket shirt and white slacks and couldn't help herself. She was like a cat with a pitcher of cream, she had to have him."

"You must be terribly upset." Isabel fiddled with her brandy snifter.

"The first night I drank a bottle of scotch and watched classic romantic movies on cable," he replied. "But then I started drawing. Have you ever heard of Gus the Cocker Spaniel?"

"The only children's books I know are the Madeline books and Harry Potter." Isabel shook her head.

"When I was a child I wanted a cocker spaniel, but my sister was allergic to dogs," he began. "I drew a cocker spaniel with fluffy ears and fur as soft as a mink coat. Then I sent him off on adventures: to the Nile to discover the pyramids, or the Amazon to hack through rainforests. Whenever I did poorly on a test or my sister threatened to tell our mother I ate the whole basket of cherries, I ran to my room and drew Gus." His face broke into a small smile. "Today I drew Gus hurling a ball at a man wearing cricket whites."

"Why are you at the Crillon alone?" Isabel asked.

"My would-be father-in-law gave us the suite as a wedding present, and we decided to use it before the wedding." He paused. "I feel terrible for Leon, he paid for the reception at the George Cinq and a classic Aston Martin. I told Celine I was perfectly

happy having a luncheon of cream of potato soup and fresh baguettes, and then renting a Mini Cooper to drive to Avignon." He ran his hands over a crystal ashtray. "Celine has very expensive taste. She brushes her teeth with Evian water and wears a diamond pendant to bed."

"It doesn't sound like you had a lot in common." Isabel studied his worn slippers and plaid pajama bottoms.

"She has eyes like sapphires and is excellent at backgammon," he mused. "And she has a wicked sense of humor. You can fall in love for all sorts of reasons, but it's wonderful to be with someone who makes you laugh."

"Rory and I used to laugh about everything," Isabel agreed. "But eventually you have to get serious. Life isn't a *Saturday Night Live* skit."

"I thought you said your fiancé's name was Neil."

"I was engaged before, I told you I'm hopeless at love." She walked to the bedroom door. "Thank you for rescuing me, but I'm very tired. Do you mind if I go to bed."

"Of course, but you might want to wait until I leave?" He grinned. "We don't want the maids whispering."

Isabel selected a hazelnut truffle from the silver tray and popped it in her mouth. She gazed at the porcelain vases filled with pink roses and the eighteenth-century tapestry lining the walls and felt her heart lift.

"That's a very good idea." Her face lit up in a smile. "I'm Isabel, it's a pleasure to meet you."

"I'm Alec," he replied. "And the pleasure is mine."

chapter two

❧

Isabel sat at the Regency desk and studied the embossed menu. Everything sounded delicious: the egg-white omelet with tomato and basil, the muesli with fresh fruit compote, the semi-skimmed milk and warm brioche.

But it was already late morning and she didn't want to wait for the maids to bring the room service table with its white linen tablecloth and selection of pastries and teas. She didn't want to stand at the window sipping café au lait when she could be strolling along the Champs-Élysées and inhaling the scent of French perfume and buttery croissants.

She glanced at her red Nina Ricci dress hanging in the closet and her ivory pumps resting on the Oriental rug and shuddered. If it wasn't for her neighbor, she might still be stranded on the balcony. She pulled a sheet of writing paper out of the desk and thought she'd scribble a thank-you. She found a pen and suddenly realized she didn't know his last name.

She folded the paper and put the lid back on the pen. She slipped on a pair of wool slacks and a cashmere sweater. She grabbed her purse and then thought she had a better idea.

"ISN'T IT A little early to make social calls?" the man asked when she knocked on the door.

"It's almost noon." Isabel entered the suite. It had wide columns and a gold inlaid ceiling. A harpsichord stood in one corner and crystal vases were filled with yellow tulips.

"Is it really? I couldn't sleep, so I started drawing," he groaned. "Then I couldn't stop drawing and didn't get any sleep."

"This is very good." Isabel picked up a sketch of a cocker spaniel wearing boxing gloves and fighting a kangaroo.

"Do you like it?" He rubbed his chin. "I thought if Gus went to Australia he should have other adventures: rappelling off the Sydney Harbour Bridge and scuba diving in the Great Barrier Reef."

"I didn't know cocker spaniels could swim." Isabel frowned.

"Gus can do anything." He studied the paper. "But you're right, I wouldn't want him getting stung by a stingray. I'll send him to Ayers Rock to play the didgeridoo."

"Alec Braxton." Isabel had noticed the scrawled signature at the bottom of the page. "I didn't know your last name. Are you famous?"

"I have my share of Twitter followers and Facebook fans." He shrugged. "Gus pays for a fifth-floor walk-up in the fourth arrondissement and an annual pass to the Musée Picasso. But he will never get me a table at Le Meurice or a charge card at Le Bon Marché." He drew back the silk drapes. "But I couldn't imagine doing anything else. Drawing is as necessary as breathing."

"That's how I feel about being an analyst." Isabel placed the sketch on the mahogany dining room table. "When I turned fourteen my friends gave me sweaters and lipsticks, but all I wanted was a calculator with more functions than an airplane cockpit. I've always found numbers so comforting."

"Comforting!" Alec exclaimed. "That's the strangest thing I've ever heard."

"It isn't when you think about it. You can always count on the square root of nine being three and the diameter of a circle being twice its radius." She stopped and her brown eyes flickered. "It's other things that are complicated: when you think you know someone and all of a sudden they behave like a complete stranger. Or when you are so happy you are as light as a balloon and the next minute everything seems as dark as the Bastille."

"I can't discuss philosophy on an empty stomach." Alec unscrewed a jar of raspberry jam. He spread it on a water cracker and took a small bite. "Would you like some?"

"You're eating raspberry jam and crackers for lunch?'" Isabel asked.

"The suite doesn't come with meals," he explained. "I could go out, but the Hôtel de Crillon occupies the most expensive real estate in Paris. The cafés on the Champs-Élysées charge ten euros for a soft-boiled egg."

"I'll buy you lunch. My boss said I must try Fouquet's." She paused. "If it wasn't for you, I'd still be trapped on the balcony."

Alec gazed at her glossy dark hair and brown eyes and wide pink mouth. He saw her slender neck and small waist and long legs.

"I'm sure someone would have rescued you, but why not?" He shrugged. "A ham-and-cheese omelet and black coffee sounds delicious."

THEY TOOK THE elevator to the lobby, and Isabel thought she had never been anywhere so beautiful. The gold-flecked marble floor was scattered with ivory silk sofas and glass coffee tables holding Lalique crystal vases. A white Christmas tree almost reached the ceiling, and boxes wrapped in silver and

gold tissue paper spilled onto the Persian rugs. Bellboys carried Louis Vuitton suitcases, and a woman in a mink jacket hugged a small dog in a cashmere sweater.

Isabel inhaled the scent of French perfume and hot cocoa and suddenly was so glad she was in Paris. She followed Alec down the marble steps, and they turned onto the Champs-Élysées. She gazed at the Arc de Triomphe on one end and the narrow Luxor Obelisk on the other and caught her breath. Everywhere she looked there were boutiques with green awnings and cafés with red umbrellas and window boxes filled with poinsettias.

They passed Chanel with its gold logo and Dior with its glittering evening gowns, and Isabel thought it was the most elegant street in the world. Women wore narrow knee-high boots and cashmere coats. Their hair was pulled into tight chignons, and they carried bright leather handbags.

"The last time I was in Paris it was so hot I spent all my time at the Louvre." Isabel gazed at a patisserie window filled with trays of vanilla custards. "It was the only place you could stay cool all day for the price of a museum ticket."

"Paris is like a fickle woman, she's either unbearably hot or intolerably cold," Alec mused. "When I was a child, my mother took me to the Centre Pompidou during the winter holidays. I thought she was interested in modern art, but she didn't know what to do with a boy in the rain."

"You grew up in Paris?" Isabel asked.

"My mother is British and married a Frenchman. I've lived in Paris most of my life." He nodded. "I attended a few different lycées. I'd turn in my science test with doodles of Gus in the margin and the headmaster would call my mother to discuss my future." He smiled. "My mother would knock on my door with a defeated expression and a list of schools that were a better fit."

"You seem to have turned out fine," Isabel laughed.

"My sister's boyfriend is a neurosurgeon." He shrugged. "I suppose I could have achieved more."

"What does your sister do?" she asked.

Alec's eyes were suddenly dark and he stuffed his hands in his pockets.

"Let's get something to eat." He stopped in front of a café. "The smell of garlic and butter is making my stomach ache."

LE FOUQUET'S HAD red-and-gold awnings and double glass front doors and waiters wearing white dinner jackets. They sat on the patio, and Isabel glanced at the wide plates of veal flanks and silver baskets of fresh baguettes and realized she was starving.

"Fouquet's has been here for more than a hundred years," Alec said. "Charlie Chaplin used to drink schnapps at the bar and Marlene Dietrich was a regular and Jackie Onassis adored the bourbon vanilla ice cream." He put down the menu. "Are you sure you don't want to eat somewhere else? I'd be happy with a warm pretzel from a food stand."

Isabel glanced at the prices and felt a bit dizzy. But then she pictured the Stuart Weitzman satin pumps she'd returned to Bloomingdale's and the Vera Wang dress that was at a designer consignment store and straightened her shoulders. She was a well-paid analyst at one of the biggest banks in America; she could afford an overpriced platter of escargots.

"Order whatever you like." She looked at Alec and her eyes sparkled. "This afternoon we'll be like Marie Antoinette and just eat cake."

"SO TELL ME about you," Alec said after they ordered lobster bisque and sides of roasted yams. "What should I know besides the fact you have very good aim and excellent taste in shoes?"

"My father loves baseball, so we attended a lot of Phillies games." Isabel blushed. "I had the most wonderful childhood: skiing in the Adirondacks and horseback riding on my grand-parents' farm. I attended an all-girls high school and went to Bryn Mawr—"

"You attended an all-girls school?" Alec interrupted, buttering a baguette.

"What's wrong with that?" Isabel bristled. "Agnes Irwin is a wonderful school and I had so many opportunities. I was president of the math club and a Future Business Leader of America."

"I'm sure it taught you calculus and physics." He looked at Isabel thoughtfully. "But you've had two failed engagements, so maybe it didn't teach you about men."

"Why should you have to learn how to fall in love? It's the most natural thing in the world," Isabel protested. "Babies need their mothers and schoolchildren form crushes on their teach-ers and old people have deep bonds with their pets."

"For love to work, two people have to want the same thing at the same time." Alec leaned back in his chair. "I've discov-ered that's as likely as a man landing on Jupiter."

"I'm sure I'll get it right next time." She nibbled a breadstick and her eyes were huge. "I love my career, but one can't live without love."

THEY ATE RICOTTA crepes with raspberry sauce for dessert and strolled along the Champs-Élysées. The sky was pale blue and the clouds were bright white and Isabel felt a tingle of excite-ment. The store windows were draped in red bows and filled with little black dresses and strands of pearls and quilted satin evening bags.

They entered the Place de la Concorde, and Isabel saw the

giant Christmas tree and wooden chalets lining the square. There were stalls selling gingerbread houses and sausages and jars of fresh preserves. She saw booths with Chinese slippers and glass necklaces.

"Would you like your fortune read?" a woman asked. She had dark hair and wore a patterned scarf and a red felt coat.

"No, thank you." Isabel shook her head. "I'm just admiring the pretty necklaces."

"It only costs twenty euros," the woman insisted.

"I'm sorry, I'm afraid I don't have time." Isabel moved away, suddenly nervous.

She and Alec paused at the next booth, and she felt someone tugging her arm. She turned around and saw the fortune-teller rubbing her hands.

"Please, I have two children and can't afford to buy them Christmas presents," she implored. "They see racing cars and dolls in shop windows and beg for something to unwrap."

Isabel opened her purse and took out a twenty-euro note.

"Please take it." She handed it to the woman. "And tell your children, Merry Christmas."

"I cannot accept charity," the woman protested. "I must read your fortune."

Isabel searched for Alec, but he was standing at the next stall, studying a selection of colored pens.

"All right, I suppose I have a few minutes." She held out her hand. "What do you see?"

The woman turned over her hand and studied her palm. She glanced up at Isabel and then traced the tips of her fingers.

"You have an important job at a large company," she began. "You'll get a promotion and have an office with floor-to-ceiling windows and a glass desk. I see a shiny gift in your near future." She looked up. "Something bright and sparkly. It will not be expensive, but it will come to have great value."

"That sounds delightful," Isabel laughed. "Thank you, you've made me happy."

"Wait, there's more," the fortune-teller interrupted. "You will fall in love with a French aristocrat and get married in an elegant château." She leaned forward and grabbed Isabel's wrist. "But there is one short line in the middle of your hand. You must be careful. You will narrowly miss being killed."

Isabel jumped as if she had been stung by a bee. She turned and saw Alec standing in front of a wooden chalet filled with gumdrops and candy canes. "I really have to go, I'll lose my friend."

"Now I have earned the money." The fortune-teller tucked the twenty-euro note in her pocket. "Be careful and listen to what I said."

"IT'S A WONDER Parisians have decent teeth," Alec said when she approached the booth. "There's enough sugar here to solve the national deficit in a third world country."

"The ricotta crepes with raspberry sauce were delicious." Isabel smiled. "But I couldn't eat another bite."

She turned and caught sight of the fortune-teller and felt a slight chill. But that was ridiculous; nothing she said could possibly come true. She was an ordinary woman wearing a patterned scarf and felt coat.

"I've always loved magicians," Isabel exclaimed, walking to the next booth, where a magician was putting on a show. "My mother hired a magician for my fifth birthday party and he made me levitate on a magic carpet."

"I once saw a magician in the Marais turn a dog into a monkey," Alec said, joining her.

"That sounds impressive," Isabel said.

"Not to the owner of the dog," Alec mused. "He wanted his dachshund back."

The magician reached into his sleeve and pulled out a brightly colored bracelet. He placed three cones on a table and searched the crowd.

"Mademoiselle will guess which cone the bracelet is under." He pointed to Isabel. "If you are correct, the priceless bracelet is yours."

"I don't think so." Isabel blushed. "Pick someone else."

"You are a beautiful woman with special powers," he said in accented English.

Isabel hesitated and her shoulders relaxed. It was Christmas and she was in Paris—why shouldn't she do what the magician asked?

"All right." She pointed to the red cone. "I choose that one."

"I'm sorry, that's not the one." He revealed the empty cone. "For five euros you can choose again."

"No, thank you." Isabel laughed. "The bracelet is lovely, but I can't afford it."

"Here." Alec reached into his pocket and handed the magician a five-euro note.

Isabel studied the two remaining cones and chose the blue one.

"The bracelet is yours." The magician removed the cone and bowed. "Merry Christmas."

"Why did you do that?" Isabel asked as they walked toward the curb. "If I picked the wrong cone, you would have paid five euros for nothing."

"He wouldn't let you choose the wrong one." Alec ate a gumdrop. "Then the other tourists would leave. Now everyone wants a chance, they're determined to win on the first try."

"It is lovely, thank you." Isabel glanced at the pink-and-blue bracelet and suddenly her cheeks were pale.

"I'm feeling a little light-headed," she stammered. "Do you mind if we go back to the Crillon?"

"Did you sample a bad piece of cheese?" Alec studied her pale cheeks. "You look a little green."

"I'll be fine," she wavered. "I'd like to lie down in my suite."

"That doesn't sound like the girl who threw her Ferragamo pumps at my balcony and insisted her first meal in Paris be at the most famous café on the Champs-Élysées." Alec frowned. "Did your ex-fiancé text and ask where you keep the instant oatmeal? It's hard to forget someone when his name keeps popping up on your phone."

"It's nothing like that." Isabel blushed. "A fortune-teller insisted on reading my fortune. She said I would receive a sparkling gift that had little real value."

"Surely you don't believe that stuff," he said. "Fortune-tellers in Paris will do anything to separate tourists from ten euros. You should have told me, she was probably in cahoots with the magician."

"Of course I don't believe it." Isabel hesitated. "But I really am tired, I just need to take a hot bath."

She shielded her eyes from the sun and stepped onto the boulevard. A car honked and the air rushed beside her. There was a grinding of metal and she fell onto the hard cement.

"Are you all right?" Alec crouched beside her. "That taxi almost ran you over."

Isabel tried to stand, but her knees buckled. She heard a car door open and the taxi driver yelled in rapid French.

"Please tell him I'm fine." She rubbed her elbow. "I just need to catch my breath."

"He was lighting a cigarette and not paying attention." He grimaced. "I should call the gendarmes and have him arrested."

"It was my fault," Isabel insisted. "I crossed the street without looking."

He scooped her up, and she wrapped her arms around his neck. He climbed the marble steps, and they entered the lobby of the Crillon. Isabel gazed at the ornate tapestries and white Christmas tree, and her eyes filled with tears. What was she doing in the arms of a strange man when she was supposed to be on her honeymoon?

"You can put me down." She bit her lip. "I'm perfectly capable of walking."

Alec carried her across the lobby and entered a room with paneled walls and dark leather booths. It had a polished parquet floor and mosaic bar. A huge ornate mirror rested above a marble fireplace, and vases were filled with purple orchids.

"What are we doing?" Isabel demanded.

"I'm not leaving until we both have a tall drink." He slid into a booth. "I don't want you to lock yourself on the balcony or fall asleep in the bath."

"I'VE NEVER BEEN much of a drinker." Isabel sipped the gold liquid. "But I do feel better, this is superb."

"It's Hennessy cognac," Alec explained. "The Crillon charges fifteen euros a shot."

"I can't let you pay for that," Isabel protested. "Put it on my bill."

"It's the least I can do, I almost got you run over." He paused. "You don't look like the kind of girl who ever jaywalked in her life. Why did you jump into the street like a horse wearing blinders in the Bois de Boulogne?"

"That woman insisted on telling my fortune," Isabel began. "She said I had an important job at a large company."

"That hardly makes her clairvoyant," Alec laughed. "You're a beautiful young American shopping on the most expensive street in Paris, and you're not wearing a wedding ring. You're either

a high-level executive or a call girl." He gazed at her pink cashmere sweater and wool slacks. "Somehow I don't think you're dressed for the part."

"Then she said I would receive a brightly colored gift that would come to have great value."

"We went over that," Alec replied. "She probably is in partnership with the magician. She tells your fortune, and then you win a prize. You are so pleased, you rush back and give her ten euros to tell you the names of your future children."

"She said I was going to fall in love and marry a French aristocrat." Isabel fiddled with her glass.

"That's like saying to every Frenchwoman who arrives in New York she's going to marry Tom Cruise or Derek Jeter." Alec sipped his scotch. "We think Americans are all movie stars or athletes, and Americans believe the French are all direct descendants of Marie Antoinette and Louis XVI. I wouldn't be surprised if American tourists assumed Paris was full of men wearing powdered wigs and pantaloons."

"I thanked her for the lovely reading, and she said there was more." Isabel felt something hard press against her chest. "I was going to narrowly miss being killed."

"Is that right?" Alec asked, leaning back in his chair. "It's a wonder more pedestrians aren't run over. Parisian taxi drivers drive too fast and whistle at pretty girls when they should be watching the traffic light."

"He didn't do anything wrong, it was my fault."

"You're in a strange city and your wedding just got canceled." He shrugged. "It could happen to anyone."

"I double majored in economics and mathematics at Bryn Mawr and was in the top three percent of my class at Wharton. I planned a winter wedding for three hundred people while overseeing a multimillion-dollar merger." She looked at Alec and her eyes were bright. "And you were right the first time, it

isn't like me at all. That's why I'm certain the fortune-teller can predict the future. You see, I never jaywalked in my life before today, but something made me do it."

ISABEL SAT ON the blue velvet sofa and sipped a cup of chamomile tea. After she and Alec finished their drinks, she returned to her suite, ran a hot bath, and soaked in jasmine bubbles. Now she nibbled a macaron and gazed at the night sky and silver lights twinkling in the Place de la Concorde.

She flipped through a travel guide and thought of all the things she and Neil had planned to do in Paris: climb to the viewing terrace of the Arc de Triomphe and look out over the Boulevard Haussmann, order Ritz Side Cars at Bar Hemingway and visit the fruit markets in Montmartre.

A leather-bound notebook lay on the coffee table and she picked it up. When Neil proposed, she started a journal to record the wonderful things that would happen during their engagement.

She knew she should have left the journal at home. She didn't have to be reminded of picking out Wedgwood china and trying on chiffon wedding dresses while she was sitting alone in the honeymoon suite of the Hôtel de Crillon.

But somehow leaving it behind made it feel as if the whole engagement never happened. She wasn't ready to put it away, like a pretty wool sweater you received as a Christmas present but couldn't wear because the fabric was scratchy.

In the beginning everything about their engagement was exciting. She and Neil were so happy and she was certain their love would last forever.

She opened it and a photo fell out. Neil had his arm draped around her and she displayed the emerald-cut diamond ring on her finger.

Dear diary,

Goodness, I haven't kept a diary since my freshman year in college! But all the wedding books say keeping an engagement journal is the best way to remember the start of your new life. And if every day is like today, I'm the luckiest girl in the world.

Neil said his boss gave him tickets to see Jersey Boys *on Broadway and he booked two nights at the Carlyle. I almost didn't go, I have a huge presentation and planned on preparing all weekend. But Neil promised we could both squeeze in time to work, and how could I resist Manhattan in the fall? The department store windows are filled with winter fashions and Central Park is a myriad of colors and the whole city buzzes with a new energy.*

The musical was wonderful and I was ready to go back to our suite and order room service. But Neil had made reservations at Jean-Georges! It has three Michelin stars and it's right on Central Park.

From the moment the maître d' meets you at the door, you feel like you've been transported to Paris. The floors are polished wood and the booths are scattered with silk cushions and the waiters have French accents and wear white dinner jackets.

We ordered the tasting menu and every course was accompanied by a Zinfandel or Chenin Blanc. The butter-poached turnips were delicious and the garlic soup with sautéed frog legs was superb.

Then the waiter brought out a plate with a mille-feuille drizzled with chocolate sauce. It was my favorite dessert when I studied at the Sorbonne. I loved the creamy custard and powdered sugar and flaky pastry.

I looked closer and realized, instead of a strawberry on top, there was a sparkling diamond ring! I gasped and Neil's face broke into a smile.

"I wanted to propose in Paris, but we're both too busy to get away," he said, taking my hand. "I love you and want to do everything with you: travel to Europe and ride horses on the farm and sail on the Delaware River. You are bright and beautiful and I can't imagine life without you. Isabel Marie Lawson, will you marry me?"

"Yes," I breathed, feeling the warmth of his palm. "Yes, I'll marry you."

The waiters clapped and the maître d' presented us with a bottle of Dom Pérignon. Neil slipped the ring on my finger and we shared the mille-feuille and I've never been so happy. Neil is caring and handsome and it was the most romantic moment of my life.

I bought this notebook at the Carlyle gift shop and promise to fill it with all the excitement of the coming year. We haven't talked about the ceremony location or number of guests, but I know two things: I want a winter wedding, and our honeymoon will be in Paris. I can't wait to arrive in the City of Light as Mr. and Mrs. Neil Harmon!

Good night, dear diary. Or I should say, bon nuit.

Isabel closed the notebook and gazed out the window. It was beginning to snow and Place de la Concorde was bathed in a golden light. It had been wonderful to be in love and certain about their future. Would she ever feel that way again?

She had read the whole passage without crying; surely she had made the right decision. If she were in love with Neil, she would be longing for him to be here in the hotel suite.

She jumped up and walked to the closet. She didn't need Neil to see Monet's water lilies at L'Orangerie or buy first edition books at Shakespeare and Company. And she wasn't afraid to sit at Le Fumoir and eat herring marinated in sherry by herself.

She noticed her beige pumps and remembered being locked out on the balcony.

"This vacation isn't going as planned," she said aloud. "First I almost freeze to death, then I come close to getting run over."

She walked to the living room and sank into a damask armchair. She gazed at the silver tray set with two porcelain demitasses and a selection of hazelnut truffles and nougats.

"I think I'll stay inside tonight." She picked up another macaron. "Paris will be here tomorrow."

chapter three

❧

Alec glanced at the sketch of a cocker spaniel dressed in board shorts and balancing on a surfboard and grimaced. Lately drawing everything Gus did—jumping out of an airplane, sailing a catamaran, wrestling a ten-pound trout on his fishing line— seemed exhausting. Sometimes he wished he could draw Gus curled up on a dog bed in front of the fire or watching cartoons on a large-screen television.

He paced around the suite and thought he just needed a good night's sleep. He couldn't keep waking up at two AM and working until midmorning. And he couldn't exist on a diet of wheat crackers and raspberry jam from the minibar.

He could usually make a check from his publisher last for months, and still enjoy a bowl of café au lait at La Poilâne and a chunk of Roquefort cheese from Pascal Beillevaire. But he had paid for the engraved wedding bands and two nights at Auberge de Cassagne in Avignon and the white angora sweater Celine adored in Le Printemps's window.

He ate a handful of cashews and wished he hadn't splurged on two glasses of Hennessey. But Isabel was so distraught. And

it really was his fault; a gentleman always took a woman's arm when they crossed the street.

He gazed down at the boulevard jammed with cars and thought it would be lovely to move to the country. He pictured a gabled cottage with an attic room for his colored pens and sketch pads. He imagined playing bowls in the village square and smoking Gauloises with old men wearing straw hats and fisherman sweaters.

But he had been raised in Paris and he thrived on museums and galleries. He hated mosquitoes, and the sound of silence was worse than the symphony of taxis and buses. And where would he get inspiration for Gus if he didn't read the headlines in *Le Monde* or watch the parade of people on the Rue de Seine?

He noticed a diamond teardrop earring on the marble sideboard and smiled. Only Celine would lose a two-carat diamond and not bother to call and ask if he found it. He pictured her honey-blond hair and long legs and groaned. God, she was beautiful, like a championship racehorse at Ascot.

He remembered when they met, at a gallery opening in Saint-Germain-des-Prés. Alec hated art openings with waiters passing around crystal champagne flutes and trays of canapés. It was impossible get close to the paintings, and if he stood in one place too long, someone was bound to step on his foot.

But his publisher believed the best way to make fashionable Parisian mothers buy his books was to compliment them on their taste in avant-garde art. Alec was young and good-looking, and it wouldn't hurt for women to imagine his dark hair and green eyes when they were purchasing a selection of bedtime stories.

"YOU AREN'T LOOKING at the paintings," a woman said, approaching him. She had violet eyes and a full red mouth. She wore a neon minidress and silver stilettos.

"It's impossible to get near the artwork without being elbowed in the ribs or hit in the thigh by a ten-kilo Hermès bag." Alec nibbled salmon and bell peppers.

"Then why are you here?" the woman asked. She had red fingernails and wore a diamond-and-ruby bracelet.

"I'm a children's book illustrator and my publisher thinks I should mingle with mothers who can afford to pay ten thousand euros for a splash of orange." Alec waved at a gold frame. "But this crowd is too young to have children. The men look like they just returned from heli-skiing in St. Moritz and the women seem like they stepped off the runway at Chanel." He studied her high cheekbones and slender neck. "Not that there's anything wrong with being a model. One of my sister's friends models for Lanvin and makes a fortune. I'm sure women see you on the runway and line up to buy a new swimsuit."

"You think I'm a model because I have thick hair and good legs?" she demanded.

"Well, yes." Alec suddenly felt sick. "Aren't you a model?"

"I'm a translator at UNESCO at the United Nations and fluent in four languages." Her eyes flashed.

"I see." Alec drained his champagne glass. He ran his hands through his hair and said feebly, "I tried learning Chinese, but studying the characters gave me vertigo."

IT WAS CELINE'S idea to drink Bombay sapphire gin at Le Bar in the George V. Waiters carried platters of foie gras and caviar, and Alec was afraid he'd have to max out his credit card. But when the bill arrived, Celine murmured to the bartender in French and he smiled and crumpled up the paper.

Alec offered to walk her home and they strolled along the Rue Saint-Honoré. She stopped in front of a stone mansion divided into four flats.

"I didn't know a translator's salary paid for a garden apartment on one of the most elegant streets in Paris." Alec gazed at the slate roof and double front doors.

"My father is a jeweler, he owns diamond mines in South Africa and Brazil." Celine fiddled with her key. "Would you mind coming inside? I hate turning on the lights by myself."

Alec glanced at her lips, which were like plump cherries, and had the sudden urge to kiss her. He followed her into the hallway and flicked the light on in the living room. The floor was polished wood and there was a floral sofa and an Andy Warhol Marilyn Monroe on the wall.

"Would you like an aperitif?" She slipped off her stilettos.

"I have to go," he mumbled. "I'm working on a deadline, I left Gus hanging off a cliff in Algeria."

The next morning Celine called and said she needed a date to *Aida* at the Palais Garnier. When he picked her up, she stood in her narrow entry in a turquoise gown and gold sandals. Her blond hair fell to her shoulders and she wore a diamond pendant around her neck. He gazed at her creamy skin and high breasts and sucked in his breath.

He drew her into the living room and kissed her on the mouth. He loosened his tie and thought he was acting like an oversexed schoolboy. Love had to be entered into slowly, or it became like a soufflé you left in the oven too long that suddenly exploded.

He ran his hands through his hair and said they didn't want to miss the opening act. Celine placed one hand between his legs and stroked the hardness beneath his slacks. He inhaled her scent of floral perfume and his last trace of willpower dissolved.

He slipped his hand beneath her panties and felt the sweet wetness and delicious warmth. When his fingers slid inside her, he felt her press against his chest. Then she dug her nails into his back and her whole body shattered.

They moved to the bedroom and tore at each other's clothes. Alec remembered the joy of new sex: discovering a birthmark on her neck and an indentation in her thigh and the glistening curve of her stomach.

She drew him onto the bed and wrapped her arms around his back. He opened her thighs and plunged deep inside her. He felt the wild rush and then the feeling of exquisite joy. She clutched his shoulders and they came together like two sprinters gasping at the finish line.

AFTERWARD THEY LAY against the quilted headboard and he wondered what he had done. The last thing he needed was to fall in love with a beautiful, wealthy girl who had first edition copies of Balzac on her bookshelf and Prada shoes at the foot of her bed. But he gazed at her long eyelashes and full mouth and wondered how he could do anything else.

THE NEXT TWO months were a frenzy of delicious sex. Alec came over after Celine returned from work, and they attempted to toss a salad or boil pasta. But Celine would brush against his chest or Alec would inhale her exotic scent, and they would turn off the pot of spaghetti or put the Camembert back in the fridge and race to the bedroom.

Sometimes they pulled on sweaters and slacks and went to the cinema or browsed in a bookstore. But what was the point of watching a romantic movie or reading a love story when what they had was better than fiction?

The only drawback was, wherever they went, men flocked to Celine like insects to flypaper. Every time Alec collected their drinks at a bar, or lingered at a newsagent while she sat at a café, he returned to find a man in his chair.

"I WAS EATING my *pain au chocolat* when Hans insisted I read *Death in Venice*," Celine explained when Alec returned from buying a packet of Mentos and found Celine sitting across from a blond tourist at Café Verlet.

"No one pulls up a chair and discusses classical literature without an invitation," Alec grumbled, popping a Mentos in his mouth.

"I was reading Goethe to practice my German," Celine said. "He must have noticed the cover."

"Then read *Madame Figaro*," Alec suggested. "No man wants to discuss bra cup sizes or the new season's style in cashmere sweaters."

"All men talk to single women, it doesn't mean anything." Celine shrugged. "The only way to stop them is to wear a diamond ring on your finger and have a round bump in your stomach."

Alec gazed at couples strolling along the boulevard and jumped up. He knew exactly how to stop men from flirting with Celine! Why didn't he think of it sooner?

He hopped on the metro and went to see his mother. He found her in the garden, bending over a row of butter lettuce.

"Alec darling!" She kissed him on the cheek. "I haven't seen you in weeks. Ever since you said you met a girl, you disappeared."

"You'd like Celine." He suddenly remembered when he arrived home from kindergarten and declared he had a crush on his teacher. He begged his mother to let him use his allowance to buy Mademoiselle Egret a glass necklace.

"Invite her over for dinner," Claudia suggested. "I'll make pumpkin soup and a summer salad."

"I wanted to ask you something." Alec wiped his brow. "You said I could have Bertie's ring when I got married."

"Of course you can have my mother's ring. I'm counting on you to give me grandchildren." She smiled. "What better reason to reread *The Little Prince* and the Paddington books?"

"I'd like to have it now," Alec continued. "I'm going to ask Celine to marry me."

"You want to give my mother's antique sapphire-and-diamond ring to a girl you just met?"

"I'm thirty and she's twenty-seven, she's hardly a child bride," Alec protested. "She's beautiful and smart and everything I dreamed of."

"But you've known her for less than two months. When you were a child you spent weeks perfecting your Christmas list and you always ordered last at a restaurant." She paused. "Why the rush?"

"Celine is like a jar of the sweetest honey or a bowl of the richest cream," he said. "Men will do anything to approach her. I thought . . ."

"That if she wore a wedding ring, they would think she was off the market?" Claudia raised her eyebrow.

"Something like that." Alec shrugged.

"That's not a good reason to marry someone." His mother frowned.

Alec pictured Celine's clear violet eyes and long legs. He saw the way she looked in the morning, with her hair in a high ponytail and her face free of makeup and her smile that was like the Cheshire Cat's.

"I have a better reason," he groaned. "I can't live without her."

ALEC SPENT THE next week in a state of giddy anticipation. It was spring and Paris bloomed with lilacs and daffodils. He

spent hours debating with himself where to propose: On the Pont des Arts, with the Louvre rising like a modern pyramid. In front of the Sacré-Coeur, with all of Paris laid out at their feet. Under the Eiffel Tower, so they could look up at the steel structure and remember they were in the most romantic city in the world.

He finally decided on Parc Monceau in the eighth arrondissement. It wasn't overrun by tourists, and Celine loved the rose gardens and willow trees and lake surrounded by Corinthian columns.

He packed a picnic of olive baguettes and Brie and capers. There were peaches and berries and a jar of whipped cream. He added a bottle of Veuve Clicquot and Celine's favorite chocolate torte.

The morning of the proposal, clouds hung low over the Seine. Alec wore a pale blue blazer and beige slacks. He felt the jewelry box in his pocket and a lump formed in his throat.

"IT'S NOT the best day for a picnic," Celine said when he picked her up at her flat.

She wore blue jeans and a navy sweater and Alec felt a twinge of disappointment. He had imagined her in a sleeveless linen dress and leather sandals. Her hair would fall loosely to her shoulders and she would smell of lavender shampoo.

Instead her hair was wound into a bun and held back with an enamel clip. She wore low boots and an orange turtleneck under the navy sweater.

"Why don't we see a movie?" she suggested. "The new *Mission: Impossible* is playing at Cinema Le Rex and we can eat popcorn and Raisinets."

"The last time we saw an American movie with French

subtitles, the actors sounded like chipmunks," Alec grumbled. "It can't rain, I bought sausages and kumquats from the outdoor market in the Marais."

The first drops fell as they entered the stone gates. They rushed under the rotunda and Alec gazed at the wet grass. He could hardly expect Celine to sit on a muddy blanket and eat soggy ham and cheese.

He took her hand and suddenly had an idea. They would go to the Passage Jouffroy and eat escargot and *baba au rhum* at one of the elegant cafés. When he was a child, he loved visiting Boîte à Joujoux with its giant erector sets and Le Petit Roi crammed with children's books and eating almond cakes at Le Valentin.

They crossed the Boulevard Haussmann and entered the iron doors. Alec saw the black-and-white marble floor and glass ceiling and let out his breath. What could be more romantic than a covered passageway built in 1836 by one of France's greatest architects?

"Let's go to Bouillon Chartier and eat carrot mousse and country terrine," Alec suggested, picturing the quaint restaurant with its red velvet walls and steaming bowls of bouillabaisse.

"I feel like pizza," Celine said. "Nick's Pizza has the best pizza margherita in Paris."

"Pizza?" Alec shuddered. He could hardly pull out the jewelry box with greasy fingers.

"When was the last time we had pizza?" Celine took his arm. "We'll share strawberry gelato for dessert."

THEY SAT ON wooden chairs and Alec glanced miserably at the menu. He could propose another day, but he was so nervous, he could barely concentrate on his work. All week he had sketched a companion for Gus: a fluffy French poodle named

Monique. Finally he crumpled it in the garbage. His readers wanted Gus to fight fiery dragons, not hold hands on a barge gliding along the Seine.

"THE WAITER ASKED you three times what you wanted to order," Celine said, interrupting his thoughts.

"Sorry?" Alec looked up. He pointed to the pizza Napoletana and handed the waiter his menu.

"Maybe we should go home." Celine sipped a glass of water. "You look like you are coming down with a cold."

Alec studied her high cheekbones and slender neck and caught his breath. Even with her mascara smudged and hair damp from the rain, she was the most beautiful woman he had ever seen. He fumbled in his pocket and brought out the velvet jewelry box.

"I wanted to ask you this with the sun streaming on the lake and the air filled with the scent of lilacs and roses," he began. "You are elegant and stunning, like a shooting star that somehow landed on my doorstep." He drew out the pear-shaped diamond ring. "Celine Du Mond, will you marry me?"

"Marry you?" Celine exclaimed. "We haven't even met each other's families."

Celine was right. Alec had wanted to ask Celine's father for his blessing, but when he called his office, his secretary said he was in Brazil until July. And he knew he should have taken her to lunch with his mother, but that would mean meeting his sister. Somehow he wanted to keep Celine away from Bettina until the diamond ring was safely on Celine's finger.

"We'll visit my mother this afternoon," he said eagerly. "She gave me her mother's ring, she can't wait to meet you."

"Are you asking me to marry you so men will stop flirting with me?" Celine asked.

"Of course not!" He bristled. "I want to spend the rest of my life with you. I want to have babies and push a pram through the Luxembourg Gardens. I want to rent a cottage in the country and play backgammon in front of the fire."

She studied the diamond ring as if she was debating what topping to put on her pizza. She looked at Alec and a smile lit up her face.

"Yes."

"Yes, what?" Alec asked.

"Yes, I'll marry you."

"You will?" Alec realized he didn't know what to do next. Did he slip the ring on her finger or kiss her on the mouth?

"You sound surprised," Celine replied. "What did you expect me to say?"

Alec glanced at the rain smudging the window and couples huddling under umbrellas and took a deep breath. The most incredible woman in Paris was agreeing to be his wife; this wasn't the time to discuss whether they would live on his salary, or if she slept under a down duvet in the summer.

He slipped the ring on her finger and gathered her in his arms. He inhaled her scent of jasmine and vanilla and thought he was the happiest man in the world.

"Yes," he whispered. "I knew you were going to say yes."

CELINE WAS THE easiest bride. Her father insisted on paying for the wedding, so Celine was happy to let her stepmother, Mathilde, plan the elaborate reception at the George V.

Sometimes Alec passed boutiques filled with chiffon wedding dresses and lace stockings and wished she wanted his opinion on the flowers or strawberry meringue. But then he pictured the glorious nights in Celine's bed and thought he was being ridiculous.

Everyone knew spending too much time planning the wedding was the fastest way to get a divorce. He should be grateful all he had to do was slip on the gray morning suit and yellow boutonniere and show up at Cathédrale Notre-Dame at three o'clock.

ALEC ATE THE last bite of wheat cracker and thought if only Patrick hadn't appeared. It seemed perfectly innocent when Celine's boss asked her to show his Australian nephew around Paris. Alec pictured a boy with sandy hair and freckles clutching a cricket bat.

He remembered when he arrived in the Place Vendôme at six o'clock. Celine asked him to meet them at a café and then they would take a dinner cruise on the Seine.

ALEC BUTTONED HIS coat and thought it really was too cold to sit on a barge at night. There was never decent heating and you could barely see out of the windows because of the fog. And why would a boy have any interest in seeing Paris after dark? Alec was sure he'd rather visit Cirque d'Hiver or to see the Christmas lights at Disneyland Paris.

He turned the corner and saw Celine sitting across from a man with wavy blond hair and blue eyes. He wore a blue cashmere sweater and gray slacks.

Alec approached the café and wondered why Celine had her hands in her pockets. Was she hiding her diamond ring or just keeping warm? And where was Patrick? Did she send her boss's nephew away so she could flirt with the guy who looked like he had stepped out of a Ralph Lauren catalog?

"God, it's freezing." Alec rubbed his hands together. "I hope Patrick didn't stop at a newsagent to buy a packet of sweets.

He won't appreciate the braised duck and sliced beets if he's stuffed with caramels."

Celine looked up and smoothed her hair. She wore a teal sweater and cream slacks and Alec thought she had never looked more beautiful. Diamond teardrop earrings glittered in her ears and she resembled an angel on top of a Christmas tree.

"This is my fiancé, Alec," she said to the man sitting across the table. She turned to Alec and her mouth puckered. "This is Edgar's nephew Patrick."

"HOW ON EARTH can that blond Adonis be Edgar's nephew?" Alec spluttered. "I pictured some knobby-kneed kid with bangs, not one of *People*'s fifty most beautiful people."

"Edgar is almost sixty, why shouldn't he have a grown nephew?" Celine retorted. They had returned from the dinner cruise and were standing in Celine's living room.

Alec thought he'd never had a more miserable evening. The Cabernet had been off, and when the waiter placed the chocolate soufflé in front of him, it collapsed. Patrick insisted on standing on the deck to see the Christmas lights, and Alec was so cold, he almost asked the woman next to them if he could borrow her mink coat.

"How can he be so tan in the middle of winter?" he continued. "I felt like a wax figure at Madame Tussauds."

"He's from Melbourne, it's the middle of summer in Australia."

"Well, someone needs to tell him to wear a hat." He scowled. "If he stands on a cricket mound without protection, he's going to get a terrible sunburn."

Celine took the ribbon out of her hair. "It sounds like you are jealous."

"Jealous?" Alec started. He gazed at her high breasts and

small waist and felt like the Wicked Witch dissolving into a puddle. "Why on earth would I be jealous?"

"You tell me," she said, unzipping her slacks and letting them fall to the floor. "You were the one who was sulking like a child who didn't receive any Christmas presents."

"I was not sulking," Alec muttered. "It was freezing, and I was trying to stop my teeth from chattering."

She took his hand and led him into the bedroom. Alec watched her unsnap her bra and forgot about the bad wine and limp dessert. He slipped his hand under her panties and thought he had discovered a hidden treasure. He pressed his fingers in deeper and watching her face open, like a flower in springtime.

She drew him onto the ivory bedspread and pulled him inside her. She urged him to go faster, and he felt the slow build and sudden terror of not being able to stop. He pulled her hands over her head and their legs twisted on the silk sheets. Then he collapsed on her breasts and heard her cry out.

God, it was incredible! Like they were the only two lovers in Paris. He waited until she stopped shaking, and then he closed his eyes and for a moment he knew perfect happiness.

"You're not a child at all," Celine murmured. "You're very much a man."

Alec suddenly felt invincible. He tucked her against his chest and whispered, "How could I ever be jealous when I get to hold you in my arms?"

ALEC SCREWED THE lid on the jar of preserves and thought that if he had known that was the last time they would have sex, he would have made it last longer. How was he to know that three days later she would board a plane to Melbourne?

And now he was alone in a honeymoon suite at the Hôtel de Crillon. He remembered Isabel stepping onto the boulevard

and was glad she wasn't hurt. It was bad enough his fiancée had deserted him; it would be terrible if he were responsible for Isabel getting run over by a taxi.

That was the thing about life. You thought everything was moving in the right direction. And then something appeared out of the blue and changed your course forever.

He thought of the night he and Celine checked into the Crillon. He couldn't get over the welcoming basket of exotic nuts and fresh fruits from Mexico. He moved around the suite, examining the Armani shaving cream in the bathroom and the heated floor in the bidet closet.

ALEC POPPED A handful of macadamia nuts in his mouth and glanced at his watch. They were meeting Celine's parents for dinner at Le Meurice and she had gone to the salon to get her hair done. But now it was almost six o'clock and they'd never get through pre-Christmas traffic if they didn't hurry.

He grabbed the key and took the elevator to the lobby. He crossed the Persian rug and approached the concierge.

"Could you direct me to the salon?" he asked. "My fiancée had an appointment hours ago, and hasn't returned."

"Are you in suite five-twenty?" The man looked up from his computer.

"Yes, how did you know?"

"The mademoiselle told me to expect a tall man wearing a red sweater." He handed Alec an envelope. "She left you a letter."

"My mother bought me this sweater," Alec snapped, stuffing the envelope in his pocket. "It's Shetland wool, hand-knit in Scotland."

Alec took the letter up to the suite and ripped it open. He scanned it quickly and groaned. How could a woman with a

degree from the Sorbonne write a Dear John letter like a bad romance author? And how could she decide eleven days before their wedding to fly to another continent?

"Who moves to Australia? It's a bunch of scrub and marsupials." He tossed the paper in the garbage. "There's no decent culture and the weather is the same three hundred sixty-five days a year."

He glanced out the window at the rain falling on the Champs-Élysées and felt a sharp pain in his chest. He knew why she had decided to spend twenty-four hours in a pressurized airline cabin when they could be sharing the marble bathtub in their suite: because she had met the only person he had ever seen who was more beautiful than Celine herself, and she couldn't resist him.

HE OPENED THE bottle of scotch and sank onto the sofa. He really shouldn't cry, Celine would think it was unmanly. Then he remembered Celine was on her way to an Australian beach and a sob escaped his throat.

He filled his glass and gazed at the silver platter of mangoes and kiwis. He picked up a slice of melon and wondered if he would ever be hungry again.

NOW ALEC MOVED to the Regency desk and studied a sketch of Gus throwing a boomerang. It had been three days since Celine left. If that had been love, he never wanted to experience it again.

For the first time since he and Celine met, he was surprised that he felt completely normal. He was like a ship passenger who has survived a transatlantic voyage and finally reached solid ground.

He thought of all the things about Celine he missed: the way she peeled an orange and read the Sunday comics out loud. How she would overhear a conversation at a café and invent a story about the couple talking.

And God, he loved the way she stepped out of the shower and lathered her body with lotion. As if she didn't know that every move she made was like the most glorious ballet.

There was a knock at the door and he stood up to answer it.

"Here you are." Mathieu entered the suite. His brown hair was slicked back and he wore a wool overcoat. "I thought you might be walking into the Seine with rocks in your coat pocket." He glanced at Alec's smooth cheeks and freshly washed hair. "You look pretty good for someone who was left at the altar. I guess sleeping under thousand-thread-count sheets and eating room service cracked lobster does wonders for a broken heart."

"I wasn't left at the altar, we never made it to the church," Alec said irritably. "And I can't afford room service, I've been eating crackers and jam."

"I was afraid of that." He examined the empty preserve jars. "Helene suggested you join us for dinner. She's making Nicoise salad with hard-boiled eggs, and strawberry melba for dessert."

"As much as I enjoy the company of my best friend and his Cordon Bleu–trained wife, I'm not ready for an evening of discussing the joys of marital sex and the pregnant woman's libido." Alec sank onto a velvet love seat.

"Helene thought you would say that." He grinned. "She authorized me to take you to Le Reservoir in Montmartre. We're going to get drunk on pomegranate martinis."

"I'd as soon stand under strobe lights in a nightclub as lock myself into a prison cell in the Bastille."

"You can't stay here eating salted nuts, you have to get on

with your life," he replied. "It's Celine's loss. Helene says if she met you before we fell in love, she would have been smitten. You're good-looking and charming and you're the only man she knows who can hang a shower curtain."

"You and Helene are childhood sweethearts, she would have had to meet me in kindergarten." Alec's face broke into a smile. "You are a good friend, Mathieu. I don't know what I'd do without you."

Mathieu took off his overcoat and folded it over a brocade armchair.

"I'm not just here as your friend, I also came as your attorney."

"I see." Alec felt something hard press against his chest.

"In two weeks it will be the first anniversary of your father's death," he began. "You will be quite a wealthy man."

"Who goes parasailing at the age of sixty-five?" Alec's eyes glistened. "He should have celebrated his birthday like a normal Frenchman by eating beef bourguignon made with too much butter and drinking too many glasses of port."

"His doctor said his heart could have given out anywhere," Mathieu replied.

"Have you ever gazed down at the Mediterranean from six hundred feet?" Alec asked. "My mother tried to dissuade him. She told him the Greek myth about Icarus and he insisted it was perfectly safe. He said a ninety-year-old man went up the day before."

"Your father led a wonderful life. Two handsome children, a successful business, a beautiful house in Paris's most exclusive arrondissement."

"You forgot the two wives." Alec bristled. "The first one who deserted him and the second one whose stepdaughter never let her forget she wasn't the love of his life." His eyes narrowed. "Stepmothers are vilified, but stepdaughters can be worse. Was

it my mother's fault that Bettina's mother left my father for a farmer who lived in a thatched cottage like Mellors in *Lady Chatterley's Lover*?"

"Family histories can be as convoluted as abstract paintings at the Centre Pompidou." Mathieu shrugged. "But it doesn't change the law."

"Ah, yes, French inheritance laws." Alec walked to the bar and poured a glass of scotch. "It's no wonder the French are the most unfaithful race. What wife wants to devote thirty years of her life to a man, only to be kicked out into the street the moment he's dead?"

"The laws were created to protect the children," Mathieu explained. "And to dissuade mistresses of wealthy patrons from demanding a wedding ring."

"My mother was the most caring wife and mother," he sighed. "Bettina is behaving as if she was a stray dog that didn't work out."

"The law says you and Bettina inherit two-thirds of Alain's estate and your mother receives a third. She is allowed to live in the family home for a year after his death and then she must relinquish it to his children . . ." Mathieu paused. "Unless she gives up her portion of the estate in exchange for living there for the rest of her life. But then she couldn't afford to live in the house."

"You know that's all she wants. Forty Rue de Passy has been her home for thirty years." Alec fiddled with his glass. "She has her vegetable garden and rooms filled with Alain's favorite things. If she leaves, estate taxes will eat up her principal and she'll end up in a walk-up in Pigalle."

"Your father stipulated in his will that whichever child marries first could live in the house." Mathieu poured a glass of soda water. "He wanted the gardens filled with children playing on swings and catching butterflies."

"We wouldn't have lived there, I would never make my mother leave." Alec shook his head. "Celine's father gave her the flat on the Rue Saint-Honoré. It has a sunny front room that would have made a perfect nursery."

"Now Bettina has an equal claim." Mathieu sipped his water. "Alain's will is ironclad, you couldn't tear it apart with a crowbar."

"I can't imagine what Bettina will say when she discovers the wedding is canceled and she can evict my mother." Alec shuddered. "She'll be so happy, it will be like Santa Claus coming twice."

"You haven't told her the wedding is off?" Mathieu spluttered.

"I was waiting for the right moment." Alec shrugged. "Hopefully after she spent a thousand euros on her couture gown and designer shoes." He paused. "The only high point of Celine's defection would be to see my sister's face when she steps out of her mint-green Jaguar and realizes Cathédrale Notre-Dame is empty."

"But you told Helene and me the wedding was canceled." Mathieu frowned.

"How am I supposed to remember to call everyone?" Alec refilled his glass and sighed. "I suppose I couldn't stand Bettina gloating that Celine traded her ivory Oscar de la Renta wedding gown for a nylon swimsuit."

"Bettina can't be that bad," Mathieu insisted. "You are related and you're one of the most generous people I know."

"When I was five years old, I snuck downstairs early and opened my Christmas stocking. I reached inside and all I found was rocks." Alec downed his scotch. "The next day I discovered a packet of colored pencils and English toffees under Bettina's pillow. She had taken out my stocking stuffers and replaced them with rocks from the garden."

"Her mother left when she was three years old," Mathieu mused. "That couldn't have been easy."

"My mother tried so hard, once a month she took Bettina to the Ritz for afternoon tea." Alec paused. "I was quite jealous, I adored the petits fours and chocolate éclairs."

"Unless you find another woman to marry in the next two weeks, you have to tell her." Mathieu gathered his overcoat and walked to the door. "If you don't want to have dinner, I should go. I promised I'd bring Helene dill pickles and horseradish."

"I'm never getting married," Alec said. "I stuck my head in the mouth of the beast once and that was enough. I'll be the godfather who shows up with a football and lacrosse stick."

"You hate organized sports." Mathieu grinned. "You said at school you spent all your time doodling in your math book."

Alec glanced at Celine's diamond teardrop earring on the sideboard and grimaced. "I won't let my godson make the same mistakes. If I'd learned to play cricket, everything might be different."

ALEC SCOOPED UP a handful of Brazil nuts and picked up his colored pencil. It had been nice of Mathieu to stop by, but he didn't want to think about Bettina and the house on Rue de Passy.

He washed the nuts down with soda water and decided he really should go for a walk. He could stop in a café and have a plate of ratatouille and a bowl of café au lait.

But he had bought Isabel the glass of cognac, and even an espresso was ten euros on the Champs-Élysées. He thought fleetingly of giving up the suite and returning to his flat. But then his feet touched the white carpet and he remembered the steaming hot shower and wondered why he would trade a four-poster bed and marble bath for a fifth-floor walk-up.

He sat at the desk and drew Gus standing next to a guillotine. He sketched the wood scaffolding and pale faces in the crowd.

"You're drawing for bloody six-year-olds." He tossed it in the garbage. He selected a fresh sheet of paper and tried again.

chapter four

~∾~

Isabel inhaled the scent of dark coffee and fresh croissants and thought the Hôtel de Crillon really was beautiful. Everything about her suite was wonderful: the satin slippers she discovered in the closet and the wooden hairbrush on the dressing table and the silver platter of pastries and fruit salad that arrived at the door.

But she had woken up feeling slightly odd. As if she'd had a dream she couldn't remember. Now she picked up the phone and put it down. She was in Paris; there was no point in calling Neil to ask if he found his warm socks or took down the Christmas tree.

She opened her leather-bound journal and ran her fingers over a photo of an ivory satin wedding dress. The bodice had pink pearls and the veil was Venetian lace. She sat on the upholstered love seat and began to read.

Dear diary,
 Today I wished we decided to run off and get married in a chalet in Switzerland. Just a minister and Neil and me

wearing fur boots and saying, "I do!" Afterward we would drink schnapps by the fireplace and think we were so clever to skip the church with the huge urns of pink and white roses and the reception with five different entrées and a band that played long after you felt like dancing.

We've only been engaged for three months, but already I feel like we're behind in choosing the caterer and cake and flowers. And the date is more than a year away: we finally settled on a Christmas wedding!

This afternoon I was supposed to meet my mother at the Bijou bridal salon in Ardmore. Models would show us the latest designs by Nicole Miller and Yves Saint Laurent and there would be French champagne and hazelnut truffles.

But my presentation ran late and I couldn't break away to leave my mother a message. It would take weeks to get another appointment and I knew she'd be terribly disappointed.

I finally sent her a text and went home to the condo. Neil was working late, so I expected to heat up a bowl of pumpkin soup and flip through Martha Stewart Weddings.

But when I opened the front door, I smelled garlic and butter and roasted chicken. I entered the dining room and the glass table was set with a white linen tablecloth. There were flickering candles and a silver breadbasket.

"You're home." Neil appeared from the kitchen. His dark hair was brushed over his forehead, and he wore navy slacks and a white collared shirt. "I was afraid the spinach salad would wilt."

"What's this?" I waved at the crystal wineglasses and enamel soup tureens.

"Your mother called," Neil explained, taking my briefcase and setting it on the sideboard.

"She did?" I gulped, hoping she'd gotten my texts and wasn't still at the bridal salon. "What did she say?"

"She said it must be so stressful working and planning the wedding and she was sorry she suggested shopping on the Main Line. She's going to find a salon in the city and come and meet you."

"She said all that?" I whispered.

"She also said she hopes we are enjoying ourselves. The whole year shouldn't be about dress fittings and tastings and trying to pare down our guest list."

"Of course we're enjoying ourselves," I wavered, thinking about the dance lessons we needed to sign up for and honeymoon we should start planning and work files I hadn't opened on my computer.

"I decided we should spend one night eating a rosemary chicken and autumn vegetables and talking about books and movies," he continued, pouring two glasses of a Kenwood Chardonnay.

"Is that all we're going to do?" I laughed, feeling like a child who had been let out of school early.

"We're going to do a lot more than that." He kissed me. "But first we have to eat my roasted chicken."

Neil brought out plates of chicken and baked eggplant and scalloped potatoes. There were berries and whipped cream for dessert. My diamond ring glinted in the candlelight and I felt warm and happy.

Oh, diary, we're not getting married so I can wear a couture gown or so we can eat raspberry fondant wedding cake. We're in love and have so much fun together. It is a long time until next December, but I know we're going to enjoy every minute of it!

Isabel closed the notebook and walked to the window. She and Neil had seemed so perfect. When had things started

to go wrong? But she had made the right decision. She wouldn't have canceled the wedding if she hadn't been absolutely certain. Reading the journal was like rethinking a stock trade that had already happened. You had to trust you knew what you were doing, or you could never follow your instincts at all.

She pulled back the curtains and saw the wide boulevard and yellow taxis. She was in Paris and had the whole day ahead of her. She could walk across the Pont Alexandre III or take a tour of the gardens at the Royal Palace.

She ate a bite of a croissant and remembered receiving the glass bracelet and almost getting run over by the taxi. She pictured the fortune-teller saying she was going to fall in love and marry a French aristocrat. Of course, that's why she had trouble sleeping! Suddenly everything was as clear as a winter sky after a snowfall.

She walked to the closet and selected a cream blouse and navy slacks. She pulled on a wool jacket and leather boots.

"Always better to bring a gift." She grabbed a plate of croissants and closed the door behind her.

"DO YOU ALWAYS appear unannounced?" Alec asked when she knocked on the door. "You don't look like the kind of woman who shows up at her neighbor's door with fresh-baked cinnamon rolls."

"I haven't baked since I was a teenager." Isabel entered his suite. A fire flickered in the marble fireplace and there was a silver coffeepot and enamel demitasses. "My mother said cooking was as easy as following a recipe, but I was too impatient to preheat the oven. My oatmeal cookies always ended up with soft centers."

"I thought you dreamed of a big house in the suburbs with two children and a golden retriever." Alec raised his eyebrow.

"Not all mothers fill lunch boxes with crustless sandwiches and homemade blueberry muffins." She handed him a croissant. "I wanted to say thank you for carrying me back to the Crillon and buying me a drink."

"You paid for lunch at Fouquet's, we're even." He walked to the Regency desk. "If you'll excuse me, I'm working on a new sketch."

"Then why are the papers crumpled in the garbage?" she asked.

"I keep wanting to draw Gus doing something drastic," Alec sighed. "My readers don't mind if he slays dragons because they're not real. But this morning I almost drew Gus chopping off someone's head with a guillotine."

"You said you were getting over Celine." Isabel tried not to laugh. "You don't want to be with someone who isn't in love with you."

"It's a bit complicated." Alec ate a bite of croissant. "This is delicious. I almost forgot there's nothing better than Parisian pastries."

"And there's nowhere better than Paris." Isabel's eyes sparkled. "I slept wonderfully, and I woke up with an idea."

"I hope it doesn't involve tossing your shoe off the balcony or stepping in front of a taxi."

"Do you ever wake up and realize you figured out something in your sleep?" she continued. "The end of the novel you're reading, or a calculus problem you couldn't solve."

"I stopped doing math in sixth form," Alec said. "That's why they invented calculators and iPhones."

"I've always been able to do it. I'd go to sleep figuring out an equation and in the morning it would be worked out in my head," Isabel said.

"You should set up a booth in the Christmas market," Alec murmured. "You could charge ten euros to decipher people's dreams."

"Last night I went to sleep worrying about the fortune-teller's prediction." Isabel perched on a velvet love seat. "I can't spend my life walking around ladders or looking up to see if something is falling from the sky."

"I'm sure you're perfectly safe." Alec grinned. "She said you'd narrowly miss being killed and you were. She didn't say anything about a repeat performance."

"That's the thing." Isabel jumped up. "She was right about the glass bracelet and about almost being run over; she was probably right about the other thing."

"What other thing?" Alec felt suddenly nervous, as if there was a spider creeping up his leg.

"She said I'm going to fall in love with and marry a French aristocrat," Isabel exclaimed. "That's why I came to Paris, to fall in love! Now all I have to do is find a French aristocrat and everything will be perfect."

"That's the craziest thing I ever heard." He whistled. "Maybe you bumped your head when you hit the pavement. You should go back to bed with a hot compress and a bowl of chicken soup."

"Don't you see? I study the markets in Asia and Europe and then decide where my clients should put their money," Isabel continued. "JPMorgan Chase pays me a large salary to predict the future."

"By using graphs and algorithms, not by getting your palm read by a gypsy."

"Ever since I was a girl, I dreamed of a husband and children." She fiddled with a cushion. "I adore my career, but I don't want to wake up when I'm forty with a penthouse apartment and an empty guest room. But I've had the worst luck with men; I

can't seem to get it right. Maybe it's time to listen to someone else."

"Not to a woman wearing red slippers and a multicolored scarf," Alec spluttered.

"Why not? She was right about me receiving a gift and almost being killed. The chances are she is right about me falling in love with a French aristocrat."

"That sounds like it makes sense, but it doesn't." Alec rubbed his forehead. "Love is random, you can't order it up like a soufflé."

"I'm almost thirty, I spent the last two years eating rainbow trout and rib eye steak at wedding receptions at the Philadelphia Club and Rittenhouse Hotel," she began. "Now my mailbox is full of announcements with yellow ducks and blue soccer balls and baby names written in cursive. If I don't find a man and get married soon, I never will."

"I know what you mean, every couple I know is pregnant," Alec grumbled. "It makes you wonder if anyone listened in health class. All that talk about safe sex and abstinence was useless."

"Sometimes when I discover a new stock or see a dip in a foreign market, I know something big is going to happen," she mused. "It's like a sixth sense. I get a tingling in my fingers and it creeps through my whole body."

"That's carpal tunnel syndrome," he said. "I get the same thing when I hold a pencil too long."

"I have that feeling now," she continued. "I'm sure the fortune-teller is right, I just need to find a French aristocrat."

"That all sounds fine." Alec shrugged. "Why are you telling me?"

Isabel stood up and walked to the window. She gazed at the gold-and-silver Christmas tree in the Place de la Concorde. She turned around and her brown eyes sparkled.

"Because you're going to help me."

"Me?" Alec laughed. "How would I do that?"

"When I was looking for things to do in Paris, I read about the Red Cross charity ball," she explained. "It's held every year at the Petit Palais and it's the most important ball of the season. Tickets are two hundred euros and the attire is formal. It sounds glorious: men in white dinner jackets and women in glittering evening gowns and a sit-down dinner of veal sweetbreads and strawberry Chantilly for dessert." She paused. "I checked with the concierge and tickets are still available. You're going to take me."

"That's a month's rent!" he exclaimed. "And I'm a terrible dancer, I always step on my own foot."

"I can't go by myself," she insisted. "A single American tourist would be as welcome as a bad cold. I'll pay for the tickets. You must own a tuxedo, you were getting married."

"I did buy a white dinner jacket for the rehearsal dinner." Alec hesitated. "But you're not planning on spending four hundred euros on a few glasses of fizzy champagne and a plate of overcooked meat and buttery vegetables."

"It's an investment." Isabel's eyes were huge. "My whole future is riding on it."

"You're serious about this?"

"When I was in college, I took the Eurostar from Paris all the way to Vienna by myself. I'm perfectly capable of balancing a checkbook, and my father taught me how to change a tire." She paused. "But I can't make oatmeal for one person without burning the bottom of the pot, and whenever I throw only one pair of socks in the dryer, they never seem to dry. I might be old-fashioned, but everything is more fun when you share it with someone. I don't want to miss out."

"Everything does seem to come in pairs. The maid left two hazelnut truffles on the pillows even though Celine's side of the

bed is empty," he sighed. "All right, I'll do it. But I'm not staying past midnight. I have to catch up on sleep or I'll never finish drawing Gus fighting a shark on the Great Barrier Reef."

"I thought you weren't going to have Gus swim in the ocean." Isabel frowned.

He stuck a pencil behind his ear. "I changed my mind."

ISABEL STROLLED DOWN the Boulevard Haussmann and stopped in front of a stone facade. She glanced at the striped awnings and thought of all the afternoons she'd spent browsing in Le Printemps during her semester in Paris. It was the most beautiful department store she had ever seen, with creamy turrets and a slate-gray roof.

Now she paused in front of a window with a mannequin perched on an elephant. The plastic figure wore an orange sweater and khaki slacks and carried a pair of binoculars. The mannequins in the next window were dressed in chiffon evening gowns. Silver balloons were scattered over the floor and a gold ball hung from the ceiling.

She entered the double glass doors and gazed at marble counters filled with bright lipsticks and expensive lotions. Salesgirls wore ribbed sweaters and pencil-thin skirts, and she remembered when she first came to Paris and wondered how the women all looked like racehorses when the croissants were so buttery and the café au laits were frothy.

She took the escalator to the fourth floor and entered the Givenchy boutique. There was a stack of pastel-colored pashminas, and suddenly she remembered the first time she met Rory, at the Saks in Bala Cynwyd. She had just graduated from Wharton and was staying with her parents until she started working at JPMorgan Chase.

She stroked the soft cashmere and thought it was easier to

think about Rory; her engagement to Neil was too recent. It was like when you burned your hand on the stove and thought it was fine. It was only when you typed on your computer or tied your running shoes, you realized you were in pain.

But Rory! It was so long ago, like a romantic movie you loved but couldn't remember the ending. They had been so young, and he looked like a film star with his blond curly hair and wide shoulders. She picked up the pashmina and remembered his green eyes and smile that could light up a room.

ISABEL SIFTED THROUGH a rack of cotton dresses. It was early summer and she was staying with her parents in Ardmore. The weather was humid and she needed light dresses and sandals. She looked up and saw a man examining a pile of pashminas.

"Which do you prefer?" He looked up. "The turquoise is a little bright, but the pale pink looks like a packet of cotton candy."

"It depends on your girlfriend's coloring," Isabel replied. "The turquoise is pretty on a blonde, but the pink could make her look washed out."

"It's for my mother. Her hair is that color that's impossible to describe but is the result of a monthly appointment at John Frieda in New York." He paused and looked at Isabel. "Perhaps you could model them and help me decide."

"Do you really expect me to drape a pashmina around my shoulders and twirl around like a runway model?" Isabel laughed.

"I didn't ask you to twirl. And I'm sure you'd make an excellent runway model." He studied her long legs. "You'd be doing me a favor. My mother's sixtieth birthday party is tonight and I haven't got a present. I've been on assignment and I only got back in town this morning."

"That sounds exciting. Do you work for the CIA like a character in *Homeland*?" Isabel asked.

"Society columnist for the *Philadelphia Inquirer*," he corrected. "It ranks only slightly higher than the obituary page. But I grew up on the Main Line, so I don't spell anyone's name wrong." He fiddled with his collar. "Spelling is important, no one wants to read their name with a missing *y* or an extra *e*."

"Shouldn't you buy her something more summery?" Isabel suggested. "These linen blazers are lovely and the floral dresses are beautiful."

"I wouldn't dare buy a woman actual clothing." He shuddered. "If you buy it too small, you are implying there has been a recent weight gain. And if you buy a size too large, you didn't notice the regime of vegetable smoothies paid off and now she's a size six. I only buy wraps and purses."

"It sounds like you have a lot of experience." Isabel's cheeks flushed. "Why didn't you bring your girlfriend to help you decide?"

"I don't have a girlfriend, I don't even own a cat. I'm sort of the prodigal son." He moved around the display table. "Youngest child of a prominent steel family. The oldest, Brian, has an office next to my father, and the middle child, Emmy, is married to a junior senator. Tabitha disappeared to Oregon after her Smith graduation and my parents worried she'd joined a commune. But she showed up at Thanksgiving engaged to a senior executive at Microsoft." He grinned, and Isabel noticed his eyes were the color of emeralds.

"That leaves me, doted on as a child for my blond curls and ability to run. Attended Milton Academy and had a brush with fame when I was state cross-country champion. But I realized I couldn't make running a career and turned down acceptance to Brown. I ended up at Marlboro College in Vermont." He looked at Isabel. "I don't know what was worse, the endless

green fields or the white cheeses. The minute I got my diploma, I moved into my parents' pool house." He smiled mischievously. "Other young men have John Glenn or Babe Ruth as their heroes, mine is Benjamin Braddock in *The Graduate*. I'm waiting for someone to tell me what my future is."

"It's not writing the society column at the *Philadelphia Inquirer*?" Isabel tried not to laugh.

"I never thought I could get tired of liver pâté or buttercream filling," he sighed. "But it seems I have a limit."

"My mother adores Chanel silk scarves." Isabel picked up a teal scarf. "You can wear them during the day with a two-piece suit or at night with an evening gown."

"Done," the man exclaimed. He studied Isabel's diamond earrings and Tiffany locket and suddenly his eyes sparkled. "Would you come with me? The Radnor Hunt Club is the oldest foxhunting club in the country. The chef prepares a delicious grilled venison and they have a cellar of vintage French wines."

"You want me to be your date?" Isabel exclaimed. "I don't even know your name."

"Rory Danford." He held out his hand. "It really would help, an odd number at the dinner table can be awkward."

"Did you say the party is at the Hunt Club?" she asked.

"Yes, my family has been members for almost a hundred years."

"I'm Isabel Lawson and I'm already invited," she replied, a smile flickering across her face. "Our mothers are co-chairwomen of the Ardmore garden committee."

ISABEL STOOD IN the paneled ballroom and gazed at the ivory tablecloths set with bone-white china and yellow calla lilies. A sixteen-piece band stood in the corner and silver lights twinkled above the dance floor. She fiddled with her ruby necklace

and wondered why she'd agreed to attend Peggy Danford's party.

Her parents received dozens of invitations and she rarely accompanied them. And she'd promised herself she wasn't going to think about dating until she finished her trainee session at Chase. There would be plenty of time to meet men after she secured a position as junior analyst.

"Here you are," Rory said as he approached her. He wore a white dinner jacket and his blond hair touched his collar. "It's so crowded, I couldn't find you."

"What a wonderful party, all the women look beautiful." Isabel gazed at women wearing satin evening gowns and Jackie O–style dresses.

"I hadn't noticed." Rory studied her red cocktail dress and silver sandals, and his eyes were suddenly serious. "I've been standing at the bar, asking Oscar to refresh my martini and waiting for you to walk through the door."

"What would happen then?" Isabel asked, feeling as if she'd forgotten to button a button.

He put his martini glass on the bar and took her hand. He led her onto the dance floor and put his arm around her waist.

"I'd wait for the band to play 'What a Wonderful World,' " he murmured. "And then I'd never let you go."

THEY STOOD ON the porch and gazed at the green fields and thick hedges. It was early evening and a dew was forming on the grass. Isabel sipped chilled champagne and inhaled Rory's cologne and felt almost giddy.

"It is one of the most beautiful spots in Chester County." Rory rested his elbows on the deck. "It's too bad most of the members enjoy it holding a shotgun. I don't think my father has ever forgiven me for not enjoying hunting. I love a juicy burger

and have a weakness for rib eye steak, but I try not to picture my dinner racing through the fields, being followed by men on horseback."

"I know what you mean," Isabel sighed. "I guess our fore-fathers didn't have the luxury of spending their leisure time playing video games or watching movies."

"I think it's more that men love competition." Rory frowned. "From the moment we enter preschool, we are trying to get ahead. My mother was furious when my teacher promoted Johnny Pearce to be a penguin, while I was left being a zebra." His face broke into a smile. "Personally, I'm quite content to sit by the pool with a thick book and a bottle of Coke."

"Don't you think about a career?" Isabel asked.

"Should I?" Rory turned to her.

"Everyone does." Isabel was suddenly flustered. "You have to build something, that's what's important."

"My contribution isn't going to make a dent in the family coffers." Rory shrugged. "We have the thirty-room estate in Ardmore and ski cabin in the Poconos. I couldn't use up my trust if I bought a Jaguar once a month and spread caviar on my morn-ing toast."

"My parents provided me with everything I needed, but that doesn't mean I don't want to achieve things of my own," Isabel insisted.

"What sort of things?" Rory asked.

"The important things," Isabel said hotly. "A career and a happy home and a family."

"Are you saying it's more noble to sit in an office than read Thackeray by the pool?"

"Well, yes." Isabel nodded. "You have to have a reason to get up in the morning."

"I have plenty of reasons. To eat my mother's Belgian waf-fles and stand under a hot shower and watch Jimmy Fallon on

late-night television." He put his hand under her chin. "And right now I have the best reason of all. I'm standing next to the most beautiful woman at the party and have an irresistible urge to kiss her."

Isabel knew she shouldn't let him kiss her—he was completely opposite from everything she looked for in a man—but his cheeks were golden brown and his hair was soft and when his lips touched hers she shivered.

She kissed him back and tasted coq au vin and champagne. He put his hand on the small of her back, and suddenly she forgot about getting her final grades from Wharton and finding an apartment to rent in the city. She wanted to stand on the stone porch with the band playing "At Last" and kiss him again.

"We should go inside." He pulled away finally. "I can't run off with my date and miss my mother's party."

"I'm not your date," Isabel said stiffly, afraid to read too much into the kiss. "I came with my parents."

"We'll have to fix that. I'll introduce you to my mother." He kissed her again. "She'll be thrilled to meet the girl I'm going to marry."

ISABEL GAZED AT the rack of Givenchy dresses and thought about the Red Cross charity ball. It was nice of Alec to take her—he hardly knew her at all. But she was paying for the tickets, and he couldn't mope around his suite forever.

She remembered him saying love was impossible and knew he was wrong. Being in love was like diving into a pool on a hot summer's day. There was nothing better than the sudden rush and cool water.

The summer with Rory, they couldn't get enough of each other. It was the beginning of August and they had spent the

last three weeks lying in the garden and eating corn on the cob and slices of fresh watermelon.

"We can't go on like this," Rory said, blocking out the sun. It was late afternoon and Isabel was stretched out on a chaise longue with a damp paperback book and glass of iced tea.

"You're the one who said there's nothing noble about working." Isabel gazed at his broad shoulders and tan chest. "I don't report to JPMorgan Chase for twenty-nine days and I haven't finished the first of Elena Ferrante's Neapolitan novels."

"I work every day," Rory said, suddenly irritable. "I can't help it if my job description involves nibbling mini quiches with congressmen and reporting what Buffy Stuyvesant wore to the Fireman's Ball."

"I'm not complaining." Isabel smiled, remembering his mouth on hers. "I'm quite enjoying myself."

"Well, I want something more." He perched on the chaise.

"You do?" Isabel's heart hammered. They hadn't talked about the end of the summer, but Isabel knew she'd be working too much to drive out to Ardmore. And she couldn't imagine Rory drinking Singapore slings with earnest young analysts who tried to see who could rack up the most overtime hours.

He untied her bikini top and ran his fingers over her breasts. His fingers moved farther down her body, and Isabel felt like she had been jolted by an electric current.

"I want this." He leaned forward and kissed her. One hand brushed her bikini bottom and she caught her breath.

"Not here," she murmured. "Someone might see us."

He picked her up and carried her into the pool house. Isabel stood with her legs apart and her hands pressed against the wall. He undid her bikini top and kissed his way from her neck down the middle of her back. She gasped and turned around and kissed him.

"God, I've never wanted anything more in my life," he moaned, drawing her onto the bed.

She lay on the cotton sheets and watched him strip off his board shorts. His cheeks were chiseled and his chest was toned and he looked like Leonardo DiCaprio in *Titanic*.

He kissed her hair and her neck and her breasts. She felt the waves build until her whole body trembled. She waited for him to carry her over the edge and suddenly he paused.

"Wait for me," he whispered into her ear. "Let's do this together."

She clung to his back and he picked up speed. His chest pressed against her breasts and she felt his slick thighs on her legs and suddenly the warmth became a bright light and her body dissolved in an exquisite release.

The sun streamed through the French doors and Isabel listened to his even breathing. Was it really so terrible that he didn't aspire to carry a briefcase or work in an office? Weren't you supposed to love someone because he made you laugh, not because of his job title?

Her body pulsed and she knew she wasn't thinking clearly. She closed her eyes and thought she'd worry about it in the morning.

ISABEL LOOKED UP and flushed, as if other shoppers could tell she'd been thinking about Rory. Maybe this whole idea was ridiculous; she should give up on falling in love and finding a husband. It hadn't worked out with Neil, and she had been sure they were perfect for each other. She should be content with her career and trips to Europe or the Caribbean.

She didn't know anything about the French aristocracy besides what she had learned in her college French courses. What

would she even talk about without getting names and dates wrong and admitting she had never felt much sympathy for Louis XVI and Marie Antoinette?

But then she remembered the glass bracelet and screeching taxi and smell of burning rubber. The fortune-teller had been right about her receiving a gift and almost being killed, and she was right about her falling in love. Isabel was as certain as when she had discovered a correction in the price of artichokes and knew it would lead to big returns for her investors.

"Oh, this is gorgeous," Isabel said aloud, recognizing a dress she had seen in *Vogue*. It was a striped taffeta and had been featured in the runway shows in Milan.

"Nobody buys a dress that was worn on the runway," a woman said.

Isabel looked up and saw a glamorous woman wearing yellow wool slacks and a cropped sweater. Ruby earrings dangled from her ears and she had a French accent.

"They don't?" Isabel asked.

"The designers slap on price tags they couldn't imagine in their wet dreams," she explained. "And the clothes are outrageous— have you ever seen a woman walking down the street in a silver lamé dress held together by paper clips?"

"Well, no . . ." Isabel hesitated.

"Valentino and Yves Saint Laurent and Tom Ford all do the same thing," she continued. "They fill the runways with outfits they wouldn't put on their standard poodles so when a woman discovers the designer's other dresses—the green tulle that costs double her clothing allowance—she feels like she got a bargain." She held up a teal dress with a pleated skirt. "She buys a diamond pin or a bottle of perfume because she saved so much money, and everyone is happy."

"I'm guessing her husband isn't happy," Isabel laughed.

"No French husband is happy when his wife comes home with bags from Le Printemps." She shrugged. "But that is the price of sending one's wife out with a charge card."

"I need a gown for the Red Cross charity ball and I don't know where to start. I bought the most gorgeous Vera Wang for my wedding and a Nina Ricci dress for our honeymoon, but this is different," Isabelle explained. "There will be dozens of women at the ball, I need to stand out."

"When are you getting married?" the woman asked.

"Oh, I'm not getting married. We called off the wedding because we couldn't agree about anything," Isabel said. "I gave the dress to a consignment store and came to Paris by myself. Now I'm going to the Red Cross charity ball to find a new husband."

"What did you say?" the woman raised her eyebrow.

"I know it sounds silly, but I have it on good authority that I'm going to fall in love with a French aristocrat and I need to look the part." She studied the woman's elegant pumps and gold bracelet. "Will you help me?"

"Help you buy a dress to find a husband . . ." The woman frowned. "You can't really believe in love at first sight?"

"I tried every other kind of love. The handsome dilettante you meet in your last semester of business school, only to discover that love and lust are two different things. The man you are so positive you are going to spend the rest of your life with, you start dreaming about a house with an enormous kitchen and a pantry filled with jars of Skippy peanut butter—" She stopped and her eyes glistened. "Until three days before the wedding you realize your goals are worlds apart and you tell the florist to donate the flowers to charity and end up in Paris at Christmastime by yourself." She stroked a gauze dress. "This time I'm going to get it right, but I need help."

"I'm sure one of the salesgirls will assist you." The woman glanced at her watch. "I have an appointment."

"In Philadelphia the only object of a winter coat is to keep you warm; in Paris every woman dresses like Marion Cotillard," Isabel pleaded. "I want to find something sexy and sophisticated that only a Frenchwoman would wear."

"I suppose I have a few minutes," she wavered, and a smile crossed her face. "You do have a wonderful neck, I think you'd look fabulous in Givenchy."

Moving from boutique to boutique, Isabel tried on Lanvin and Balenciaga and Dolce and Gabbana. She stepped out of the dressing room in a red Oscar de la Renta gown. One shoulder was bare and the fabric was the softest silk.

"That's the one," the woman exclaimed. "You look like Audrey Hepburn in *Breakfast at Tiffany's*."

"But she wore a black cocktail dress." Isabel frowned, turning around.

"A dress isn't about the color or the fit. It's about how it makes you feel," she replied. "I see a beautiful woman who is about to discover her powers of attraction."

Isabel gazed in the mirror and thought her hair looked shiny and her skin was creamy and the light freckles on her nose almost disappeared.

"I see her too, I'll take it." She hugged her chest and her eyes sparkled. "Now, where will I find a pair of stilettos?"

She paid for her purchases and waited while the salesgirl lined boxes with tissue paper. She turned around and noticed the woman walking to the escalator.

"I didn't thank you!" Isabel ran after her. "Can I buy you an espresso or pastry?"

"Another time," she called back. "I have a lunch date, I have to go."

Isabel clutched her packages and watched the woman run onto the boulevard.

"People say the French are rude," she said aloud, stepping onto the escalator. "But I think they are the nicest people in the world."

ISABEL SAT IN a booth in the Brasserie Printemps and nibbled an almond-milk brioche with blueberry cream. She gazed up at the blue mosaic dome and the view of the Eiffel Tower and wondered why anyone would want to be anywhere else.

Why couldn't she marry a French aristocrat and live in Paris? JPMorgan Chase had branches all over Europe.

They would fly to Philadelphia every Christmas and celebrate with her parents. In the summer she'd invite her mother and father to their château in Provence and they'd eat fondue and local cheeses.

She tore apart the brioche and thought Paris really was a magical city. First Alec rescued her from the balcony and then the fortune-teller predicted her future and now a strange woman appeared in the department store and chose the perfect ball gown. She tasted blueberry and almonds and thought all you had to do was believe in love: everything else would follow.

chapter five

❧

Alec fiddled with his bow tie and sank onto the blue velvet love
seat. It had been the most disastrous day, and now he had to
dress for the Red Cross charity ball.

Why on earth had he said yes? He'd as soon visit the dentist.
But Isabel had been determined and he felt somehow responsi-
ble for her. Isabel wouldn't have met the fortune-teller if they
hadn't explored the Christmas markets.

He thought briefly of calling the front desk and asking for
a suite on the sixth floor. There would be no answer when Isabel
knocked on his door. But what if she searched the whole hotel
until she found him? He couldn't explain why he'd switched
suites without lying or hurting her feelings.

He scooped up a handful of pistachios and thought about
Mathieu's visit. He knew he should tell Bettina the wedding was
canceled, but every time he pictured her smug smile a pit formed
in his stomach.

He picked up a sketch of Gus wearing scuba gear and
thought if only it was as easy to solve his own problems as it
was for Gus to discover a treasure chest. He could beg Bettina

to let Claudia stay in their father's house. But she was as likely to do as he asked as Santa Claus was to land in the Place de la Concorde.

Mathieu said he should find someone else to marry, but that was impossible. Celine had broken his heart and wounded his pride and depleted his bank account. He would as soon go down that road again as lie under a guillotine.

The first time Celine and Bettina met was at the house on the Rue de Passy. Celine insisted she meet his whole family and he grudgingly set up a luncheon. It was early summer and he wore a blue blazer and tan slacks. He drove through the iron gates and saw Bettina's Jaguar in the driveway and shuddered.

"DARLING," HIS MOTHER called, standing on the stone steps. She wore a floral dress and held two bottles of wine. "I was just down in the wine cellar. I can't decide whether to serve a Pétrus Merlot or Château Latour Bordeaux."

"I'll drink them both," Alec grumbled, opening Celine's car door.

Celine and his mother had met over afternoon tea at the Ritz and hit it off. Celine admired Claudia's vintage Hermès clutch, and Claudia gushed over Celine's taste in shoes.

"Don't be silly, it's going to be a lovely afternoon." Claudia kissed Alec and Celine on both cheeks. "I made *boeuf bourguignon* and summer squash and apple flan for dessert."

"I'm not concerned about the food, I'm worried about the company." Alec followed his mother into the foyer. "Did Bettina bring Schatzi, her miniature schnauzer, or does she plan on doing the biting and snapping herself?"

"Your sister is excited to meet Celine." Claudia straightened a vase of calla lilies. "She and Édouard are waiting in the grand salon."

Alec ran his hands through his hair and thought Édouard was part of the problem. He and Bettina had been dating for four years, but he was no closer to proposing than he had ever been. Bettina always had an excuse: he'd just completed his residency; he worked twenty-four-hour rotations at the hospital.

But now Édouard was an established neurosurgeon with a practice in the eighth arrondissement and an apartment near the Palais Bourbon. He took six weeks' annual vacation and bought Bettina sapphire earrings for her birthday.

Alec walked to the bar and poured a glass of scotch. He downed it quickly and thought he would go to church every Sunday if they made it through the entrée without Bettina offending Celine. He pictured Celine tossing the diamond ring on her salad plate and wished he were home eating a bowl of cereal.

The grand salon was scattered with paisley sofas and Louis XIV chairs. Oriental rugs were stretched over wood floors and a crystal chandelier hung from the ceiling.

Claudia kept the bar stocked with the finest liqueurs and the cigar box filled with cigars, as if Alain would appear any minute and hand her his briefcase and demand a glass of sherry.

His father had been loud and sometimes rude, but he loved his family. Alec remembered admitting he wanted to go to art school instead of following his father into the business and his father examining his sketches and saying who was he to judge what would make his son happy. He was halfway down the hall when his father called out to him.

"The sketches are very good, you must get your talent from your mother."

NOW ALAIN WAS dead and had left his family in a mess. His mother would have to leave the ornate dining room with its

mahogany table and faded tapestries. The kitchen had never been remodeled, but Claudia loved drinking creamy coffee in the breakfast nook and filling the enamel vases with cut flowers.

If only he had accepted his father's offer of an allowance when he turned twenty-one. He didn't want to be like Bettina, living in a chic apartment he couldn't pay for himself. But he could have saved that money and offered it to his mother now. How was he to know that Alain would write in his will that 40 Rue de Passy went to his children and Claudia would have nowhere to live?

"There you are," Bettina said. Her brown hair was cut in a pageboy, and she had long red fingernails. "You've grown your hair, I thought you were the pool boy."

"Celine likes it." Alec touched his hair. "And it saves money at the barber."

"I've always thought long hair was for boys." Bettina nibbled a mushroom quiche. "Like in that book your mother read when we were children. It was so silly, but you adored it." She paused and looked at Alec. "No wonder you grew up to be an illustrator."

"*Peter Pan* is one of the most beloved children's books," Alec spluttered. "I'd give anything for Gus to affect children the way I was influenced by Tinker Bell and Captain Hook." He took Celine's hand. "Celine, this is my sister Bettina and her boyfriend, Édouard."

Bettina studied Celine's blond chignon and high cheekbones. She wore a yellow crepe dress and silver sandals.

"It's a pleasure to meet you. Alec never mentioned you and now he's engaged." Bettina looked pointedly at Celine's small waist. "Unless there's a reason for a hasty wedding."

"I didn't mention Celine because we rarely see each other besides Christmas and birthdays." Alec refreshed his drink.

"And the wedding won't be until Christmas. At which time Celine will wear a wedding dress with a twenty-six-inch waist." He downed the scotch. "If you'll excuse us, I promised I'd show her the rose garden before lunch."

"YOU DON'T HAVE to speak for me as if I'm a department store dummy," Celine said as they strolled through the garden. "And I've seen your mother's roses."

"We'll go back inside, I just needed to cool off." Alec loosened his collar. "Bettina makes me feel like a schoolboy."

"You're acting like one," Celine retorted. "It's not very sexy."

"I was afraid . . ." Alec glanced at Celine's violet eyes and full lips, and his voice trailed off. How could he tell her he was terrified Bettina would say something to threaten their engagement?

He ran his hands through his hair and thought he was acting like a frightened puppy. The most spectacular woman in Paris had agreed to be his wife and nothing was going to stop them.

"I was afraid she'd ask to be your maid of honor and you wouldn't know how to refuse," he said weakly. "I'm sure you have your own idea for attendants."

"Your sister would be as likely to stand behind the bride as the prime minister would be to attend our wedding." Celine's face softened and she kissed him. "Now let's relieve your mother of that bottle of Pétrus Merlot."

THEY SAT AT the long table and ate leek soup and Nicoise salad. There was a Limoges platter of potato salad and creamed cauliflower.

"You hardly need a full set of china," Bettina mused, cradling her wineglass. "You should sell some pieces at Sotheby's. They would fetch a good price."

"Your father loved giving dinner parties." Claudia buttered a baguette. "I would never part with the china."

"It will be hard to find an apartment big enough to fit twelve soup tureens," Bettina continued. "And the style is so old-fashioned, the whole house needs to be updated. One of Édouard's patients is an interior decorator. I'll ask him about replacing the carpets, they're quite dusty and I'm prone to hay fever."

"It's only June," Alec interrupted. "Claudia can live here until January and then . . ."

"We can discuss this later." Claudia stood up and turned to Celine. "I made ratatouille with tomatoes from the garden. Perhaps you can help me bring out the plates."

"PERSONALLY I THINK a spring wedding is nicer," Bettina said when they were all eating cream of potato soup. "You can take photos in the Luxembourg Gardens and drive away in a Bentley convertible."

"Celine's father's sixtieth birthday is New Year's Eve," Alec explained, wishing the lump in his throat would disappear so he could enjoy the mushrooms in wine sauce. "We're going to have a double celebration."

"We'll have to cancel our vacation." Bettina turned to Celine. "Every year Édouard and I go to Mustique the day after Christmas. Paris can get tedious with the tourists trampling through the Place Vendôme. Mustique has white sand beaches and colorful restaurants. Basil's Bar is built on stilts and serves a delicious rum punch."

"We used to go to Mustique every January," Celine replied.

"My parents have a house overlooking Britannia Bay. It's not elaborate like Mick's, but you can see the tortoises and coral reefs."

"Mick?" Bettina asked.

"Mick Jagger. He and my father play checkers." Celine smiled. "He says he lets Mick win, but my father has always been a terrible loser."

"Alec never told me how you met," Bettina said, suddenly changing the subject.

"At a gallery opening." Alec squeezed Celine's hand. "My publisher sent me to rub elbows with the upscale clientele."

He wished he'd made up a secret code with Celine—her cat was ill and they had to go home and give her medicine—so they could leave. A silver coffeepot stood on the sideboard, and Alec thought they'd have to get through dessert and, if they were really unlucky, a glass of his father's aged cognac.

"How interesting." Bettina studied Celine's long eyelashes. "Are you an artist's model?"

Celine's eyes darkened and Alec wished he could crawl under the table.

"Celine is a translator for the United Nations. She's trying to teach me Afrikaans." Alec drained his wineglass. "But I've always been all thumbs when it comes to languages."

"BETTINA TALKS TO Celine as if she were one of those wedding Barbies you see in the children's section of Le Bon Marché," Alec groaned, taking a bowl of whipped cream from the fridge.

Claudia had asked for help with the apple flan and Alec jumped at the chance. Celine was in the powder room, and Alec was afraid if he was alone with Bettina and Édouard he would do something drastic.

"It went fine, they even have something in common." Claudia

sprinkled powdered sugar onto white plates. "They both have vacationed on Mustique."

"How could she ask if Celine is an artist's model?" Alec demanded. "Just because Celine has a body Degas would have loved doesn't mean she spends her days draped in velvet and eating grapes."

"You thought she was a model when you met," Claudia reminded him.

"I'm a man, we're born to make mistakes. Bettina has a degree in medieval history from the Sorbonne," he sighed. "Not that she's ever used it except to boast about her knowledge of the Crusades."

"Bettina thinks it is silly to have a career when they are going to get married and start a family," Claudia replied.

"Somebody better inform Édouard," Alec muttered and his eyes were serious. "I don't know why you defend her. She treats you like an unwelcome guest in your own home."

"She was a child when her mother left." Claudia shrugged. "And she is right. The house belongs mainly to you and her."

"If Celine and I get married by January third, you won't have to leave," Alec said slowly. "Alain's will says that whichever child gets married first has control of the house."

"Of course I'll leave—40 Rue de Passy is the perfect place for a family," Claudia insisted. "You'll fill the nursery with Enid Blyton and the Hardy Boys mysteries. On weekends you'll cook strawberry crepes and the children will bring in daffodils and get mud all over the wood floor." She paused. "You'll start to say 'When will you learn to wipe your feet?' and then you'll inhale the scent of baby shampoo and fresh cut flowers and realize you wouldn't have it any other way."

"You belong here," Alec insisted. "Celine's father gave her an apartment on the Rue Saint-Honoré that is steps from the

Tuileries Gardens. If we run out of bedrooms we'll buy a flat on a leafy street in Saint-Germain-des-Prés."

"I do love this house," Claudia sighed. "When I sit in the library, I can still hear your father yelling at the politicians on the television. No matter who was elected prime minister, he always wanted someone else . . ." She hesitated. "I hope your sudden marriage has nothing to do with Bettina and me."

"Of course not. Marriage is the most impossible institution," Alec scoffed. "What chance does love have when every day you are presented with land mines: When are you supposed to take out the garbage? Did she ask you to pick up a jar of mustard or salad dressing? Who would want to spend their life with the person they want to please most?"

"Then why are you getting married?" Claudia asked.

Alec pictured the way Celine ate spaghetti without getting sauce on her napkin. When she stepped onto the boulevard, taxis lined up to pick her up. And when he caught sight of her reading a magazine at the newsagent, he wondered who this exquisite creature was until he moved closer and realized she was his.

Alec clutched the bowl of whipped cream. "Because I can't do anything else."

THEY RETURNED TO the dining room and ate apple flan and berries and whipped cream. Bettina and Celine discovered they both got their hair done at Christophe Robin on the Rue de Rivoli and had the same art history professor at the Sorbonne.

Alec glanced at his watch and thought they could say their good-byes. Édouard looked like he needed a nap and his mother enjoyed watching the BBC on Sunday afternoons.

"I really don't understand," Bettina said, stirring cream into a Limoges demitasse.

"Don't understand what?" Alec asked.

Bettina turned to Celine and her lips were pursed. "What you could possibly see in Alec."

"HOW DARE SHE say that?" Alec bristled, taking off his blazer.

It was early evening and they were standing in Celine's living room. Alec had walked straight to the bar and poured a large sherry.

"Say what?" Celine slipped off her sandals.

"That she doesn't know what you see in me. I may not perform cerebrovascular surgery like Édouard, but Gus influences the lives of children in sixteen countries," Alec replied. "Yesterday I got a letter from a boy in Guam who wasn't allowed to have a dog so he named his hamster Gus. He's teaching him how to play fetch."

"A hamster can't play fetch," Celine laughed.

"That's the point, Gus isn't just a children's book. It's a springboard for their imagination." His eyes flickered. "They read about Gus fighting bulls in Pamplona or parasailing in the Maldives and realize they can do anything."

"I'm going to bed," Celine announced. "I have to be at work early."

"But it's only seven PM," Alec protested, watching her take off her diamond earrings.

He clutched his glass and thought Bettina wasn't the only one acting like a child. He behaved as if she still had the power to deprive him of the last vanilla custard. It didn't matter what Bettina said; he and Celine were madly in love.

He followed her into the bedroom and closed the door. He walked over to her and kissed her.

"What are you doing?" she asked.

"That dress has a difficult zipper," he whispered. "I'm going to help you take it off."

He unzipped her dress and slipped the other hand around her waist. His fingers explored the warm flesh at the top of her thigh, and suddenly Bettina and 40 Rue de Passy disappeared like a genie's bottle. God! She was sweet and wet, and when he slid his fingers inside her, her whole body shuddered.

He caressed her, pulling her against his chest. Celine cried out and he lifted her up and wrapped her legs around his thighs. She leaned down and kissed him and he thought any minute he would explode.

"I love you," he whispered. "You're the only thing that matters."

"I love you too," she murmured, a small moan escaping her lips.

He laid her down on the floral bedspread and unbuttoned his shirt. She unsnapped her bra and her breasts were two golden pieces of fruit. Alec slipped off her silk panties and slid inside her and she clung to his back. He slowed his rhythm until Celine whispered his name and then he picked up speed and they came together in one dizzying thrust.

The sky outside the window was pink and purple, and Alec draped his arm around Celine's waist. Was there anything as terrible and magical as love? And once you found it, could you ever live without it?

NOW ALEC ATE another handful of pistachio nuts and wondered why he was even thinking about Celine; she was in a different hemisphere. But if he called Bettina, he would have to explain why Celine left. Bettina would purr like a kitten with a warm bowl of milk.

He straightened his bow tie and heard a knock on the door.

He opened it and saw an unfamiliar figure in a red satin gown. Her hair was knotted in a chignon and she wore long white gloves.

"Hello," he said uncertainly.

"That's not a very enthusiastic welcome." Isabel smiled, entering the room.

"It's you," Alec gasped. "I didn't recognize you."

"Were you expecting another woman to go dancing with?" Isabel glanced at his white dinner jacket and tan slacks.

"Of course not, I don't want to go dancing at all." Alec bristled, studying her slender shoulders. "You just look different, like a movie poster."

"Do you think the gloves are too much?" Isabel asked and laughed. "The woman was right. The price tag on this dress was less than the ones in the window, so I thought I was getting a bargain. The gloves are Italian silk and were only an extra fifty euros. I felt like I came out ahead."

"What woman?" Alec walked to the desk.

"I met a strange woman in the couture section of Le Printemps. She said no one buys the designs in the window. They're overpriced and the styles are outrageous," Isabel explained. "She showed me the dresses in the back and said this Oscar de la Renta was perfect."

"It is lovely," Alec admitted.

"She was like a fairy godmother." Isabel's brown eyes sparkled. "I looked in the mirror and knew I couldn't wear anything else."

"First you believe in fortune-tellers and now you have a fairy godmother." Alec frowned. "You're the most unlikely financial analyst."

"Being an analyst is all about hunches and superstitions." Isabel fiddled with her diamond clip. "I know an analyst who wore a striped tie on the day the stock market crashed, so he

refuses to wear a striped tied again." She paused. "It's only the numbers that are constant. How they end up on the screen is a combination of magic and voodoo."

"I'll remember that if I ever hire a stockbroker," Alec laughed.

"Is this your latest drawing?" Isabel stood at the desk. "Gus looks very pleased with himself."

"He just discovered a treasure chest and he's going to give the jewels to the local children." Alec picked up the drawing. "Except to the boys who play cricket, they have their pressed white slacks and shiny black balls. They don't need anything else."

"Not all cricket players go around stealing other men's fiancées," Isabel laughed.

"A friend was here and reminded me I haven't told my sister, Bettina, that the wedding was canceled," Alec said. "It brought up old memories, like a toothache that won't go away."

"Why don't you call Bettina?" Isabel asked.

"She thought I wasn't good enough for Celine." Alec poured a glass of scotch. "She didn't know why she was marrying me."

"Why would she say that?" Isabel wondered.

"Celine does look like the female lead in a James Bond movie, she could stop traffic by stepping out of a taxi." He rubbed his brow. "But it's more complicated. A bit like those nighttime American soap operas you see on television with French subtitles."

"It sounds fascinating." Isabel perched on an ivory love seat.

"Bettina's mother left my father and ran away with a farmer when she was three years old," he began. "She never forgave my mother for marrying Alain, she wanted him all to herself."

"But she was a child," Isabel murmured. "Surely your parents made her behave."

"My mother was determined for Bettina to feel loved, and my father was more comfortable with his newspapers and boxes

of cigars." He sipped his drink. "When Bettina was four, she marched into my father's study with her favorite Madeline doll. She said he could have it as long as he sent me back wherever I came from."

"Older sisters are often jealous of little brothers." Isabel grinned. "But that was ages ago, you're both adults."

"Bettina has a memory like an elephant. And it doesn't help that Celine and I were engaged after three months and she and Édouard have been together for four years," he sighed. "Édouard seems as eager to propose as Queen Elizabeth is to give up the throne."

"You have to tell her," Isabel insisted. "She won't be happy if she shows up at an empty cathedral with a set of Villeroy and Boch demitasses."

"I'll call her tomorrow." He put his glass on the sideboard. "You paid a fortune for these tickets, we don't want to be late."

"We're going to have a wonderful time." Isabel rubbed her lips. "I read an article about the ball in *Paris Match*. It's attended by *ducs* and marquises and viscounts."

"It sounds like a chapter from *The Three Musketeers*." Alec grimaced, walking to the door. "I'll be happy with a glass of Dom Pérignon and a plate of veal sweetbreads."

"Wait," Isabel called.

Isabel walked toward him and put her hands around his neck. He inhaled her scent of jasmine perfume and felt slightly dizzy.

"Your tie was crooked." She stepped back and her face lit up in a smile. "Now it's perfect."

"Thank you," he said, and realized he had been holding his breath. "I've always been hopeless at tying my own tie."

THEY CROSSED THE Place de la Concorde and Alec felt a rush of pride. Paris in the winter could be damp and bitter, but the

Christmas tree glittered like an elaborate charm bracelet, and the obelisk was a shimmering beacon, and the stone facade of the Petit Palais took his breath away.

"It's magnificent." Isabel gazed up at the wide columns and gold inlaid doors. "It's like a scene from *The Arabian Nights*."

"The Petit Palais was built for the world's fair in 1900," Alec explained. "It was designed in the Beaux Arts style and takes up a city block. The columns are pink Vosges granite and the mosaic floors were imported from Italy."

The interior courtyard had a domed cupola and sweeping murals and a glass bar lined with crystal bottles. There was an ice sculpture and platters of black-truffle brioche and smoked eel and pork rillettes.

"I thought the Red Cross was all about thick bandages and those little white hats." Alec whistled. "This looks like a scene from the *Decameron*."

"Parisian women are so sophisticated." Isabel glanced at women wearing sapphire pendants and shimmering cocktail dresses. "How am I supposed to compete with baronesses wearing emerald brooches inherited from the Duchess of Mont-pensier?"

"You're an American, it's the most competitive race on earth." Alec took a champagne flute from a passing waiter. "Is that the way you behave before a client presentation?"

"That's different. When I walk into a conference room, it's like one of those sand puzzles that you shake and it falls into place," Isabel said. "No matter how nervous I am, I relax."

"Getting a viscount to ask you to dance is easier than predicting the consumption of chia seeds in Japan," Alec insisted.

"Picking the right husband isn't easy at all . . ." Isabel's voice wavered. "I thought Neil and I were in love. He looked handsome in a tuxedo and we enjoyed doing the fox-trot and the waltz." Her eyes were huge. "Until a month before the wedding,

when he decided to quit his job and insisted we move to his grandparents' farm so he could spend his days in cowboy boots." She smoothed her skirt. "I didn't expect to attend black-tie galas every week, but it is nice to get dressed up and feel young and pretty."

"You're going to do fine." He pointed to the circular foyer. "All you need to do is hold a glass of champagne and stand over there."

"Why should I do that?"

Alec studied her brown eyes and dark eyelashes and slender neck.

"Because you'll be the first thing a man sees when he hands his wool overcoat to the coat-check girl." He paused. "And he won't look anywhere else."

ISABEL SIPPED CHAMPAGNE under a framed Pissarro, and Alec's shoulders relaxed. She really was striking in the red satin gown, like a ballerina on one of Bettina's music boxes. He really had to stop thinking about his sister; she was like Maleficent at Aurora's christening.

The sideboard was filled with silver platters of caviar dumplings and baked sea bass and onions au gratin. He looked up and saw Isabel talking to a blond man in a silk tuxedo. She caught Alec's eye and a smile lit up her face. He grabbed a plate and noticed a familiar figure wearing a black tuxedo and gold watch.

"What are you doing here?" Mathieu approached him. "You usually avoid any occasion that requires shirt studs and cuff links."

"I'm doing a favor for a friend," Alec explained. "No wonder your rates have gone up if you're hobnobbing with barons and *comtes* at a two-hundred-euro-a-plate ball."

"Helene's boss gave her the tickets for Christmas." Mathieu sipped his champagne. "She wanted to wear her Pucci gown while she could still do up the zipper."

"I have to thank her for the watercolor you gave us as a wedding present. I tried to return it, but the gallery owner said fine art wasn't returnable." Alec nibbled steamed mussels. "The art world can be so pretentious. If it's not a commercial commodity, why was it for sale in the first place?"

"You should keep it," Mathieu suggested. "It would look fine above your desk."

"I don't need any more reminders of Celine," Alec grumbled. "I'm sure she didn't fill her carry-on with silver salt shakers or a ceramic fruit bowl. She's probably forgotten that next Friday was supposed to be her wedding day."

"You'll get over her." Mathieu put his hand on Alec's shoulder. "It just takes time."

"No one wants to be with someone who doesn't feel the same," Alec said slowly. "I'm just afraid I won't get over the idea of her: That you could live the rest of your life with someone you loved. That you could wake up every morning and see her slip on her stockings and think you were the luckiest guy in the world."

"There are plenty of spectacular women at the ball. You're good-looking and entertaining when you're not moping like a basset hound." He pointed to a woman wearing a blue cocktail dress. "Strike up a conversation with that brunette."

"Basset hounds don't mope, they were born with droopy cheeks," Alec corrected. "And I'd rather sample the bay prawns in warm mayonnaise than make conversation with a woman." He paused. "They all look lovely in their designer gowns and clouds of expensive perfume. But just when you get comfortable enough to wear plaid pajamas to bed and drink orange juice out of the carton, they trample all over your heart."

"Helene would kill me if I drank juice out of the carton," Mathieu laughed.

Alec looked up and saw a woman in a green chiffon gown walking toward them. Of course Bettina was at the Red Cross ball! Why hadn't he thought of that, and how could he sneak away without her seeing him?

"Where are you going?" Mathieu asked.

"She can't see me here." Alec put his plate on the sideboard.

"It's a charity function, not the red-light district of Montmartre." He stopped and looked at Alec. "You haven't told her the wedding is canceled."

"Not exactly." Alec shifted his feet. "I was going to call her tomorrow."

"Unless you become the invisible man, you're telling her tonight." Mathieu turned and smiled. "Bettina, how nice to see you. Alec was just commenting on how beautiful you look in that green dress."

"My brother and his attorney, what a surprise," Bettina murmured. "Who would have thought the scrawny teenager who used to sneak my father's port would become an important lawyer."

"We did not sneak Alain's port, he offered it to us," Alec retorted. "We may have finished the bottle after he went to bed, but eighteen-year-olds have done worse."

"I'm surprised to see you and Celine out so close to your wedding," Bettina replied. "Shouldn't you be rehearsing your vows or packing for your honeymoon?"

"Celine's not here," Alec mumbled.

"You came alone?" Bettina raised her eyebrow.

"Excuse me, I have to join Helene," Mathieu cut in. "The doctor said she shouldn't drink more than one glass of champagne."

"When will you and Celine start a family?" Bettina asked.

"Though I can't imagine Celine ruining that perfect waistline." She ate an escargot. "Maybe you'll adopt."

"Celine talks about children all the time." Alec bristled. "She wants a boy who plays the flute and a little girl who loves ballet."

They had imagined a boy with Celine's high cheekbones and small nose. The girl would have his dark hair and her violet eyes and red mouth.

Except now the boy would have Patrick's floppy blond hair and the little girl would be so breathtaking, she would make your heart ache. Two stunning people shouldn't fall in love—what was left for everyone else? Beauty should be distributed evenly, like crustless sandwiches at a child's birthday party.

He pictured Patrick's chiseled jaw and blue eyes and knew he'd never had a chance.

Bettina peeled prawns with her long fingernails, and Alec thought he had nothing to be afraid of; he was a grown man with a fifth-floor flat and a membership to the Louvre.

"Celine isn't in Paris." He took a deep breath. "She's in Australia."

"Why is she in Australia?" Bettina asked.

"That's what I wanted to know." Alec rubbed his brow. "Why would anyone rather be in a country where the oldest building is only two hundred years old, and it's so hot and sunny you have to spend Christmas on the beach?"

"When is she coming back? Your rehearsal dinner is in six days."

"She's not coming back." Alec picked an imaginary piece of lint from his dinner jacket. "The wedding is canceled."

"Are you all right? I was afraid she'd call it off!" Bettina gasped. "She is quite beautiful and her father owns diamond mines in Brazil and South Africa. She could have her pick of Saudi oil magnates or even European royalty."

"Not every woman calculates her fiancé's net worth when she's considering marriage proposals," he snapped. "Celine picked me. She may have traded me for an Australian cricket player, but there was never an Arabian prince or ruler of a minor European country in the picture."

"A cricket player," Bettina repeated.

"Apparently he has an excellent arm," Alec sighed. "And he looks like David Beckham, but with better hair and leaner muscles."

Isabel walked over to join them and Alec inhaled her jasmine perfume.

"There you are! My throat is parched and I'd give anything for a glass of Dom Pérignon." She turned to Bettina. "We haven't been introduced, I'm Isabel Lawson."

Alec flinched and thought the last thing he needed was to explain Isabel to his sister.

"How do you know each other?" Bettina wondered.

"We are staying at the Hôtel de Crillon," Isabel replied. "Well, not in the same suite, though we practically share a terrace. I was supposed to be here on my honeymoon, but it fell through. Alec rescued me from being locked out on the balcony.

"He poured me a brandy and put me to bed, and we've been inseparable ever since," she continued. "We ate lobster bisque at Fouquet's and drank cognac at the Crillon bar and visited the Christmas markets." Her face lit up in a smile. "I've never attended a ball with viscounts and *ducs,* it was so sweet of Alec to bring me."

"Isabel is a financial analyst from Philadelphia," Alec explained. "She's never been to Paris at Christmas."

"How delightful." Bettina studied her diamond earrings and white silk gloves. "How long are you staying?"

"I haven't decided. I want to go shopping in the Marais and

dance at the clubs in Montmartre." She paused and her eyes were bright. "Alec said there's nothing more romantic than standing under the Arc de Triomphe at night. The Champs-Élysées glitters like a thousand fireflies."

"WHAT WAS THAT about?" Alec exclaimed after Bettina went to find Édouard. "Lobster at Fouquet's and cognac at the bar at the Crillon? And I never suggested standing under the Arc de Triomphe, it's a good way to get run over."

"I couldn't let her picture you sitting alone in your suite, contemplating throwing yourself off the balcony."

"I'd never jump off the balcony, I'm afraid of heights," Alec fumed. "You made it sound like one of those romantic movies where the couple spends twenty-four hours traipsing through Paris and the camera goes in on a kiss at the end."

"You brought me to the ball and I met a handsome *comte*. His name is Antoine de Villoy and his family has a château in the Loire Valley." She smoothed her skirt. "I wanted to do something nice for you. I thought you'd want Bettina to think you have a new love interest."

"I suppose it doesn't hurt. She looked like she swallowed an ostrich egg," Alec laughed. "Where is this *comte*? He sounds too perfect—are you sure he doesn't have a wooden leg or a mistress hidden in the attic?"

"He's a banker with an apartment off the Rue de Rivoli." Isabel smiled. "He likes American movies and Stephen King and he keeps a boat in Antibes." She grabbed a glass of champagne. "I should go find him, I told him I had to talk to a friend."

Isabel disappeared into the crowd, and Alec thought no French aristocrat liked American movies; they were full of explosions and car chases.

There was a sudden pain in his foot and he gasped.

"I'm sorry, I must have stepped on your foot," an older woman said, holding a plate of vanilla custards.

Alec rubbed his shoe and thought he shouldn't have come. He'd much rather be at home drawing Gus. He imagined Gus wearing a black mask and riding a horse, like a four-legged Count of Monte Cristo.

Taking Isabel to the ball was the right thing to do; he was helping a friend. He filled his plate with petits fours and thought, even if he refused to fall in love, someone had to. If no one did, the human race was doomed.

chapter six

Isabel strolled along the Boulevard Saint-Michel and glanced at the distant spires of Notre Dame Cathedral. She had loved exploring the fifth arrondissement when she studied at the Sorbonne. The outdoor cafés were crowded with girls in floral skirts and young men carrying leather backpacks. They all drank endless espressos and pored over copies of Flaubert and Sartre.

The Place Saint-André-des-Arts was littered with colorful sketches and she spent hours in the Cluny Museum gazing at the tapestry of the Lady and the Unicorn. But mostly she loved sitting under the cherry blossoms and watching all of Paris walk by.

Even now, with the tables pushed inside and a soft rain falling on the pavement, she adored the Latin Quarter. The boulevards were lined with galleries, and the alleys were filled with wine bars and old men playing backgammon.

She turned on the Rue de la Bûcherie and remembered the Red Cross ball at the Petit Palais. The whole evening had been glorious: the sixteen-piece orchestra and ice sculptures and platters of lamb cutlets. The crème brûlée that melted in her mouth and the selection of chocolate tortes.

Antoine had been handsome and charming, like a character in a French novel. He explained he never carried his phone in his tuxedo and wrote her number on a napkin. He tucked it in his pocket, and Isabel suddenly felt the champagne sink to her toes. She had met a French aristocrat and he'd asked for her phone number!

The rain fell on her umbrella, and she wanted to dance like Fred Astaire and Audrey Hepburn in *Funny Face*. All she had to do was listen to the fortune-teller and her dreams would come true.

She pictured Alec in his white dinner jacket and frowned. He might think believing in the fortune-teller was silly, but he knew nothing about her. She had tried to fall in love with the right man and failed.

Isabel didn't want to come home at night longing to talk about the surge in Facebook's stock price. Or wishing someone would greet her with a chilled Chardonnay and baked chicken because she had been sitting at her desk all day and hadn't eaten anything except a tuna sandwich.

Isabel wanted to be part of a couple—that's what made working so hard worth it. Even if she could afford her own house, what was the point of having a sitting room and a formal dining room if she curled up every evening with a bowl of instant oatmeal and *The Economist*?

She reached 37 Rue de la Bûcherie and caught her breath. She had spent hours at Shakespeare and Company when she lived in Paris, and just seeing the three-story bookstore with its narrow shelves and piles of books made her happy.

The first time she entered the double brass doors when she was studying at the Sorbonne, a young Frenchman gave her a tour of the seventeenth-century former monastery. In 1951 an American named George Whitman opened the bookstore and

invited authors and playwrights to spend the night. Beds were scattered among the shelves so they could sleep.

He reeled off the names of writers who had been regulars—Anaïs Nin and William Styron and Henry Miller—and Isabel wanted to stay there forever.

Now a young couple held hands, and she remembered when she and Rory spent a week in San Francisco. Every evening they visited City Lights bookstore in North Beach. Isabel tried to read the latest Armistead Maupin, but Rory pulled her close and kissed her.

Why was she thinking about Rory again? Neil was the fiancé she had left in Philadelphia. But it was still painful to think about Neil, like a recent sunburn that left a blister.

Rory was so long ago, and their romance was the first time she had given her heart away. They had been like the young couple with their hands tucked in each other's pockets. When you were twenty-four and in love, you had the wisdom of Socrates and the energy of Michelangelo.

She remembered when Rory announced he was leaving. It was early September and she was sorting boxes in her parents' attic. The leaves were turning orange, and she felt their relationship changing, like the new chill in the air.

"THERE YOU ARE." She looked up. "I'm finally going to bring my books with me. I haven't seen my collection of Edith Wharton and Tom Wolfe since I was in high school. The new apartment has built-in bookshelves in the bedroom."

In a week she started working at JPMorgan Chase and had rented a one-bedroom apartment on Rittenhouse Square. Rory made excuses not to see it: he had to finish a piece about the Bryn Mawr hound show; he was asked to cover the Concours

d'Elegance. But Isabel felt a distance between them, like the width of the Delaware River.

"I'm moving too." Rory perched on a box. He looked handsome in blue jeans and a white button-up shirt.

"Moving?" Isabel repeated.

"An old roommate from Milton founded a start-up in San Francisco," Rory said. "He's got a penthouse on Nob Hill with views of the Oakland Hills and Bay Bridge." He fiddled with his collar. "I'm going to stay with him."

"But what are you going to do?" Isabel felt her heart beat faster.

"Get up in the morning and explore Fisherman's Wharf." He shrugged. "Sit at a café in North Beach and eat a calzone and strawberry gelato." He paused. "I'm sure I could write a few society pieces for the *San Francisco Chronicle*. All those dot-com millionaires showing up at the symphony in jeans and sneakers."

"I see." Isabel examined the stack of books so he couldn't see the tears in her eyes.

"Your trainee program ends in December, so you can come in January," he continued.

"You want me to come to California?" Isabel asked.

"Of course, San Francisco is the banking capital of the West Coast," he said. "And the wedding will be in December, so it will be perfect."

"What wedding?"

"Our wedding," Rory replied. "Have you forgotten? I said at my mother's birthday party that she would be thrilled to meet the woman I'm going to marry." He paused. "We'll have the rehearsal dinner at the Radnor Hunt Club and the reception at my parents' house—" He stopped and smiled. "One of the benefits of having a thirty-room estate is you don't have to deal with hotel staff when you host a party for four hundred people."

"We're too young to get married," Isabel said, suddenly flustered. "I just graduated from business school and you . . ."

"Don't have a proper job?" he finished. "Marriage isn't a contract about who takes out the garbage and who stops at Kroger's to pick up the laundry detergent." His green eyes flickered. "You get married because everything is brighter when you're together and you'd rather have chicken pox than be apart.

"I'm doing this all wrong, I haven't formally proposed." He got down on one knee and took Isabel's hand. "We haven't known each other long, but it only took a moment to realize I wanted to spend the rest of my life with you.

"I'm not the best with words, that's why I write society pieces instead of the great American novel." He pushed his hair off his forehead. "But I love you and I'll do anything to make you happy."

He reached into his pocket and drew out a green velvet box. Inside was a square emerald surrounded by diamonds on a platinum band.

"Isabel Marie Lawson"—he took out the ring—"will you marry me?"

"Do you always carry antique engagement rings in your jeans pocket?" She tried to laugh, but her legs were shaky and she couldn't breathe.

"I wanted to propose on our weekend in the Adirondacks, but our cabin smelled like fish," he began. "Tonight Alice, our cook, offered to make us a romantic dinner. But I didn't want my mother to forget her pashmina and return early from the theater." He leaned forward and touched her hair. "I like proposing in the attic. We're all alone and that sweater is practically see-through."

"I wasn't expecting company." Isabel glanced down at her fishnet sweater and beige slacks.

"Well, I found you," Rory whispered. "And I'm asking you to marry me."

Isabel inhaled his musk scent and thought they were too young to get married. She barely had started her career, and Rory didn't know what he wanted besides his daily swim and cup of Peruvian coffee.

And could she really move to San Francisco? She loved her parents and their big house in Ardmore. She adored the change of seasons and the giant Christmas tree in Rittenhouse Square.

But she looked at Rory's chiseled jaw and knew she had to marry him. Marriage wasn't about having a joint 401(k) and planning for a golden retirement. It was about laughing together and never wanting to be apart.

"Yes," she whispered.

He slipped the emerald ring on her finger and kissed her. One hand undid her zipper and slipped beneath her panties.

"What are you doing?" she gasped, feeling the delicious heat.

"I'm kissing the bride," he murmured, pulling her sweater over her shoulders.

She lay on the thick carpet and drew him on top of her. He slid out of his jeans and pushed her legs open. The carpet was soft and she inhaled his musk aftershave. She wrapped her arms around his back and he plunged deep inside her.

"I'm not the bride yet," she said, feeling her body reach and tip.

He moved faster and she didn't think about anything except the delicious glow and her body being wrenched apart. The endless waves carried her over the edge and she wondered how anything could be so good.

"WE HAVE TO practice for the wedding night," he murmured, draping his arm around her waist.

Isabel thought of Rory's lack of a job and moving to San Francisco. The emerald ring glittered in the afternoon sun and she thought she'd worry about it tomorrow.

NOW ISABEL GAZED at the tables piled with books at Shakespeare and Company and thought she really had to concentrate on Antoine.

"Excuse me, mademoiselle," a male voice said. "Can I help you?"

Isabel looked up and blushed, as if the bookseller could tell what she was thinking.

"I'm looking for a book on the French aristocracy." She smoothed her hair. "I need to know everything, from the Middle Ages to Napoleon. I took French in high school and at Bryn Mawr, but they never teach you anything except the French Revolution." She paused. "There must be other interesting facts besides how many dresses Marie Antoinette wore every day and who was allowed in Louis XVI's bedchamber.

"Though that period is fascinating. Have you ever seen *Dangerous Liaisons*? It's one of my favorite movies. All those gorgeous châteaux with elaborate gardens perfect for clandestine meetings," she sighed. "These days you can't hide anywhere, we all have GPS on our iPhones."

"We don't have anything at the moment." The man clicked through the computer screen.

"This is Shakespeare and Company, it's the most famous bookstore in the world." She pointed to the shelves that reached the ceiling. "Surely you have something on the feudal system or the court of the Sun King?"

"All our books are in English, and there is not a great demand for works on the French aristocracy."

"That's the problem with Americans, they're only interested

in themselves," she sighed. "I learned about the Civil War every year from the fifth grade, but I never studied the Wars of the Roses."

"Perhaps come back tomorrow, we get used books every day."

"If you don't have a single book on the aristocracy, one is hardly going to walk in off the street." She frowned. "It's very important, I met a French *comte* and he asked for my phone number." She stopped and her eyes were huge. "But if I don't know the difference between *noblesse de lettres* and *noblesse d'épée,* he might not be interested in me at all."

"You seem to know a lot about French history." He grinned. "I'm sure you have nothing to worry about."

"I always read the part of the textbook the teacher didn't go over in class." She nodded. "But it's not enough, I have almost a thousand years to cover."

Isabel was about to walk onto the street when she heard a voice behind her. She turned and saw an old man with gray hair. He wore a faded blazer and tan slacks.

"I overheard you saying you needed a book on the French aristocracy," he said. "I think I can help."

"How could you do that?" she asked.

"Come with me." He led her to the back of the store. He climbed a ladder and pulled a thick book off the shelf.

"*The Noble Regime* was written by a professor at the Sorbonne and translated into English." He handed it to her.

"How did you find it?" she gasped.

"Young people think the answer to everything is in a computer." He shrugged. "But some things exist even if they're not in a database."

"This is wonderful." She flipped through the pages and her face broke into a smile. "How can I thank you?"

He hesitated and then he looked at Isabel. "Can I tell you a story?"

"Of course," she said. "You just gave me a wonderful gift."

"Forty years ago I fell in love with an American who was living in Paris as an au pair," he began. "She wanted to get married, but I was a struggling writer and had nothing to give her. The day she was supposed to leave she appeared at my door.

"She said she didn't care if we lived in a two-room flat in Montmartre and could never afford a holiday, we had to be together," he continued. "Our lives were no great success story, I became a teacher and she worked as a florist. She died six months ago, but she left me with memories that will last forever. If you found true love with this *comte*, hold onto it."

"That's a wonderful story." Isabel's eyes glistened. "I'm sure she was beautiful."

He walked to the door and turned around. "I never even noticed."

ISABEL STROLLED ALONG the Boulevard Saint-Michel and hugged the book to her chest. The rain had stopped and a thick mist settled on the roofs.

Paris really was a magical place. First she met the fortune-teller, and then the woman at Le Printemps suggested the perfect gown to wear at the ball, and now a complete stranger discovered a book about the French aristocracy.

Couples held hands on the sidewalk and Isabel inhaled the scent of cigarettes and fresh baguettes. All she had to do was go back to her suite at the Crillon and wait for Antoine to call. Then her future would begin.

chapter seven

Alec sat on the blue velvet sofa and tucked the napkin under his chin. The silver tray held waffles with maple syrup and strawberry jam. There was a fruit salad and warm brioche with melted butter. He ate a bite of poached Scottish salmon and thought nothing had ever tasted so good.

HE HAD WOKEN up early and sketched until lunchtime. Then he glanced at the rain falling on the Place de la Concorde and decided he wasn't going to risk getting pneumonia for an over-priced crepe at a crowded café. The room service menu lay before him and he picked up the phone.

NOW HE FIDDLED with his fork and glanced at the sketch of Gus standing in a forest. A witch appeared with a basket of apples. Gus chose the green apple but realized it was poisoned and switched it behind his back. He handed the poisoned apple

to the witch, and she took a bite and collapsed onto the forest floor.

He ate a bite of grapefruit and thought Bettina was probably on her way to 40 Rue de Passy right now. He couldn't let her evict Claudia, but he didn't know how to stop her.

If only Celine hadn't run off to Australia, Claudia could be picking out new carpets instead of worrying how she was going to get her antique bedroom set into a fourth-floor flat. That's if Bettina let her take her own bed—she probably would stand at the door with a checklist of items that belonged in the house.

It was his fault. If he had told Celine about his father's will, she might never have left. But what if she thought he was marrying her to protect his mother? And families didn't share their secrets; it wasn't right.

The salmon got stuck in his throat, and he remembered when they received a dinner invitation from Bettina. It was a few days after the luncheon at his mother's house and he and Celine were having breakfast in his kitchen.

ALEC GLANCED AT the ivory card stock and frowned. Bettina had never invited him to anything in her life, and now she was requesting his and Celine's presence at an intimate soiree. He pictured making conversation about the prime minister and the plans to expand Disneyland Paris and choked on his coffee.

"Are you all right?" Celine looked up from her soft-boiled egg. "You're quite pale."

He stuffed the card in the envelope and tossed it on the table. It was rare that Celine stayed at his flat, and he hoped they'd spend the day eating berries and making love in bed.

"Bettina invited us to dinner at her town house." Alec grimaced. "I've only been there once. She has a houseboy who takes

your shoes, and after you leave she checks the artwork for fingerprints."

"She was perfectly nice at lunch," Celine said. "I don't know what you're worried about."

"Bettina is like a fox. She'd look good as a coat, but you wouldn't want to meet her in the forest."

"We should go." Celine peeled an orange. "I want to get to know your family."

He poured cream into his coffee and flinched. What if Bettina tried to cause a rift between them so they called off the wedding? But how could he admit his fears to Celine when he'd never told her his mother's situation in the first place?

His falling in love with Celine and wanting to get married was just a lucky coincidence.

"I'll RSVP that we'd be delighted," Alec sighed, sipping the coffee and wondering when the cream went sour.

ALEC CLUTCHED HIS wineglass and glanced at the salon, with its white silk sofas and silver wallpaper. He should have asked Bettina for a Chardonnay instead of the Burgundy. If he got red wine on the white wool carpet, she'd drag him to the Bastille.

No wonder Édouard hadn't proposed. He was probably afraid he'd track in a bit of dirt and Bettina would serve him divorce papers. The marble bar was set with silver goblets and Alec felt like he'd wandered into a restricted area of the Louvre.

He'd have to drink three glasses of wine to get through the evening, and he'd wake up tomorrow with a pounding headache. But then he glanced at Celine in a yellow silk dress and sapphire earrings and his heart lifted. Nothing terrible could happen while she was sitting beside him.

"I want you to meet our friends Gil and Elaine." Bettina

brought out a platter of spinach canapés. "Gil is the head of the neurology department at Édouard's hospital, and Elaine works at the Swiss embassy." She paused and her smile was bright. "She doesn't speak as many languages as Celine, but I think you'll have a lot in common."

"What do you do?" Elaine turned to Alec.

"Alec draws pictures of dogs for children's books," Bettina explained, handing Alec a plate.

Alec opened his mouth, but he caught sight of Celine chatting with Édouard and gulped. He promised himself he wouldn't respond to Bettina.

"His name is Gus." He stuffed a canapé in his mouth. "And he's a cocker spaniel."

They moved into the dining room and sat at the long mahogany table. A crystal chandelier hung from the ceiling and the chairs were purple velvet. Alec peered at the framed Matisse and cabinet filled with Lalique crystals and wondered why a single woman wanted a dining room that belonged in Versailles.

"Tell us about the wedding," Bettina said, ladling cream of asparagus soup into porcelain bowls.

"The ceremony will be at Cathédrale Notre-Dame, and the reception will be in the Salon Louis XIII of the George Cinq." Celine tore apart a baguette. "Did you know that during World War II the hotel built a secret wine cellar and kept it safe from the Nazis? Now they have almost fifty thousand bottles and the oldest is a 1792 Madeira." She stopped and laughed. "I had to convince my father we didn't need a two-hundred-year-old bottle of sweet wine at our wedding."

"Celine and I both studied history at the Sorbonne," Bettina said to Elaine. "Higher education is so important. When we have children, we might send them abroad to St. Andrews or even Oxford."

Alec almost blurted out that both universities would be even more ancient by the time Bettina and Édouard had children, but he took a long gulp of wine.

"We would like to host an engagement party," Bettina said, turning to Celine. "Nothing fancy, we'll take over a private room at Tour d'Argent. Perhaps you could give us a guest list."

"How thoughtful, we'd love to," Celine beamed.

"It's important to be a family, especially since our father died." Bettina smoothed her hair. "When will you move into 40 Rue de Passy?"

"Why would we move there?" Celine asked. "I'm fond of Claudia, but I can't imagine living together."

"Celine works long hours, she doesn't want to come home to a big house with cracked plaster and temperamental heating." Alec gripped his wineglass so tightly he thought it would shatter. "The apartment on the Rue Saint-Honoré has a lovely garden and the location is so central."

He reached for a baguette and caught his sleeve in the soup tureen. The bowl teetered and splattered green soup on the floral rug.

"God, I'm terribly sorry." He crouched down and dabbed the green stain with his napkin.

"Now I remember why our father made us eat in the kitchen during dinner parties." Bettina appeared beside him. "You were always clumsy."

"You can hardly see it," Alec said hotly, staring at the rug. "It looks like an extra leaf."

"THAT WAS WORSE than sitting through a Truffaut retrospective," Alec said, sipping a glass of scotch.

They had finally gotten through the roasted duck with aubergine and strawberry flambé for dessert and were sitting in Celine's living room.

"Bettina's apartment is beautiful." Celine took off her sapphire earrings. "And the peach sorbet was delicious."

"If you like living inside a Fabergé egg," Alec snapped. "I knew we shouldn't have gone. She handpicked Gil and Elaine to belittle me."

"What do you mean?" Celine asked.

"Elaine is not as pretty or as accomplished as you, but she is dating the head of the neurology department. With your looks and qualifications, you should be engaged to the minister of health," he spluttered. "And she never lets me forget she attended the Sorbonne and I went to arts school." He paused. "As if we sat around coloring with crayons."

"She is planning our engagement party." Celine smiled.

"That's another thing. She knows I don't have any friends besides Mathieu. And she still thinks of him as the grungy teenager who smoked my father's Gauloises."

"What do you mean you don't have friends?" Celine asked.

"Men don't have friends," he explained. "They don't talk when women aren't around, they just grunt at the television."

"You're imagining things. You are not children anymore, you're both adults." Celine took off her stockings. "But why did she ask if we were moving into 40 Rue de Passy?"

Alec gulped and thought he should tell Celine the truth. She would understand his sister was poisonous and they would stay away from her. But was it any way to start a marriage to show his own family's imperfections? And how would she feel about him if she knew his sister was a wolf in sheep's clothing?

He put the scotch on the side table and crossed the room. He drew Celine to her feet and kissed her.

"We've talked about Bettina enough." He slipped his hand beneath her dress. "There are more important things to do."

"Like what?" Celine said and laughed.

He brushed her inner thigh with his fingers and kissed her collarbone. She clutched his shoulders and murmured his name, and suddenly he felt like he could do anything.

He unzipped his slacks and let them drop to the floor. He picked her up and laid her on the sofa.

"Somebody will see us," she whispered. "We should go to the bedroom."

But he stroked her nipples and didn't care about anything except her luscious breasts and smooth thighs.

She leaned against the cushions and guided him inside her. The sensations built up and he pushed so fiercely he was afraid she might break. Then she cried out and her body shook and he collapsed beside her.

Celine stood up to grab a robe, and he waited until his breathing was even. He had been acting like a child. From now on he would be a man.

THERE WAS A knock at the door and Alec got up to answer it.

"You look like the king of Spain during his exile." Mathieu entered the suite and shook out his umbrella. "A roaring fire in the marble fireplace, brandy snifter on the coffee table, selection of international newspapers laid out on the sideboard."

"The hotel maids are excellent," Alec admitted. "I'll recommend them for a Christmas bonus."

Mathieu glanced at the plate of Scottish salmon and sliced kiwi and whistled.

"A three-course room service meal instead of crackers and jam?"

"It's pouring rain and I'm going to get scurvy if I only eat

crackers," Alec protested. "It wasn't that expensive. The basket of pastries was no extra charge."

"Good, I'm starving." Mathieu selected a croissant. "You are allowed to spend money. In a week you're going to inherit a third of your father's estate."

"Why do you think I didn't take any allowance from my father when I turned twenty-one? I'd never be a kept man." Alec bristled. "Anyway, I live perfectly well off Gus's earnings." He glanced at the silver coffeepot. "And coffee tastes the same whether you drink it in a porcelain demitasse or a paper cup."

"You don't want the French government to eat it up in taxes," Mathieu said. "You could give some to Claudia."

"My mother is British. She'd rather sell her vegetables at the market than take money from her son." Alec paused. "Did you ever hear Churchill's speech to the House of Commons when World War II broke out: 'I have nothing to offer but blood, toil, tears and sweat. We have before us an ordeal of the most grievous kind.'" He paused and ate a bite of salmon. "Now that was a leader. Our Vichy government spent the war smoking cigars and drinking cognac with the Nazis."

"That's very noble, but it's not going to help Claudia stay in 40 Rue de Passy," Mathieu mused. "Are you sure you can't find a girl to marry? That would solve everything."

"I told you, I'm never getting married." Alec poured a cup of coffee.

"You'd be surprised how enjoyable it is." Mathieu walked to the window. "I come home to baked chicken and roasted potatoes every night. And Helene is marvelous at the laundry, she never mixes up the colors or loses a sock."

"You sound like something out of a Flaubert novel," Alec gasped. "No wonder the French inheritance laws are despicable, if that's how French husbands think of their wives."

"I love Helene." He smiled. "And you have to get married, you're a children's book illustrator. You can't miss out on having a family."

"I'll be like Hans Christian Andersen and gather local children in the park," Alec said. "We'll read fairy tales and blow bubbles and then I'll return them to their parents."

"What's this?" Mathieu picked up a white silk glove from the love seat.

"That's Isabel's. She left it in my coat pocket." Alec looked up. "A fortune-teller said she is going to fall in love and marry a French aristocrat. She met some *comte* at the ball and thinks he's perfect." He put down his coffee cup. "These days, it's hard to tell who are impostors. His ancestors might have been given the title by Napoleon."

"The girl in the red satin gown and diamond earrings?" Mathieu asked.

"She did look lovely," Alec sighed.

"That's it!" Mathieu exclaimed. "You should marry her. She's quite beautiful and she's dying to marry a French aristocrat. Claudia can stay in the house and you'll get Bettina off your back."

"That's the craziest thing I ever heard," he spluttered. "We only met three days ago. So far she's locked herself on the balcony and stepped into oncoming traffic. That's hardly a recommendation for a life partner."

"She has eyes like a young Audrey Hepburn and a mouth like Kate Moss," Mathieu said. "Americans are quick learners, you could teach her how to maneuver around Paris."

"I wouldn't consider it, and you know our family never uses our title." Alec paused. "My father wanted to chuck the whole thing after his first wife ran off with a serf."

"Feudalism was abolished under Louis XVI." Mathieu grinned.

"Well, he was a farmer." Alec shrugged. "Isabel is charming, but I don't know anything about her. And I told you, I'd rather paddle a rowboat in the Luxembourg Gardens during a downpour than get down on my knee in front of a woman ever again."

"I'm trying to help." Mathieu pointed to the sketch of Gus and the witch in the forest. "That woman looks a lot like Bettina."

"I'm an artist." Alec scooped it up. "I draw from personal experience."

"I hope you're not thinking of poisoning Bettina." He scowled. "I'm terrible at criminal law and you're no help to your mother in prison."

"I'm not murderous!" Alec insisted. "It's not illegal to wish she'd come down with adult measles."

Mathieu gathered his umbrella and walked to the door.

"I have to go, Helene and I are attending a Lamaze class." He turned around. "Think about what I said. Can you imagine Bettina's face if you appeared on the steps of Notre Dame with Isabel?"

ALEC STIRRED HIS coffee and thought Isabel did have a lovely laugh, and when she smiled her brown eyes sparkled. But he couldn't afford to date. His bank account was still recovering from the cuff links he bought for the rehearsal dinner and Celine's wedding gift.

He remembered walking into Chopard's and handing over a month's salary for a heart-shaped pendant and flinched. He was never again going to open himself up to heartache and penury.

His sketch pad lay on the coffee table and he picked it up. He drew Gus standing on a yellow brick road under a rainbow.

There was a witch in a black dress and glittering red shoes. He sketched a door falling on the witch and flattening her on the pavement.

He selected a warm brioche and ate it in one bite.

chapter eight

Isabel stood on the stone balcony and inhaled the damp air and scent of expensive perfume. The Christmas tree sparkled in the Place de la Concorde and the lights twinkled on the Champs-Élysées and all of Paris looked like it was going to a party.

She leaned over the railing and wanted to blow kisses to the doormen in their gold-and-blue uniforms. In an hour, the *comte* was picking her up and taking her to the most famous restaurant in Paris.

A soft mist settled on her shoulders and she stepped inside. Her hair was pinned with a gold clip and she wore red lipstick. She glanced at the pink-and-blue glass bracelet on the dressing table and put it on. Antoine would never know it wasn't made of diamonds and sapphires, and it might bring her luck.

Now she had to decide between her silver stilettos and satin ballet slippers. She couldn't remember how tall Antoine was, and she didn't want to get anything wrong. She scooped up both pairs and hurried down the hallway.

"I HOPE I'M not disturbing you," Isabel said when Alec answered the door. "Isn't it a little early for bed?"

"I was taking a nap," Alec explained, knotting the silk robe around his waist. The plush drapes were closed and the Tiffany lamps were turned on low. "Central heating always makes me sleepy."

"You should open the curtains." She entered the suite. "The rain stopped and the Champs-Élysées looks like a Monet painting."

"Where are your shoes?" Alec asked, glancing down at her stockings. "Don't tell me you locked them on the balcony."

"They are right here." She smiled and held up the stilettos and ballet slippers. "I thought you could help me."

"Help you do what?"

"Choose which to wear." She perched on a brocade armchair. "Antoine invited me to dinner at Tour d'Argent, and I don't know whether to wear the slippers or stilettos. I must have drunk too much champagne, I can't remember how tall he is."

"Aren't you about five foot four?" Alec asked. "I'm sure he's taller than Napoleon."

"You're right, I'm just so nervous." She smoothed her skirt. "How do I look?"

Alec glanced at her black velvet cocktail dress and glossy hair and thick mascara.

"You look lovely." He smiled.

"Black is a safe color, and I don't want to take any chances," she explained. "What if an old girlfriend dumped him wearing a green dress or a pink miniskirt?"

"You need a shot of this." He walked to the bar and poured

two glasses of scotch. He handed one to Isabel and sat opposite her. "So, the *comte* asked you out?"

"I waited all day for him to call, I'd finally given up," she said, sipping her drink. "An hour ago I stepped in the bath when the hotel phone rang. Antoine said his maid took his tuxedo to the dry cleaner's with my number in the pocket. He tried to get it back, but they had tossed it in the garbage." She paused. "He was terribly angry, he said he'd take his business elsewhere."

"How did he find you?"

"It's so romantic," she sighed. "He called the Ritz and the George Cinq and Hôtel de Crillon."

"But you could have been staying anywhere." Alec rubbed his brow. "There are hundreds of hotels in Paris."

"He said a beautiful girl could only stay in a five-star hotel and there weren't many to choose from."

"He got lucky," Alec mumbled.

"Ever since I met the fortune-teller, wonderful things have happened." Her brown eyes sparkled. "Today I went to Shakespeare and Company to buy a book on the French aristocracy, but there weren't any." She fiddled with her glass. "As I was leaving, an old man appeared and handed me the perfect book."

"You can't think that has anything to do with the fortune-teller?"

"I know it does, and I'm sure Antoine and I are going to fall in love." She touched her chest. "I can feel it here."

"Probably heartburn, I get it from eating too many salted nuts," he murmured. "They shouldn't allow minibars in hotel rooms. They're all fat and calories without any nutrition."

"We're going to have a candlelit dinner at Tour d'Argent," she began. "I've read about it for years, it's one of the most renowned restaurants in Paris. I looked up the menu and it has

roasted fillet of duckling and multicolored beetroots and vanilla clementine for dessert."

"It sounds wonderful." Alec smiled. "I'm happy for you."

"Look at the time, I have to go!" She jumped up. "He's meeting me in the lobby."

"Isabel, wait," Alec called.

"What is it?" She turned around.

He pointed to her stocking feet and grinned. "You forgot your shoes."

ISABEL GAZED AT the gold-and-white marble floor and blue velvet wallpaper and thick marble columns. Rich tapestries lined the walls and crystal chandeliers dangled from the domed ceiling. She pictured the building when it first opened in 1758 and welcomed kings and queens and courtiers. Now she was standing in the lobby, waiting to go to dinner with a *comte*!

What if they had nothing to talk about or she wasn't attracted to him? The glass bracelet glittered on her wrist and she remembered the fortune-teller. This was the moment she had been waiting for and everything was going to be perfect.

The double doors opened and a man entered the lobby. He had dark blond hair and brown eyes and narrow cheekbones. He wore a navy suit and clutched a bouquet of flowers.

"Isabel?" He approached her.

"Yes?" Her heart hammered in her chest.

"I'm glad I picked the red roses." He handed her the bouquet. "Nothing else could match your beauty."

THEY SAT AT a window table at Tour d'Argent and ate lobster bisque and goose foie gras with brioche. Isabel gazed at the moon glinting on the Seine and tall spires of Notre Dame Cathedral

and shivered. It really was beautiful, like an impossibly elegant coffee table book.

"I've wanted to eat here since high school," she said, cradling her wineglass. "It's the oldest continuous Parisian restaurant and was listed in Baedeker's guide to Paris in 1860.

"They have a wine cellar of four hundred fifty thousand bottles, and after you finish your meal, they give you a postcard with a picture and the serial number of your duck," she finished. "I can't wait to send the card to my parents."

"You know a lot about French restaurants." Antoine smiled.

"I've always loved everything about Paris: the food and fashion and art—" She stopped and blushed. She sounded like a schoolgirl instead of a sophisticated Parisian.

"It's the greatest city in the world." Antoine nodded. "The museums are breathtaking and the public parks are spectacular. Where else can you leave your office at midday and pop into the Louvre to see the *Mona Lisa*?"

Isabel glanced up from her soup and noticed his blond hair flopped over his forehead and the dimple on his chin.

"I agree completely," she said, her eyes sparkling. "Everything is perfect when you're looking at the *Mona Lisa*."

"HOW DID YOUR family receive their title?" Isabel asked, eating potatoes with caviar seeds.

They ate pressed duck cooked in its own blood and multicolored carrots. There were platters of rice pilaf and small ravioli. Isabel sipped a Louis Jadot Pinot Noir and felt happy. Antoine was handsome and charming, and when he brushed her sleeve, a tingle ran down her spine.

"My ancestor fought for Henry IV in the Wars of Religion," Antoine explained. "When he returned from battle, Henry rewarded him by making him a *comte*."

"So it was a *noblesse militaire*," she said.

"Do you know much about French nobility?" he asked.

"Just a little." She fiddled with her napkin. "It's wonderful that men with families devoted their lives to the king. France might not be here today if they weren't willing to go into battle." She paused. "Can you imagine going off to work and not seeing your family for years?"

"I hadn't thought about it like that," Antoine laughed.

"But it really was a good system. When they returned, they received land and animals and were invited to court." She paused. "These days you work for a company for thirty years and only receive a gold watch."

"You are very refreshing," he said, finishing his wine.

"I am?" Isabel asked, the color rising to her cheeks.

"In France, the old families are so bored, they fall asleep in their soufflé," he mused. "And other people pretend they don't care there's a '*de*' in your name, but they treat you differently."

"It's the same in America with the Kennedys and Kardashians. People say terrible things about them, but often they're jealous."

"I don't want to be a Kennedy," he said.

"Why not?" she asked.

He touched her hand and his eyes were serious.

"Because then I wouldn't have had the good fortune of attending the Red Cross ball and meeting you."

"I'm glad I went to the Red Cross charity ball too." Isabel felt the warmth of his palm and a tingle ran down her spine. "I can't think of anywhere I'd rather be than sitting here with you."

"TELL ME ABOUT you," Antoine said, sipping a glass of cognac.

After the waiter cleared the duck, he brought gold plates of crepes with powdered sugar and an orange sauce. The crepes

"Belle Époque" were a Tour d'Argent specialty, made with Cointreau and flaming Grand Marnier.

"I grew up on the Main Line in Philadelphia," Isabel began. "It's very different from Paris. When you stand on my parents' porch, you see trees and fields."

"I know the Main Line well," Antoine replied. "My roommate at Le Rosey was from a town called Haverford."

"That's next to Ardmore!" Isabel exclaimed. "They have a wonderful library and in winter there is ice-skating on the pond."

"My roommate told me the oldest families in America live on the Main Line," he continued. "Their ancestors built railroads and banks and factories."

"My school was filled with McDowells and Sinnotts," she mused. "But I never thought about it. They were just labels on lunch boxes."

"I knew when I saw you in the red satin gown and long white gloves that we had a lot in common." He covered her hand with his.

"I supposed you're right," she said and smiled. "We do."

"There's one thing Paris doesn't have." He leaned forward. "It doesn't have any women as breathtaking as you."

AFTER DINNER THEY strolled along the Pont Neuf and gazed at the Île de la Cité. Isabel saw the barges gliding down the Seine and twinkling lights of the Eiffel Tower and felt light and happy.

"Pont Neuf means 'new bridge,' but it is actually the oldest standing bridge in Paris," Antoine explained, leaning against the stone railing. "Henry IV ordered its completion to celebrate the victory of the Wars of Religion. It was the first bridge with a pavement, and citizens used it as a gathering place."

"It's beautiful," she murmured.

"Now I am boring you." Antoine shrugged. "I'm being a typical Parisian boasting about his city."

"Of course not, I want to hear more."

"You must be cold." He glanced at her black velvet dress and bare shoulders. "Would you like to wear my jacket?"

She nodded and her eyes were bright. "Yes, thank you. That would be lovely."

"I had a wonderful time." He draped it over her shoulders. "It's not often you meet someone you feel close to so quickly. But there's something about you that I can't stop thinking about."

Isabel pulled the jacket around her and tried to stop her heart from racing. "I know exactly what you mean."

ISABEL ATE A macaron and gazed at the giant Christmas tree in the Place de la Concorde. It was after midnight, but she was so excited, she couldn't fall asleep.

The whole night had been wonderful: the bouquet of roses and the pressed duck at Tour d'Argent and the stroll along the Pont Neuf. Stopping at the bar at the Crillon for a late-night drink.

There was the moment when Antoine waited with her at the elevator and she was afraid she might not see him again. But then he asked if he could call her tomorrow and kissed her.

She took her hair out of its clip and had an uneasy feeling. Was it wrong that they hadn't talked about their careers? Then she glanced out the window at the stone obelisk and Petit Palais and thought she was being silly. Of course they talked about Paris! There would be plenty of time to discuss their goals and dreams.

She noticed her leather-bound journal on the coffee table and picked it up. She had been so certain she and Neil were in love—what if she was wrong this time too?

She sat on the ivory love seat and began to read:

Dear diary,

Can you believe it's only nine months until the wedding? Today the apple blossoms were in bloom and the slush disappeared and it felt like the first blush of spring. I pictured everything we have to look forward to: attending engagement parties and registering for gifts and sending out invitations, and wanted to skip through Rittenhouse Square! Love is the greatest drug, Neil and I are so happy.

We did have a little hiccup yesterday, but we straightened it out. We decided to go to Tiffany's to pick out our wedding rings. I know we have plenty of time, but everything else seemed so daunting: deciding whether to serve cream of asparagus soup or lobster salad as an appetizer, debating whether to take formal photos before the ceremony or during the cocktail hour. I thought it would be fun to go to Tiffany's and admire the gold and platinum wedding bands.

And it was fun! We met after work and the salesman served us French champagne and petits fours. He admired my diamond engagement ring and I couldn't help but smile. Neil chose the most beautiful ring! When you hold it up to the light, it leaves you breathless.

I picked out a platinum band with a row of tiny diamonds. I tried it on and Neil and I both thought it was gorgeous. Then the salesman brought out a tray of men's rings. To be honest, I didn't know there was such a selection. There were plain gold bands and platinum rings set with diamonds. There was even a band made of rubies! Finally the salesman suggested a thin platinum band and Neil tried it on.

"It's a little tight," he said, wiggling it on his finger.

"All the fiancés say that at first," the salesman laughed. "It's supposed to be tight, you don't want it to slip off."

"I'll have to take it off when I play squash or go sailing." Neil frowned. "Perhaps I should try something a little bigger."

I got this funny feeling in my stomach, as if I'd eaten too many chocolate truffles.

"You never take your ring off," I explained, trying to keep my voice steady.

"Of course I'll take it off," Neil replied. "How can I play basketball if it's rubbing against my fingers? And it would be impossible to wear it skiing if I'm using mittens."

"My father never takes his ring off," I insisted. "You'll get used to it."

"But that's silly," Neil protested. "I take my watch off when I go to the gym. I never forget to put it back on."

I saw the salesman watching us and bit my lip. I couldn't make a scene in the middle of Tiffany's. But how could Neil not understand?

The salesman put the ring back in the case and straightened his tie.

"Would you excuse us for a minute?" he asked. "I'd like to show your fiancé something."

They walked to another part of the store and I brushed tears from my eyes. I knew I was being silly; Neil's love for me had nothing to do with a piece of gold jewelry. But then I glanced at my diamond engagement ring and thought it did feel different. You can't help thinking about the person you love when you are wearing his ring on your finger.

The salesman and Neil returned and Neil pointed to the platinum band.

"I'd like to try that one on again," he said.

The salesman took it out of the case and Neil slipped it

on his finger. He turned to me and smiled. "Actually it fits perfectly. Should I get it?"

I looked at Neil's blue eyes and my heart swelled.

"I love it." I kissed him and whispered, "And I love you."

"Please wrap it up," he said and handed it to the salesman.

We went to Lacroix to celebrate and ate guinea hen with chanterelles and white chocolate mousse for dessert. We held hands across the table and it was so romantic.

Oh, diary, I'm sure the salesman said something to Neil about wearing the ring all the time, but it doesn't matter. What's important is he understood how I felt. We're in love and we're going to have a wonderful marriage!

Isabel closed the leather-bound journal and sighed. She had been sure that she and Neil were right for each other. How did she know what she had with Antoine would last?

The fortune-teller said she was going to fall in love and marry a French aristocrat and she had to believe her. They had a wonderful dinner; even Antoine said he felt something special.

If she was going to concentrate on Antoine, she had to tuck the journal into her suitcase. But could she really just forget her failed engagement? She suddenly took a deep breath and picked up her phone. She pressed send and waited while it rang.

"Isabel?" Neil's voice came over the line. "What a surprise, are you still in Paris?"

"I'm sitting in the suite at the Hôtel de Crillon . . ." She hesitated. "I hope I didn't disturb you. I know you are on vacation."

"I was just headed out the door," he answered. "How are you?"

"I'm fine," she wavered, suddenly wondering why she'd called.

She couldn't tell him about Alec rescuing her from the balcony or the fortune-teller's prediction or meeting Antoine. But she had to make sure he was all right. She was the one who had called off the wedding.

"I visited the Eiffel Tower and went shopping on the Champs-Élysées and ate dinner at Tour d'Argent," she began. "There's still so much to do. I want to take a barge on the Seine and visit the Louvre and see the Grand Palais."

"I'm glad you went," Neil replied. "It's good for both of us."

"It is?" Isabel clutched the phone.

"We needed the break. In the new year we'll both get a fresh start," he continued. "It's been snowing since you left. I'm going skiing in Vermont with some old fraternity brothers."

"I hope you have a good time," Isabel said and suddenly felt awkward.

"I really have to go." Neil paused. "Don't forget to do what I asked."

"What was that?" Isabel wondered.

"Send me a postcard," he answered. "I promise I'll do the same."

Isabel pressed end and placed the phone on the side table. She felt strangely empty, like when you opened a box of chocolate pralines and discovered they had already been eaten.

She opened the French doors and stepped onto the balcony. She wanted to tell Alec about Antoine and the pressed duck at Tour d'Argent. But the curtains in his suite were drawn and the lights were off.

She walked inside and climbed into the four-poster bed. Her hair rested on the silk pillowcase and she thought she'd tell Alec tomorrow.

chapter nine

Alec stuck the pencil behind his ear and studied the sketch of Gus standing before a firing squad. A handkerchief was tied around his floppy ears, and his paws were tied with an orange ribbon.

He tossed the paper in the garbage and sank onto the velvet sofa. These days you couldn't use guns in an illustration. But how dramatic would it be if Gus's enemies pelted him with fruits and vegetables?

He thought about the Red Cross charity ball and Mathieu's visit and sighed. He had no choice; he had to see Bettina and beg her not to evict Claudia.

He could invite Bettina to lunch in his suite and order bouillabaisse and baked cod and warm chocolate mousse. But then she'd see the antique furniture and Impressionist paintings and gold harpsichord. He pictured her saying Celine's father had been so generous to pay for the suite and it was a pity Celine had left. He would rather face a firing squad himself.

The morning sun filtered through the window and he grabbed

his jacket. He stuffed his wallet into his slacks and opened the door.

"WHAT ARE YOU doing up?" Isabel asked, standing next to the elevator. "I've never seen you in anything but a robe before lunchtime."

"I've been an early riser my whole life," Alec replied, fixing his collar. "But if Celine's father is paying a thousand euros a night for a suite, there's no point in rushing out."

"Why are you going out now? It's freezing and looks like it might rain." She paused. "It's a perfect day to sit by the fire and illustrate your books."

"I needed to take a break," he sighed. "I wanted Gus to be shot by the firing squad, but my editor would prefer he be pelted by tomatoes."

"I'm sure Gus would agree with your editor." Isabel grinned.

"Besides, I have an errand to run." He stepped into the elevator. "I'm going to buy my sister a Christmas present."

"Christmas is today!" She frowned. "And you don't get along with your sister. When you were a child, she asked your father to send you away."

"This is different." He rubbed his brow. "I need to talk to her about something."

"You're trying to bribe her into doing what you want." She smiled. "People do it all the time. My boss offers free tickets to the Phillies when he needs the associates to work on weekends. It softens the blow when you spend Saturday night eating pizza and preparing spreadsheets."

"I do believe in the spirit of giving," Alec said hotly. "Anyway, haven't you heard the expression 'Keep your friends close and your enemies closer'?"

"She must have done something terrible," she murmured.

"I don't have time to talk about it," he said as they entered the lobby. "I'll see you later."

"Wait," Isabel ran after him. "I want to buy souvenirs for my parents. I'll come with you."

"I can't afford the department stores, I'm going to visit the boutiques in the Marais."

"Even better." She beamed. "I haven't been there since I studied at the Sorbonne."

"All right." Alec shrugged and walked down the steps. "But look both ways before we cross the boulevard." He smiled. "So I don't have to rescue you from being run over again."

THE MARAIS STRETCHED from the third to the fourth arrondissement and was filled with cobblestone streets and winding alleys. There were bright window boxes and elegant galleries and quaint cafés.

"What would Bettina like?" Isabel asked, entering a boutique on the Rue de Sévigné.

"I have no idea." Alec sifted through cashmere sweaters and wool scarves. "All her clothes look like they belong in a military museum, and the only jewelry she wears is probably a chastity belt."

Isabel laughed. "I met her at the ball and she was quite attractive."

"If you admire Cruella de Vil." He scowled. "If she saw a wet dog on the street, she'd poke it with her umbrella."

"She can't be that bad," she protested, examining a silk blouse.

"I told you she brings out the worst in me," he sighed. "Celine said she made me act like a child and she was right."

"Then why are you buying her a present?"

Alec thought it would be nice to tell Isabel about his mother

and 40 Rue de Passy. But there was nothing she could do to help, and he didn't want to reveal his family's secrets.

"It is Christmas," he said finally. "I'll buy this scarf, and we'll go to a café and have tartines and café au lait."

"Oh, look!" Isabel exclaimed, reaching into the window and picking out a pink ostrich purse. "It's a vintage Hermès clutch! My father gave the exact same purse to my mother for their tenth anniversary.

"The airlines lost it last year, and she was devastated. She'll be thrilled that I found a replacement."

"I'm glad your shopping is a success." Alec took the scarf to the counter.

"Don't you see, it's just like the woman at Le Printemps and the old man at Shakespeare and Company," Isabel explained. "Everywhere I go in Paris, something wonderful happens."

"You don't believe a genie made the purse appear just so you could buy it for your mother?"

"Ever since the fortune-teller made her predictions, magical things have occurred," she insisted. "Antoine and I had a lovely date, and we're going to see each other again."

"You almost got run over by the taxi," Alec reminded her.

"But that was part of her prediction." She handed the Hermès clutch to the cashier. "As long as I follow her advice, everything will fall into place."

"You are in Paris, there are hundreds of Hermès purses," he said. "Let's get some air. All this talk about genies and fortune-tellers gives me a headache."

THEY SAT AT a window table at La Poilâne and ate crusty French bread with melted goat cheese and sliced tomatoes. A soft rain fell and the cobblestones looked slick and wet.

"I live across the street and come here every morning for warm apple turnovers," Alec said. "Often I have to wait in line, but it's the best pastry in Paris."

"You live there?" She peered out the window at a narrow building with a florist and butcher.

"It's not the Crillon, but it's perfectly adequate." He bristled. "Though sometimes the smell from the butcher can be over-powering. Then I just ask the florist if I can buy some day-old peonies. I put them next to the window and the smell goes away."

"I think it's charming," Isabel mused. "Everywhere in Paris is like a storybook."

"Celine didn't think so," Alec grumbled. "She thought the Marais was an embarrassing leftover from the pre-Napoleonic era."

"Last night Antoine took me to the Pont Neuf and we watched barges glide down the Seine," she sighed. "They were decorated with Christmas lights and it was so romantic."

"How was the rest of the date with Antoine?" he asked, stirring sugar into his café au lait.

"He brought me red roses and we drank French wine and ate pressed duck at Tour d'Argent," she replied. "When we walked back to the hotel, he kissed me."

"I'm glad it went well." He nodded.

"Tonight he's taking me to the opening of an exhibit at the Musée Rodin and then to dinner at L'Arpège," she continued. "But I'm only here for four more days, so he has to propose soon. If I go back to Philadelphia, we might never see each other again. My mother said long-distance relationships are impossible and she's right. You can't keep a romance going when you live in different time zones."

Alec almost choked and dropped his spoon. "You can't just move to Paris, you have a home and a career."

"Paris is full of banks, and someone would hire an American-educated analyst. I'd have to refresh my French, but I've been watching French movies in my suite." She paused. "Catherine Deneuve is glorious, I could watch her all night.

"To be honest, I don't want to live in Neil's and my condo." She fiddled with her napkin. "It's like rereading a paperback book when you know the ending."

"But you and Antoine just met." He ran his hands through his hair. "You can't expect him to propose."

"He has to," she insisted. "I wouldn't move to Paris unless we were engaged, but long-distance romances don't work. Rory and I tried, and it was a disaster."

"You keep mentioning Rory when you were supposed to marry Neil." Alec frowned.

"Rory was like the bright red coat you see in a department store window: completely impractical for winter but you can't resist buying it. You wear it all November until you realize the wind whips through the fabric and it's not the slightest bit waterproof."

"And Neil?" Alec asked curiously.

"Neil is the Burberry you find at Neiman Marcus," she said. "It's navy or black so it will go with anything. You know it will last for decades and won't look a bit different from the day you bought it." She stopped and her eyes were bright. "Until you see it in your closet and realize you never wanted to wear it at all."

"Poor Neil." Alec grinned. "I've never heard anyone being compared to a coat."

"What kind of coat is Celine?" Isabel asked.

Alec pictured her blond hair and violet eyes and slender cheekbones. He remembered her light laugh and the way her lips always looked wet.

"She was a mink."

AFTER THEY LEFT La Poilâne, they visited Victor Hugo's house in the Place des Vosges and bought warm croissants at a patisserie on the Rue Saint-Antoine. The rain fell harder as they approached the Hôtel de Crillon and Alec opened his umbrella. Isabel took his arm and he inhaled her scent of floral perfume.

"God, I look like a wet cat. I have to take a bath and get ready for Antoine," she said when the elevator stopped at the fifth floor. "I had a lovely time, thank you for showing me Paris."

Alec wanted to say she didn't look like a wet cat at all; she was very pretty. She shouldn't chase after love; if she waited, it would find her. But his track record was worse than hers and he didn't know a thing about love.

"It was my pleasure." He shrugged. "I hope you have a lovely evening."

ALEC ENTERED HIS suite and poured a glass of scotch. He drank it quickly and sank onto the silk love seat. The pleasant buzz of eating tartines and walking in the rain with Isabel had worn off, and suddenly he was angry.

How dare Celine run off and leave him eleven days before their wedding? And how could his own sister take 40 Rue de Passy from his mother? He placed the glass on the coffee table and thought it was no wonder the world was full of alcoholics; once you hit puberty you were doomed. There was always some woman to make you miserable.

Suddenly he remembered the only real fight he and Celine ever had. It was in early September and her father hosted an engagement party. He had a top-floor apartment in the Faubourg

Saint-Germain. The elevator doors were brass plated, and there was a marble bust in the entry.

ALEC GLANCED AROUND Celine's father's grand salon, with its Louis XVI chairs and priceless Ming vases. An Oriental rug covered the marble floor and a gold candelabra rested on the sideboard. He almost knocked over a Baccarat vase and flashed on a sketch he had drawn of Gus bounding down a circular staircase on Christmas morning.

Everything in the illustration looked perfect: the giant Christmas tree littered with sparkling ornaments, the plate of cookies on the fireplace mantel, the stack of presents wrapped in shiny paper. But Gus was only a puppy and couldn't help himself. He tore open the presents and nibbled the cookies and tugged at an angel until the tree tipped over. On the last page, Alec drew Gus outside with his wet nose pressed against the window, looking forlornly at a boy and girl opening their stockings.

"The women all look like models or actresses," Alec said to Celine, pulling his mind away from Gus. "I've never seen so many miniskirts and beehive hairdos. And the men resemble South American gangsters, they're all wearing gold chains and suede loafers."

"The women are actresses and models. Everyone wants to wear Leon's sapphires and emeralds." She paused. "And my father would never associate with gangsters, they are international businessmen involved in export and import."

"That fellow has a bulge in his slacks"—Alec pointed to a man with dark hair and tan skin—"and he isn't happy to see me."

"Just relax." Celine kissed him. "I have to help Mathilde with the vichyssoise."

Alec walked to the sideboard and filled his plate with chicken liver pâté and olives. An older woman stood beside him, wearing a Courrèges dress.

"You must be the fiancé," she said, eating cheese gougères. "How did you and Celine meet?"

"At a gallery opening," he replied. "Celine was much more interesting than the paintings."

"Are you an artist?" she inquired.

"I'm a children's book illustrator." Alec spread pâté on toast. "Have you heard of Gus the Cocker Spaniel?"

"Of course! I gave my nephew *Gus and the Sphinx* for his sixth birthday."

"That's one of my favorites." He beamed. "Gus should never have gone back to the pyramid alone after the guided tour."

"I always buy books as presents," she continued. "It must be hard to keep children's attention with iPads and smartphones. My niece hadn't even heard of Harry Potter until it was in the cinema." She looked at Alec. "Will Gus become a movie or television show?"

Alec put the pâté on his plate and winced. "I'm afraid not. There was a company in London that produced a line of Gus mugs, but they weren't microwave-safe."

He loosened his collar and wondered why he felt like he was in a steam room. All he had to do was smile and shake hands, and then he could go home and have a very large scotch.

"You could look like you are enjoying yourself," Celine said as she approached him. "Mathilde hired the best caterer in Paris."

"I didn't know your father was friends with the French mafia," Alec hissed. "I'm afraid someone is going to try to sell me a gold watch."

"Have a drink." She handed him a gin and tonic. "My father asked you to give a toast."

"A toast!" he exclaimed.

"He's going to give a speech and it would be nice if you said something too." She pursed her lips. "You are marrying his daughter."

"I've only met him twice." He wiped his forehead. "I hope he gets my name right."

They sat at a glass table in the Art Deco dining room and ate smoked salmon with *fromage blanc*. There was a warm chestnut-and-apple salad and leeks vinaigrette. Alec skewered an oyster with his fork, but it slipped onto the plate.

"Mathilde and I want to thank everyone for coming," Leon began. His dark hair was slicked back and he wore a pinstriped suit. "You can imagine my surprise when I returned from Brazil to find my little girl was engaged. But Celine was always head-strong, I remember when she rode a pony out of the Tuileries Gardens because she wanted her own horse." He paused. "Luck-ily the gendarme was a friend or we may have ended up at the police station.

"Alec seems like a fine young man and I'm sure he will make Celine happy." He paused. "The caterer prepared peach Melba for dessert, but first Alec would like to say something."

Alec stood up and wished he'd had either much less or much more to drink.

"The last speech I gave was in lower school when I had to talk about my weekend with Henri, the class guinea pig." He cleared his throat. "First I want to thank Celine for agreeing to be my wife. I never gave much thought to God, but now I pray every night. When you are bestowed with an amazing gift, you want to thank the person responsible.

"I also want to thank Leon and Mathilde for raising a won-derful daughter." His eyes flickered. "I hope we do half as good a job with our children.

"Lastly, I want to thank Gus. If my publisher hadn't sent me

to the gallery in Saint-Germain-des-Prés, Celine and I wouldn't have met.

"Ever since I drew Gus in the margins of my high school science book, he's been part of my life. At times I've been jealous of him sailing down the Euphrates or discovering the gardens of Babylon. But today I can say I wouldn't trade places with him." He gazed at Celine. "Marrying Celine is going to be the greatest adventure I could imagine."

There was a polite round of applause and Alec took his seat. Celine was staring at him as if he was the family dog and had just chewed her father's slippers.

"Excuse me." He stood up and the room tipped. "I have an appointment with the lavatory."

"YOU THANKED AN imaginary dog!" Celine exclaimed, opening her front door.

She hadn't said a word since they left her father's apartment. Alec was tempted to drop her off and go home, but he was still woozy from the wine.

"Gus isn't imaginary." He followed her into the living room. "If you open the first page of *Gus and the Mummy,* you'll see he exists."

"Are you telling me he has thoughts and feelings?" she demanded.

"Is Anna Karenina or Madame Bovary imaginary?" he snapped. "And what about when we go to the cinema? You cried at the end of *Doctor Zhivago.*"

"Those are people." She removed her earrings. "You're talking about a dog."

"Have you heard of Lassie?" he said and suddenly felt bad. Maybe he shouldn't have mentioned an imaginary cocker spaniel to her father's closest friends.

"I'm not some crackpot who argues with Gus in the shower," he fumed. "But he has to be real to me, or he wouldn't come alive on the page. Leonardo da Vinci's *Mona Lisa* has the most famous smile in the world, and she exists behind a gold frame at the Louvre."

Celine looked up and suddenly he was reminded of her beauty. Her blond hair tumbled over her shoulders and her violet eyes were coated with thick mascara.

"I'm going to bed," she said. "We'll discuss it in the morning."

She closed the bedroom door, and Alec slipped his hands in his pockets. He could follow her into the bedroom and kiss her. He imagined unzipping her dress and cupping her ripe breasts. A small moan would escape her lips and she would rub against his chest.

But you couldn't solve everything with sex; sometimes you had to take a stand. He picked up a cashmere blanket and lay down on the floral sofa. His eyes closed and he fell asleep.

ALEC GAZED OUT the window at the rain falling on the Place de la Concorde. When would he stop missing Celine? She was like a sliver of glass that got stuck under his skin.

He remembered telling Isabel that Celine was a mink coat and knew he was wrong. She was an impossibly luxurious angora sweater. It was only after you wore it for a week that you developed a small rash.

What would it be like to fall in love with someone who didn't make him feel like he needed to be better?

Suddenly he remembered the way Isabel's face lit up when he rescued her from the balcony. He pictured carrying her into the Crillon after she missed being hit by the taxi. Her brown eyes were huge, and she always looked like she had a wonderful secret.

He picked up the crystal decanter and placed it on the coffee table.

"Oh God, no," he murmured. He sank onto the ivory love seat and refilled his glass.

chapter ten

～ஃ～

Isabel stood at the window and watched the rain fall on the Place de la Concorde. It was early evening and the lights on the Champs-Élysées glowed like embers in a fireplace. She walked to her closet and bit her lip. A soft drizzle was romantic when you were sipping hot chocolate in your suite at the Hôtel de Crillon, but Antoine was taking her to the Musée Rodin and she wanted to wear her new satin pumps.

She wondered why she wasn't nervous; she was going on a second date with a handsome French *comte*! But all she had to do was listen to the fortune-teller and everything would be perfect. She suddenly pictured the strange woman at Le Printemps asking how she could believe in love at first sight. Of course she did—it was as common as chicken pox.

They were going to see the Matisse and Rodin exhibit and stroll through the museum's lush gardens. Afterward, he was taking her to L'Arpège and they'd eat crepes and discuss books and movies. By the time they walked back to the Crillon, they'd be dying to go up to her suite. But she would kiss him and gently turn him away.

Could she really expect Antoine to ask her to marry him without sleeping together? The French thought Americans were terrible prudes; he probably wouldn't expect anything different. And sex turned everything upside down, as if you saw the world from the top of a Ferris wheel.

She would give her boss notice right away and move to Paris. She imagined an apartment in the seventh arrondissement with lacquered window boxes and a small garden. Every morning she would stop at a patisserie for *pain au chocolat*, and after work she and Antoine would meet for aperitifs.

She slipped on diamond earrings and remembered when she visited Rory in San Francisco. It was early November and they had been apart for two months. Rory suggested she stay with him at his roommate's apartment. But Isabel said she couldn't possibly stay with someone she'd never met and booked a room at the St. Francis Hotel.

ISABEL STOOD AT the window of her room at the St. Francis Hotel and gazed at the palm trees in Union Square. It had been almost balmy when she walked off the plane and she tucked her cashmere jacket into her carry-on.

Now she looked down at women in knit dresses and men in light wool suits and wondered how you could celebrate Christmas without fierce blue skies and snowdrifts. What was Thanksgiving without piles of orange and yellow leaves and homemade apple cider?

Rory called and told her all the things he loved about San Francisco: jogging on the Marina Green and eating pot stickers in Chinatown. Visiting the Palace of the Legion of Honor and watching classic movies at the Roxie Theater.

Isabel replayed their phone conversations and tried to get excited. But getting married and moving to San Francisco seemed

like a movie she'd watched on an airplane. She knew it had been gripping, but she had been distracted by the flight attendant offering peanuts and couldn't remember the story line.

The first month they were apart, she existed in a state of anticipation. She loved sitting at her desk and conjuring up Rory's white smile and getting that giddy feeling. Lately he was a vague outline and she couldn't fill in the details.

Now she gazed at the crystal vase filled with tulips and thought she was being ridiculous. He would arrive any minute and they would fall into bed. After they made love, they would order room service Cobb salad and talk about her Vera Wang wedding dress and the Tiffany favors.

There was a knock at the door and she answered it.

"God, I'm sorry I missed your plane! I can't believe I forgot what time it arrived." Rory entered the room and kissed her. "I've been in Carmel and thought today was Sunday." He stopped and smiled. "Don't you remember during the summer when every day felt like a weekend?"

Isabel wanted to say it wasn't summer; it was almost Thanksgiving. If you looked out the window at men and women carrying leather briefcases, you would know it wasn't the weekend. But his blond hair flopped over his forehead and his cheeks glistened with aftershave and a tingle ran down her spine.

"What were you doing in Carmel?" she asked.

"Teaching golf at a charity event." He walked to the minibar and opened a bag of M&M's. "It was at an estate on Seventeen Mile Drive with its own helicopter pad and views of the Pacific."

"That's interesting," Isabel said and stopped. What did it matter what Rory did as long as he did something?

"I was a championship golfer in high school. I'm still writing society pieces too." He shrugged. "A lot of people in San Francisco have two jobs. They work at a start-up where no one takes a salary and everyone eats microwave popcorn for lunch.

At night they park cars at Gary Danko's and go home with a wad of hundred-dollar bills and leftover prime rib."

"I just thought . . ."

"That I had been sowing my oats and I'd settle down and choose a career?"

She looked out the window at the silver stretch of Bay Bridge and decided she hadn't flown across the country to argue about how Rory filled his days. She turned to him and smiled.

"That you would discover something you were passionate about."

He tossed the wrapper in the garbage and kissed her. She kissed him back and wrapped her arms around his chest.

"God, I've missed you," he whispered. "What were we thinking, being apart?"

He pulled her sweater over her shoulders and unsnapped her bra. She stood in her silk panties and thought she had been waiting for this moment for months.

He drew her onto the bed and buried his face in her breasts. She inhaled his citrus aftershave and thought everything was going to be all right. He would kiss her nipples and stroke her thighs and her body would dissolve in endless ripples.

But suddenly he opened her legs and plunged inside her. His breathing was ragged and his chest was slick with sweat. He called out her name and came in one long, frantic thrust.

Isabel stood up and walked to the window. The first time you made love after being apart was always rushed. It was like eating a chocolate-dipped ice cream cone on a hot day. The vanilla ice cream was delicious, but you had to eat it quickly so the chocolate coating didn't melt, and you couldn't enjoy it at all.

In the morning they'd wake up and have long, leisurely sex. The Fairmont would pack a picnic lunch of sourdough bread and local cheeses. They'd hike to Coit Tower and watch the sailboats on the bay.

She climbed into bed and pulled the sheets over her shoulders. Her skin was damp from the sex and central heating, but she still felt a slight chill.

ALL WEEK THINGS were slightly off. Rory purchased tickets to *Kinky Boots* at the American Conservatory, but she had already seen it. She bought him the latest John Irving novel, but he had just finished it. When they made love, Isabel felt like she had a cold she couldn't get rid of. The sensations were there, but she couldn't quite feel them.

On the last day, she sat at Enrico's on Columbus Avenue in North Beach. She adored North Beach, with its Italian restaurants and gelato stands and City Lights bookstore. The weather had turned cold, and she huddled over a bowl of clam chowder and a sourdough baguette.

"I'm sorry I'm late." Rory approached the table and kissed her. "My roommate wanted to discuss something and I lost track of time."

Isabel wondered how she'd never before noticed Rory was so often late. But she pictured the glorious summer of lying by the pool and making love in the guesthouse and realized they never had to be anywhere then.

"Was it something important?" she asked.

"He offered me a job at the start-up, managing their blog." He sat opposite her. "They received a second round of funding and created some new jobs. I'd have my own office and stock options and season tickets to the Giants."

"That sounds wonderful," Isabel replied, wondering why there was a pit in her stomach.

"I turned him down, I don't want to stay in San Francisco. The buildings are all white and there are too many flowers."

He smiled. "Cities should be gritty and crowded and have plenty of history."

Isabel felt the air leave her lungs. Once Rory returned to Philadelphia, they would regain their rhythm. They'd buy a small Christmas tree and celebrate Christmas by themselves. Then they would drive out to Ardmore and join their parents at the Hunt Club for venison and plum pudding.

"I want to travel for a while," Rory said. "Spend the winter in Sardinia and the spring in Ibiza."

"The JPMorgan Chase trainee program is very competitive." Isabel frowned. "I wouldn't have a job when I returned."

"I was actually thinking of traveling for a year," he said slowly. "I have enough money for a couple of generations. Why shouldn't we have fun?"

"Fun," Isabel repeated, something hard clamping her chest.

"It's not a four-letter word," he said and smiled.

Isabel wanted to say they weren't children whose only task was to learn to spell and play with their dog Spot. Adults had to do something important, or there was no point in any of it.

"And you want me to come with you?" she asked.

Rory looked up, and his eyes had never seemed so green, like the emeralds in Shreve's on Post Street.

"Only if you want to."

Isabel remembered when he proposed and she had to say yes. Her body was drawn to him like a magnet and she couldn't imagine being apart. But now she felt strangely still, like damp firewood in a fireplace.

"I don't think so." She shook her head. "I should go back to Philadelphia."

"We can postpone the wedding for a year," Rory suggested.

"You don't know where you'll be next Christmas. Maybe

you'll be sailing in Portofino or snorkeling in the Maldives."
She paused and looked at Rory. "It's all right, we'll both be fine."

"Are you sure?" Rory asked.

"Perfectly sure." She nodded, blinking back sudden tears.

"I do love you." He touched her hand. "You're the only thing
that ever held my interest."

ISABEL SPRITZED HER wrists with Lancôme perfume and thought
love wasn't just physical attraction. And it wasn't the steady
feeling she had with Neil, as if they were interlocking pieces of
a jigsaw puzzle.

Love was magical and elusive, like a number series that
seemed random but couldn't be arranged any other way. She
had been approaching it all wrong, but now she was finally
going to get it right.

It had stopped raining, and the lights on the Champs-Élysées
glittered like a diamond bracelet. She slipped on her satin
pumps and ran down to meet Antoine in the lobby.

"THIS BUILDING WAS built in 1727 for a wealthy financier,"
Antoine said, standing at the bottom of a marble circular stair-
case. "The grounds are almost two acres, and there's a chapel
and English gardens."

Isabel gazed at the black-and-white marble floors and thick
ivory columns and thought she had never seen such a beautiful
house. Gold chandeliers dangled from the ceiling, and wide
arches led to a music conservatory.

"It must have been wonderful to live in Paris in the eigh-
teenth century." She looked out the French doors at manicured
green lawns and thick hedges and gravel pathways. "All those
horses and carriages and women wearing fabulous gowns."

"The French aristocracy have always known how to enjoy themselves," Antoine mused. "My ancestor the third Comte de Villoy had a house on the Rue de la Varenne. He employed forty manservants and gave elaborate costume balls. His robes were lined with rubies and emeralds and cost more than my entire wardrobe."

"Paris really is the most romantic city," she sighed. "I would move here in a minute."

"I thought Americans love their country." Antoine smiled. "They fought so hard for their independence."

"Paris is filled with wide boulevards and elegant palaces," she said. "Philadelphia is all docks and railway stations."

"In the summer, the Champs-Élysées is so congested, the taxi drivers have shouting matches," Antoine mused. "If you try to leave the city on Friday evening, you can be stuck in traffic for hours. But if you stay you spend the weekend avoiding crowds at the Louvre."

"It sounds like people love Paris too much," Isabel laughed. "Everyone wants to be here."

Antoine's eyes were serious and he murmured, "There is always room for a lovely young American."

Isabel stumbled and tripped over an Oriental rug. Antoine steadied her and his arm brushed her chest.

"It's warm in here." She flushed. "Why don't we walk in the garden?"

"IT REMINDS ME of the dining room in a French farmhouse," Isabel said, glancing around the restaurant. Square tables were set with starched white tablecloths and Baccarat china. Paintings of purple eggplant and orange squash lined the walls, and the floor was covered with a geometric carpet.

"All the vegetables come from the restaurant's garden," she

continued. "There is a twelve-course tasting menu paired with French wines. If we are lucky, the chef will visit our table."

"You did your homework," Antoine laughed, nibbling vol-au-vent in a white onion sauce.

"Neil and I were supposed to visit Paris on our honeymoon and I researched things to do," she began. "I didn't want to miss any of the tourist attractions. People say they want to see the 'real Paris,' but there's a reason the Louvre and Eiffel Tower are so famous.

"But I wanted to dine somewhere special. So on our twentieth anniversary I could say, 'Remember that exquisite meal we had at L'Arpège? The baby turnips were delicious and the chocolate nougat was the best I ever tasted.' " She paused. "We'd realize we hadn't done anything like that in years, and fly to Paris for the weekend."

"You were supposed to be in Paris on your honeymoon?" Antoine asked.

"Neil thought the buttercream filling on the wedding cake was too dry, so we canceled the wedding." She hesitated. "Of course, there were other reasons. We couldn't agree about anything. I'm glad we called it off before the ceremony. It would have been awkward to announce things weren't going to work out while the guests were blowing bubbles at the bride and groom." She stopped and her eyes glistened. "I wanted to stay in bed for a week. But I'm happy I came to Paris, I'm having a lovely time."

"Neil made a mistake." Antoine looked at Isabel.

"What do you mean?" she asked.

"He should have eaten the cake."

THEY ATE GREEN garlic soup and vegetable ravioli. There were plates of Brussels sprouts and beetroot tartare in horseradish cream. Isabel drank a smooth Bandol and felt light and happy.

Antoine knocked the saltshaker with his sleeve and salt spilled on the tablecloth. He picked up a pinch of salt and threw it over his shoulder.

"What are you doing?" she wondered.

"It's an old superstition," he explained. "It's bad luck if you spill salt on the table unless you toss some of the salt over your shoulder."

"You don't actually believe that?" she asked.

"The French are very superstitious." He nodded. "If a pregnant woman sees an owl, she is certain to have a girl. And if you want good fortune when you move into a new house, you must bring the table in first."

"Most Americans are too pragmatic to believe in superstitions," she said. "They'll step around a ladder or avoid a black cat, but only because they saw it in a movie. I think they're wrong; the world is so mysterious. Everywhere I go in Paris, I meet someone new or something wonderful happens."

"Every year I go to Aix-en-Provence for the Christmas holidays. But this year, the hotel mixed up my reservation." Antoine ran his fingers over his wineglass. "If they hadn't made a mistake, I would be sitting in a château, staring at a damp vineyard, instead of being here with you."

Isabel remembered thinking the reason they had canceled the honeymoon and she had come to Paris by herself was so she would meet the fortune-teller. She looked at Antoine and her heart beat a little faster.

"I'm glad they mixed up the reservation too."

THEY STROLLED ALONG the Rue de la Varenne and Antoine took her hand. The street was lined with creamy stone mansions and iron latticework, and she felt like she was in a foreign movie.

Suddenly she looked up and a snowflake settled on her cheek.

"It's snowing." She turned to Antoine. "My first snowfall in Paris."

He pulled her close and kissed her softly on the lips. She kissed him back and tasted cream and cognac.

"There is a superstition that if you kiss a beautiful woman when you see the first snowflake, wonderful things will happen," he said when he released her.

"I've never heard that before," she replied.

Antoine touched her cheek and smiled. "I just made it up."

ISABEL STOOD ON the balcony and wrapped her arms around her chest. She had told Antoine she had to stop in the hotel gift shop, and said good-bye in the lobby. They were both flushed from the wine and cognac, and she didn't want to risk inviting him to her suite.

It really had been a wonderful evening; they shared an interest in history and art and French movies. She loved the way he was so comfortable in his own skin, as if he wore a white dinner jacket and dined at candlelit restaurants every night.

And she could tell he felt something toward her. When he kissed her, he didn't let her go. She remembered the soft snow falling on their hair and shivered. Was it possible that they were developing feelings for each other?

She couldn't wait to tell Alec about the Garden of Orpheus at the Musée Rodin and the fig ice cream at L'Arpège. He would be so pleased things were going well.

She stepped into the hallway and knocked on Alec's door. His light was on but there was no answer. She would have to wait and tell him tomorrow.

She walked back to her suite and unzipped her dress. She pulled on a silk robe and climbed onto the four-poster bed.

"I'm in Paris, and I'm falling love," she said aloud. "I'm the luckiest girl in the world."

chapter eleven

❧

Alec sat at the Regency desk and rubbed his neck. He had fallen asleep hunched over his notepad and had woken up in terrible pain. He flipped through the Crillon's list of services but couldn't justify spending two hundred euros on a masseuse who would probably make it worse. Celine had given him a massage for his birthday, and afterward he was in such agony, he crawled into bed with a hot water bottle and a packet of aspirin.

His sketchbook was open, and he studied a drawing of Gus and a pert cocker spaniel standing on the Pont Alexandre III. Gus wore a black beret and clutched a bouquet of red roses.

He closed the sketchbook and groaned. The last time he drew Gus romancing a dog, he was falling in love with Celine.

He remembered visiting Victor Hugo's house in the Place des Vosges with Isabel and eating goat cheese tartines at La Poilâne. It started to rain as they walked back to the Crillon and she took his arm.

His forehead was damp and he felt slightly feverish. Maybe the cream in his café au lait was sour. He couldn't have feel-

ings for Isabel; that would be worse than getting walking pneumonia.

How could he think about Isabel while he was getting over Celine? Whenever he discovered something Celine left behind—a pair of stockings in the closet, a hairpin in the bathroom—he wanted to stab himself with his toothbrush. And he was still paying off the Missoni sweater he bought her for Christmas. The salesgirl at Le Bon Marché insisted it was the must-have piece of the season, and he begrudgingly handed her his charge card.

He pictured Isabel's dark eyes and white smile and thought she was the most peculiar woman he'd ever met. She was smart and beautiful, but she trusted a Parisian gypsy with her whole future.

But it didn't matter how he felt about Isabel; she was falling in love with Antoine. He remembered seeing her light on at midnight and wondered if Antoine had spent the night.

He buttoned his shirt and thought he didn't have time to think about himself. In nine days Bettina would evict Claudia and he had to figure out a way to stop her. Bettina's gift rested on the coffee table and he knew he had to go see her.

He splashed his face with water and grabbed his coat. First he would go to Chartier in Montmartre and have a bowl of vichyssoise and roasted chicken. He pictured the *baba au rhum* with Chantilly and almost felt better.

HE STEPPED OUT of the elevator and saw a woman wearing a black wool dress and beige pumps. Her smooth pageboy curled around her shoulders and she carried a Chanel bag.

"Bettina!" he exclaimed, his cheeks turning pale "What are you doing at the Crillon?"

The elevator doors closed, and he wished he could force

them open. Why was Bettina here and what did she want? It couldn't be anything good; she was like the grim reaper with a designer purse and stockings.

"I called your phone, but it was off," Bettina said. "I thought I would come and see you."

"I was going to get some lunch," he explained, wiping the sweat from his forehead.

He couldn't face Bettina without first having a glass of Pinot Noir or a tall scotch.

"I'll join you." She walked beside him. "There's something I want to talk about."

"I'm going to Chartier in Montmartre," he replied. "I know you hate sharing your table with other diners, and the waitstaff has been known to recycle the breadbasket."

Bettina hesitated and her eyes flickered. "We'll have lunch here. I haven't eaten in the dining room since the Hôtel de Crillon reopened."

"At the Crillon?" Alec asked. "I couldn't afford a buttered radish."

"It will be my treat," Bettina said and smiled. "I never gave you a Christmas present."

THEY SAT AT a round table in the main dining room, and Alec gazed at the crystal wineglasses and pewter breadbaskets. The domed ceiling was made of blue mosaic tile, and red velvet drapes were tied with silver sashes. A grand piano stood in the corner and there was a signed Degas above the marble fireplace.

He tore open a baguette and wondered why anyone needed a gold-plated butter knife and how could they charge forty euros for a poached egg with hollandaise sauce. Maybe he should move to the countryside and keep a cow and a few chickens. Restaurant prices in Paris were outrageous.

"You said you were hungry," Bettina said when Alec ordered a bowl of pumpkin soup and frisée salad.

"I can never eat when the thermostat is too high. Hotel dining rooms are too stuffy." He wiped his brow. "It gives me indigestion."

"You should be grateful that you are staying in a suite at the Crillon." Bettina raised her eyebrow. "After all, you're not paying for it."

"The hazelnut truffles and lavender bubble bath have been delightful." He nodded. "But I'm ready to go home."

"What does Isabel think?" she asked. "Is she prepared to live in a fifth-floor walk-up in the Marais, or does she have her sights set on 40 Rue de Passy?"

"Isabel?" he spluttered. "What on earth are you talking about?"

"The young American I met at the Red Cross charity ball," she continued. "Celine was the love of your life, but you moved on so quickly. When we were children, you took hours to pick out a library book, and I couldn't stand going with you to the patisserie because you couldn't decide between a chocolate éclair and vanilla custard." She pursed her lips. "Are you planning on marrying Isabel on New Year's Eve and moving into 40 Rue de Passy?"

"I rescued Isabel from the balcony when she locked herself out," he snorted. "All that talk about romantic dinners and walks along the Seine was just an American admiring Paris. And I would never move into 40 Rue de Passy; it belongs to my mother."

Alec gasped and wished he could take back his words. He should never have said Claudia deserved to stay in his father's house; it would only infuriate Bettina. He wiped his forehead and thought he really had to ask the maître d' to turn down the thermostat.

"I know you asked Celine to marry you so Claudia wouldn't have to leave." Bettina sipped her wine. "Though I still don't understand why she agreed. Her father could buy her any mansion in Paris. And an intelligent, beautiful woman should marry someone important. It looks bad if all French politicians date actresses and models."

"I proposed to Celine because I was madly in love with her, and she said yes because she felt the same," he retorted. "Édouard is like a tortoise. Most of us aren't willing to be in a relationship that moves slower than rush hour traffic on the Boulevard Saint-Germain."

"Édouard and I want to get it right, rather than calling off the ceremony two days before the wedding," Bettina replied, skewering a lamb cutlet.

"I've given up on women and marriage." He tore apart a baguette. "I'm going to be a doting godfather who spoils his godchildren with gold coins on Christmas morning. When I'm old, I'll get a dog and people will comment we have the same facial expressions."

Alec had considered getting a dog, but it seemed disloyal to Gus. But maybe when he had arthritis and couldn't draw anymore, he would get a Saint Bernard that slept on a rug in front of the fireplace.

"I don't believe you," Bettina insisted. "I saw the way you and Isabel looked at each other at the ball."

"Then you need glasses," Alec snapped. He drizzled a sherry vinaigrette on endive leaves and sighed. "Isabel is seeing a French *comte*."

"A *comte*?" She raised her eyebrow. "I thought she was here on vacation."

"She said they're falling in love." He fiddled with his collar. "Last night they went to the Musée Rodin and L'Arpège."

"Maybe I was wrong." She ate pureed squash. "I'm sure they are a lovely pair."

"You've never even met him—how do you know he's right for Isabel?" he demanded. "Just because he's a *comte* doesn't mean he wears Armani suits and Gucci loafers like Louis Jourdan in *Gigi*."

"You need to look after yourself, you're over thirty." Bettina studied his frayed sweater and corduroy slacks. "You'll never find someone to marry if you get a soft belly and lose your hair."

"My stomach is like a board!" he fumed. "And I didn't come to lunch to get dating tips. If you'll excuse me, I have to go."

"You can't leave yet." She patted her mouth with a napkin. "I asked the chef to make chocolate *bûche de Noël*, it is Christmas."

Alec grudgingly stayed and shared their childhood dessert. He waited for Bettina to return from the powder room and stabbed a sugar cube with his dessertspoon. Having lunch with his sister was like attending a dinner party with Attila the Hun. He pictured Gus wearing a fur coat and earmuffs and eating venison with a Norwegian holding a spear.

Now wasn't the time to ask Bettina to let his mother stay in the house. She was like the croupier at the casino in Monte Carlo. She couldn't wait to sweep his chips off the roulette wheel and leave him penniless.

Bettina returned from the powder room, and he ate a large bite of chocolate and nougat. If he kept his mouth full, he couldn't say anything wrong.

"Next week 40 Rue de Passy will be ours," she said, pulling out her chair. "We'll update the kitchen of course, it's a fire hazard. And I plan on breaking the wall between the conservatory and library. Wouldn't it be lovely to have one large room with views of the garden?"

"The house is perfect the way it is," he grumbled. "I don't want anything to do with renovations."

"You don't have to." Bettina smiled and poured cream into her demitasse. "I'll just send you half the bill."

THEY STOOD AT the hotel entrance while the valet called a taxi. Alec glanced at bellboys in gold uniforms and guests wearing cashmere jackets and thought everyone looked so happy.

It was Christmas at the Crillon; he should be enjoying the free hot cocoa and gingerbread. Instead he felt like he had been to the principal's office and narrowly missed getting detention.

"Thank you for lunch," he said and reached into his jacket pocket. "I bought you a Christmas present."

"It's the least I could do now that you don't have someone to cook for you." Bettina put the package in her purse and stepped off the curb. "You didn't have to get me anything. Celine gave me the best gift I could imagine."

"If I hear from her, I'll let her know," he muttered.

"I am your big sister and I do care about you." She turned around. "Next time you fall in love, try harder to hold on to her."

ALEC SAT ON a leather stool in the Crillon bar and fiddled with his scotch glass. He shouldn't drink hard liquor when he felt feverish, but this was an exception. Bettina was like the female villain in a James Bond movie. She looked innocent until she opened her mouth and started spewing threats in Russian.

He ate a handful of cashew nuts and suddenly choked. What if Bettina didn't believe him and asked Isabel? He pictured her slinking through the lobby like Mata Hari.

There might not be anything going on between him and

Isabel, but he still didn't want her to know about his family. And what if he was falling in love with her? Bettina would ruin his chances.

He threw a ten-euro note on the table and hurried to the elevator. The only way to stop Bettina was to get to Isabel first. He pressed the button and hoped he wasn't too late.

"ALEC!" ISABEL SAID when he knocked on the door. She wore a ribbed sweater and tan slacks. She held a leather-bound book and had a yellow highlighter stuck behind her ear.

"Come in. I'm studying the plot of *Rigoletto*." She paused. "Antoine asked me to the opera at the Palais Garnier, so I'm learning the story line. It can be so embarrassing to cry when the female lead is actually happy her husband drank a vial of poison." Her brown eyes sparkled. "We are going to Café de la Paix after the performance to have oysters and French champagne."

"That's wonderful, but I need your help." Antoine sat opposite her.

"Are you ill?" She looked at him. "Your cheeks are flushed and you are holding your neck strangely."

"It's nothing, I have a crick in my neck." He flinched. "I'm going to Versailles and I was hoping you'd join me."

"Why are you going to Versailles?" she asked.

"I'm drawing a series of sketches of Gus trying to save his estate from being overrun by a murderous crowd." He fiddled with the cushion. "The French Republic may not have been fond of their queen, but Versailles was Marie Antoinette's home. It wasn't polite of the mob to pound on the gate as if they belonged there."

"I thought Gus was a male dog." Isabel frowned.

"It's not based on Marie Antoinette. I certainly don't approve

of her actions." He ran his hands through his hair. "Though I do think the guillotine was barbaric—a permanent stay in the Bastille would have been sufficient. I'm going to set it in a castle in Scotland, but I want to visit Versailles for inspiration."

"Why do you need me?" she asked.

"I want to see it through someone else's eyes, so I don't miss the little things . . ." He paused. "Like a squirrel collecting nuts in a tapestry or hand-painted doves on a teacup."

"I was going to buy a dress at Le Bon Marché for this evening." Isabel hesitated. "I can't wear the same gown I wore to the ball."

"We have plenty of time," Alec assured her. "We'll visit the L'Orangerie and Queen's hamlet and Petites Écuries." He waved at a pile of books on the coffee table. "You'll learn more about the French aristocracy than from reading history books."

"They do all say the same thing. Marie Antoinette should never have siphoned off millions of francs from the treasury to send to her brother in Austria, and if Louis XVI had more of a backbone, the French Revolution wouldn't have happened." She stood up and grabbed her jacket. "I can't wait to see Versailles at Christmas. It will be like one of those winter scenes in a snow globe."

"EVERYTHING IS SO large," Isabel said, looking up at the domed ceiling.

They had toured the gardens with their marble fountains and stone statues and chestnut trees. Alec led her through the Queen's Hamlet and showed her the vegetable patches filled with broccoli and cabbage and asparagus.

Now they stood in the Hall of Mirrors and Alec caught his breath. No matter how many times he visited Versailles, he couldn't quite believe it was real. It was like a child's fantasy

of an Arabian palace. Gold statues lined the walls and crystal chandeliers dangled from the ceiling and the parquet floor had jeweled flecks.

"Versailles was originally built as a hunting lodge for King Louis XIII," Alec said. "Later three wings were added and Louis XVI and Marie Antoinette each had their own apartments."

"I do envy Marie Antoinette," Isabel mused, gazing at the intricate tapestries.

"I'm not surprised," Alec murmured. "Most women would like a jewelry box overflowing with emerald and ruby pendants and a closet filled with couture gowns."

"I don't envy her because of her clothes or jewels." Isabel shrugged. "Though a pretty dress can make you happy when you are feeling down, and they say diamonds are a girl's best friend for a reason.

"I envy her because she was in love. The royal family planned to escape, but Louis XVI refused to leave." She paused. "Marie Antoinette could have been carried safely over the border, but she chose to stay with her husband."

"She ended up being dragged through Paris in an open cart," he grumbled. "She probably regretted her decision when the citizens threw apples at her shorn head."

"Don't you see, there's nothing more important than love. She could have started a new life in Austria. But she would rather die in the worst possible way than be without the man she loved."

"You've seen too many romantic movies." Alec grinned.

"I thought I was in love with Rory. But when he moved to California, I barely missed him," she began. "Neil and I were perfect for each other. We took the same business school courses and read the same economic journals. But you can't build a future with someone because you own the same brand of briefcase.

"It doesn't matter now because I met Antoine. Oh, I didn't get a chance to tell you about our evening. We saw Rodin's *The Thinker,* and the passion fruit soufflé at L'Arpège was delicious." She paused. "After dinner we strolled along the boulevard and it started snowing. He kissed me and I wanted it to last forever."

"That's the best way to get pneumonia," Alec said. "I hope you both came home and took a hot bath."

"I didn't ask him up to my suite." Isabel hesitated. "Somehow I didn't think it was right."

"You want Antoine to propose but you didn't want to have an nightcap?" Alec demanded. "Maybe you shouldn't listen to the fortune-teller."

"What do you mean?" she asked.

"If you're in love, you don't want to be apart," he insisted.

If he could make her see the fortune-teller was wrong and she didn't really have feelings for Antoine, they could start from the beginning. He could ask her on a date and see if they were interested in each other.

"I have to trust the fortune-teller," she said, suddenly impatient. "I've made terrible mistakes before and this time I have to get it right."

"You can't really believe this fortune-teller knows who you should marry!" Alec spluttered. "She only met you for a few minutes. Even a dating site needs more information before it can suggest potential suitors."

"People think the answer to everything is on Wikipedia, and if you spend enough time on WebMD you can cure cancer." She paused and her eyes were bright. "But there are many things we don't know. Why shouldn't a fortune-teller predict my future?"

Alec opened his mouth and stopped. If she was in love with Antoine, he wanted her to be happy. But he flashed on Bettina

saying there was something between them and wondered if she was right.

"Isabel . . ." he began.

"Yes?"

He wanted to tell her that when you were really in love, you felt it in every bone in your body. You couldn't stop thinking about the person and all you wanted was to be together. But she was desperate to believe the fortune-teller and wouldn't hear his advice.

"It's getting crowded in here." He pointed to a group of Japanese tourists. "Let's see the stables."

THEY VISITED THE private opera house and queen's bedchamber. Alec pointed out the gold ottomans where high-ranking courtiers watched the royal births, and Isabel laughed and wondered whether Marie Antoinette wore lipstick while she was in labor.

They stepped into the courtyard and thick clouds hung over the fir trees. Alec shivered and knew he was coming down with a fever. Suddenly he longed to be in his suite with a pair of dry socks and heated brandy.

"I had the most wonderful time, thank you for taking me," Isabel said.

"I'm glad we came. Though I'm looking forward to the Crillon's hot cocoa and heated floors." Alec glanced at her wrist and frowned. "Weren't you wearing your glass bracelet?"

"Of course, I wear it everywhere." Isabel touched her arm and gasped. "Maybe it fell off in the Queen's Hamlet when I took off my jacket."

"I'll look for it," he suggested.

"That would be too much trouble, it could be anywhere." She stopped and her lips trembled. "It's just the fortune-teller said it would come to have great value."

"I'll retrace our steps like in an Agatha Christie novel," he said. "Stay in the Grand Trianon so you don't freeze to death."

Alec crossed the courtyard and thought he needed his head examined. If he crouched on his knees, sifting through the winter cabbage, he'd end up in the hospital. But he was the one who had dragged Isabel to Versailles; the least he could do was find her bracelet.

The lodge had a paneled great room and stone kitchen. He peeked in the narrow bedrooms and wondered why Marie Antoinette insisted on living so simply when she had lavish quarters at the palace.

He remembered a sketch of Gus using his X-ray vision to find buried treasure in the Sahara Desert. All Gus had to do was wiggle his wet nose and he discovered an ancient coin buried beneath the sand. Gus would find the bracelet in a minute.

Alec entered the garden and searched through the vegetables. Suddenly he noticed a pink glass band draped over an artichoke. He dropped it in his pocket and hurried across the cobblestones.

"You found it, I don't know how to thank you!" Isabel reached up and kissed him on the cheek. "I told you wonderful things keep happening. Can you imagine finding one glass bracelet in all of Versailles?"

"It's my pleasure." Alec nodded. His throat burned and his forehead was covered in sweat. "I think we better call a taxi."

ALEC SAT ON the blue velvet sofa in his suite and huddled over a glass of brandy. Even after a hot shower, he felt like a woodpecker had attacked his head and his legs were submerged in quicksand.

He shouldn't have trudged through the vegetable patch when he was already sick. But Isabel looked like a child who

was afraid the Easter bunny wouldn't arrive. And she had trekked through the drafty halls of Versailles when she could have been relaxing at the Crillon.

It had been a terrible day. Bettina had made it clear she was going to evict Claudia and he did nothing to stop her. And Isabel seemed madly in love with Antoine. He wouldn't be surprised if tomorrow she announced their engagement!

But it had been fun talking about Marie Antoinette and the French Revolution. And he loved Isabel's look of wonderment when he showed her the boulle tortoiseshell cabinetry in the king's bedchamber and the Grand Canal in L'Orangerie.

He remembered her kissing him on the cheek and her scent of floral perfume and expensive lotions. God, he wanted it to go on forever!

She must realize she was being foolish. She barely knew Antoine and wasn't even ready to invite him to her suite. She couldn't get engaged just because the fortune-teller said she was going to fall in love with a French aristocrat.

He swallowed two aspirin and washed them down with brandy. He had to help his mother and win over Isabel. They both needed him, and he wasn't going to disappoint them.

chapter twelve

❦

Isabel glanced in the full-length mirror and couldn't believe she was seeing her own reflection. Her eyes were coated with sparkly eye shadow and her cheeks were lightly powdered and she felt like Audrey Hepburn in *Sabrina*.

She had returned from Versailles and walked past the boutique in the lobby. The emerald Balenciaga gown in the window was so perfect, she felt like it had her name on it. She entered the store and admired the crepe bodice and full skirt. The salesgirl suggested pairing it with jeweled pumps and Isabel handed over her credit card.

Now she fiddled with diamond earrings and knew she had been right. It was a gorgeous dress and Antoine would be pleased. She glanced at the bouquet of yellow roses on the end table and thought she was in a fairy tale. She was going to one of the most famous opera houses in the world and falling in love!

The afternoon at Versailles had been lovely; Alec was so easy to be with. But she felt at times something was bothering

him. Maybe he needed someone to talk to and didn't know how to ask.

Antoine was meeting her in the lobby in thirty minutes; she had plenty of time to see Alec and make sure he was all right. She would insist he order a bowl of tomato basil soup and side of vegetables. He couldn't get better on a diet of crackers and strawberry jam.

Her phone rang and she answered it.

"Isabel, darling," her mother's voice came down the line, "I've been calling you, but your phone goes straight to voice mail."

"I'm sorry, it never seems to hold a charge." Isabel bit her lip. "I've been meaning to call, I've been busy."

"I'm glad you're getting out and exploring." Adele's voice was soft. "I wasn't sure it was a good idea to stay in the honeymoon suite at the Hôtel de Crillon. I thought you might wish you were there with Neil."

"I am the one who called off the wedding," Isabel reminded her. "I actually called Neil yesterday. It's so strange, you can spend more than a year with someone and then not know what to say on the phone."

"It can't be easy for either of you, but I'm sure you made the right decision. You couldn't get married if you had any doubts." She paused. "I am concerned about you being alone in Paris. Your father and I went once at Christmas and everywhere you turned there were couples holding hands and kissing. It seems everyone who is in love goes to Paris at Christmas."

"I was a little lonely, but now I'm having a wonderful time," Isabel said. "I ate dinner at Tour d'Argent and visited Versailles."

She considered telling her about Antoine, but it wasn't something you discussed over the phone. There would be plenty of time to explain after he proposed.

"I ran into Peggy Danford at the florist," Adele continued. "Rory married a Flemish girl and is living in Brussels."

"Rory!" Isabel exclaimed.

"It might not be the best time to tell you, but I thought you should know," Adele said uncertainly.

"I haven't talked to Rory in years," Isabel replied. "I'm very happy for him."

"Whoever thought Rory would settle down," Adele mused. "You think you're never going to meet the right person, but eventually you do."

"I'm not sure Brussels is settling down," Isabel laughed.

"It was very brave to call the wedding off three days before the ceremony," Adele continued. "You are bright and beautiful and you will find the right person."

"Don't worry." Isabel glanced in the mirror at her diamond pendant and red lipstick. "The next time I fall in love, it will be forever."

ISABEL HUNG UP and remembered when her mother would watch her do precalculus homework in high school. Adele laughed she could conjugate a French verb and reel off the names of British poets, but trigonometry reminded her of Chinese takeout menus. Isabel replied there was nothing simpler than math; you just had to approach it logically.

How could she explain to her mother she was trusting her future to a fortune-teller? She snapped the glass bracelet around her wrist and knew she was doing the right thing. The fortune-teller had been correct about the bracelet and about almost being killed, and now she was right about Antoine.

And who wouldn't want their daughter to marry a French *comte*! Perhaps her parents could come to Paris in the spring or she and Antoine would fly to Philadelphia. She glanced at

her watch and realized talking on the phone and daydreaming about Antoine had made her late. She would have to see Alec after the opera. She spritzed her wrists with floral perfume and hurried to the elevator.

ISABEL SHIFTED IN her seat and peered at the stage. The velvet chairs weren't as comfortable as they looked, and the heating in the opera house seemed to be malfunctioning. It had been so cold in the foyer she wished she'd brought a wrap, but now it was so hot, she might faint. And the orchestra was just below them, so every time a trumpet blared, she was afraid she'd burst an eardrum.

She glanced at Antoine sitting beside her and took a deep breath. He looked so handsome in a white dinner jacket and tan slacks. It wasn't his fault the curtain went up half an hour late and now Isabel was desperate for a sparkling water.

She should be enjoying it more; she was sitting in a box at the Palais Garnier watching *Rigoletto*. But the performers traipsed around the stage shouting at each other in Italian, and the female singers wore so much makeup, they looked like they were made of plaster.

The curtain came down and Isabel stood up. It was intermission and they could go to the bar and drink a glass of Dom Pérignon. She followed Antoine down the circular staircase into the grand foyer.

"I read about the Palais Garnier in Fodor's," Isabel said. "It was designed for Napoleon III by Charles Garnier and it took fourteen painters and seventy-three sculptors to complete the exterior." She sipped a glass of champagne. "It was the most expensive structure built in the Second Empire and every opera company wanted to perform here.

"These days people build whole communities online and

they can watch operas on Netflix." She gazed at the baroque columns. "But in four hundred years, what will they have to show except a bunch of websites and phone apps?"

Isabel glanced at Antoine and blushed. The French aristocracy grew up surrounded by priceless art and marble statues. She was acting like a tourist seeing the *Mona Lisa* for the first time at the Louvre.

He leaned forward and kissed her.

"What was that for?" she asked.

"I love being with you, you make me see things in a new light. I've attended the Palais Garnier since I was a boy, but I never noticed the gold leaf on the floor or the cherubs in the murals. I was too busy wishing the program was over," he whispered in her ear. "To be honest, I still think it's a little boring."

Isabel felt a little shiver, as if there was a fan at the back of her neck. Antoine said he loved being with her and she felt the same!

"How could you say that?" she laughed, and her shoulders relaxed. "It's *Rigoletto*!"

Antoine went to the bar to get a selection of canapés and a blond woman kissed him on the cheek. She had blue eyes and high cheekbones and a wide pink mouth. He took her arm and led her across the foyer.

"This is my dear old friend Jacqueline L'Hermitte," he said to Isabel.

"You make me sound like I'm one hundred," Jacqueline laughed. "Antoine and I attended school together in Switzerland. He was terrible at following rules, he insisted on visiting the female dorms after dark."

"We were fourteen, we wanted the girls' supply of chocolates," he explained.

"You weren't always fourteen," she said, and Isabel noticed the heart-shaped mole on her cheek. "At the last school dance

you looked so handsome, the other girls whispered that you were going to be a movie star."

"Jacqueline has a selective memory." Antoine grinned. "I remember a bad haircut and shaving nick on my chin."

"We must catch up, I haven't seen you the whole holidays," Jacqueline continued. "Are you coming to Chamonix? Pierre and Gustav rented a chalet for the month of February."

"I wouldn't miss it." Antoine nodded. The bells chimed and he turned to Isabel. "Shall we go inside? The second act is beginning."

Jacqueline kissed Antoine on both cheeks, and Isabel inhaled Chanel No. 5. She gulped the rest of the champagne and wondered who Pierre and Gustav were and how Antoine could take a month off from the bank.

The bells chimed again, and Isabel thought she couldn't worry about that now. First she had to get through the last act of *Rigoletto*.

ISABEL SAT IN the floral booth and sipped a Kir Royale. She gazed at the hanging potted plants and red velvet wallpaper and felt impossibly Parisian. She had attended the opera, and now she was having supper at one of the most famous cafés in Paris.

She had read in the guidebook that Café de la Paix opened in 1862 across from the Palais Garnier. Patrons lingered over French onion soup and almond sponge cake and glasses of Campari. Oscar Wilde had been a regular, and Marlene Dietrich had her own table.

The third act of *Rigoletto* was mesmerizing, and when Rigoletto collapsed over his dead daughter's body, Isabel brushed away tears. Antoine clasped her hand and she smiled and moved closer.

Now she glanced at women in glittering cocktail dresses and remembered Antoine's friend Jacqueline. She was the kind of woman who slipped on a turtleneck sweater and loafers and ran into the street looking like a supermodel.

Antoine probably knew countless Jacquelines and Aimées and Chantals. Isabel had never been jealous, but she didn't live in a city where all the women had smooth chignons and pouty lips and smoky eyes.

"Jacqueline is charming." She ate a bite of veal kidney. "What does she do?"

"Jacqueline doesn't do anything besides buy lipsticks and handbags," Antoine laughed. "Her family is a *noblesse de cloche* and their title dates back to the fourteenth century."

"She must do something," she insisted.

"She skis in the Alps and sails on the Riviera and squeezes in cooking classes." He shrugged, nibbling oysters on the half shell. "I'm sure she would say she is terribly busy."

"It sounds refreshing, but I'd get bored if I spent all my time on the ocean or tossing vegetables into a skillet." She paused. "I've wanted to be an analyst since high school."

"I dreamed of being an Olympic skier after I graduated from Le Rosey," he said. "But I broke my leg and spent an entire season reading detective novels. The surgeon said I'd never be able to race and my father asked me to join the bank."

"Does your father work at the same bank?" Isabel asked.

"It's the family bank," he explained. "My great-grandfather opened the first office on Place Vendôme. I'm the client liaison. I have a pleasant secretary and paneled office and healthy expense account."

"You don't actually work with numbers?" She felt something hard press against her chest.

"My job is to make sure the automaker from Munich leaves Paris with a stack of postcards and bottle of eau de cologne for

his wife." He smiled. "It's quite enjoyable, though too many dinners of cheese soufflé makes you fat."

Isabel ate new potatoes and her thoughts swirled in her head. Antoine had never said he was an analyst; she just assumed they held similar positions.

And what did it matter if his family owned the bank? He wasn't like Rory, who flitted from one interest to the next, or Neil, who was ready to give up his career for bundles of hay and a bucket.

She had to trust the fortune-teller. Antoine was perfect and she should relax and enjoy herself.

They ate chocolate with praline for dessert and talked about the French Alps. Every year a group of school friends rented a chalet in Megève or Courchevel. They skied off piste and spent the evenings eating fondue and complaining about their knees.

"I bought you a gift," Antoine said, reaching into his pocket.

"You took me to dinner and the opera," Isabel protested. "You don't need to get me a present."

"It's Christmas and I'm with a beautiful woman." He placed a red velvet box on the table. "How could I not buy something special?"

Isabel gazed at the square jewelry box and gasped. Was Antoine going to propose? Everything about her stay in Paris had been magical; now the fortune-teller's last prediction was coming true.

"Are you going to open it?" he interrupted her thoughts.

"Of course." She snapped it open and discovered a pair of silver earrings. She looked at Antoine and her voice wavered. "Oh, they're lovely."

"They're silver snowflakes. I saw them in the window at Cartier." He noticed her expression and faltered. "If you don't like them, I can exchange them."

"I'm just overwhelmed," she said quickly. "I'm sitting at the Café de la Paix eating Belgian chocolate and raspberries." She looked at Antoine and her face broke into a smile. "There's nothing else I want, and I'm having a wonderful time."

THEY STROLLED ALONG the Champs-Élysées, and Isabel thought Alec was right; she had to invite Antoine to her suite. What could be more romantic than gazing at the Christmas lights on the Place de la Concorde and sipping aged cognac?

"See that star in the sky?" He pointed at the night sky. "When I was a child, I received a telescope for Christmas and spent all my time studying the stars and the moon. I thought the stars were made of precious jewels and wanted to launch myself in a rocket ship and grab them," he continued. "Then I got older and put the telescope away and concentrated on tennis and skiing." He took her hand. "When I met you at the Red Cross charity ball, I realized I didn't need to go to space to find a treasure. It was right here on earth. You're the loveliest woman I've ever met."

"When I was six I saw a rainbow from my bedroom window and followed it into the garden," she began. "I discovered a birds' nest and was sure the leprechauns left eggs filled with emeralds and rubies. Magic is everywhere if you let yourself believe in it."

Antoine drew her toward him and kissed her. His lips were warm and he tasted of praline and almonds.

"That's the wonderful thing about life," he whispered. "Sometimes the greatest gift shows up when you least expect it."

She kissed him back and a shiver ran down her spine. She pressed against his chest and suddenly thought the world was spinning.

"I'm terribly sorry, but I have to go," Antoine sighed, tuck-

ing her hair behind her ear. "I promised a client I would take him to the top of the Eiffel Tower, and I can't get out of it."

"Of course." Isabel kept the disappointment out of her voice. "I had a wonderful evening."

"I'd like to see you tomorrow night," he said, kissing her again. "Perhaps we could take a boat cruise down the Seine."

She kissed him back and her chest expanded. "I can't think of anything I'd like better."

ISABEL TOSSED HER purse on the coffee table and sank onto an ivory love seat. The oysters at Café de la Paix were delicious and the walk along the Champs-Élysées was like being in a Cary Grant movie. And everything Antoine said had been so romantic. He was honest and warm, and when they were together she felt as if she was a glass of sparkly champagne.

Then why did she feel wobbly, like when she went outside for the first time after a bad flu?

Did she really belong in a chalet in the French Alps or on a yacht on the Riviera? Could she learn European customs and chat with Antoine's friends as if she'd attended a Swiss boarding school? And was she ready to give up her position at JPMorgan Chase and Sunday brunches at her parents' estate in Ardmore?

But then she remembered the empty feeling when she canceled the wedding. She couldn't bear eating a carton of Greek yogurt and Caesar salad for dinner. And what was the point of going apple picking if you had no one to share it with?

It didn't matter if she had to learn to use the Paris metro and negotiate with the butcher. Even if her children grew up with French accents and a hazy knowledge of American history, she would have a husband and family.

Antoine was the man she was going to marry; she just had

to figure out how to get him to propose. She glanced at the red Cartier box and suddenly her heart beat faster. How was Antoine to know she would consider moving to Paris unless she told him?

She remembered when they were at Musée Rodin and she laughed that she would move to Paris in a minute. But all tourists said that; it was like saying you wish you could spend every day at Disneyland when you arrive in Los Angeles. Tomorrow night she would tell him she always had dreamed of living in Paris.

A bowl of fruit sat on the coffee table, and she wondered if Alec was feeling better.

"I hope it's not too late to take him an orange and bunch of grapes," she said aloud. She walked to the window and peered at his balcony. "His light is on and I can't wait to tell him my good news."

"YOU CAN'T KNOCK on someone's door at midnight," Alec said when he answered the door. "I could be half naked and asleep."

"You don't look half naked, you're wearing a suit." Isabel placed the fruit basket on an end table and looked at Alec. He wore a navy suit and white shirt and red tie. "I didn't mean to intrude, are you going out?"

"Where would I be going in the middle of the night? I'm not a Midwestern tourist who has to see the lights on the Arc de Triomphe," he asked. "I put on a suit when I get blocked. I pretend I'm sitting in an office, and if I don't finish my illustrations, my boss is going to breathe down my neck."

"I thought authors get writer's block." She ate a bite of a peach. "I've never heard of artists suffering the same thing."

"It took Michelangelo six years to paint the Sistine Chapel,"

he replied. "Creating art isn't like building a house, it doesn't come with a set of blueprints."

"It looks like you're still blocked." She picked up a sketch of Gus leaning over a princess lying in a coffin. The princess had long black hair and Gus kissed her on the mouth. "Isn't this a scene from *Sleeping Beauty*?"

"There are only so many stories in the world." He snatched the paper. "Everyone relates to fairy tales. How many family situations remind you of Cinderella, and how many women think they need to be rescued by a handsome prince like Rapunzel was?"

"I don't need rescuing," Isabel said sharply. "I just want to fall in love."

"Ah, yes," Alec said. "How was the opera?"

"We ate chocolate pralines at Café de la Paix and saw *Rigoletto* at the Palais Garnier." She paused and her eyes were bright. "The men wore elegant tuxedos and the women were dressed in jeweled evening gowns and it was like a scene in *Casino Royale*."

"Then why aren't you drinking Drambuie with Antoine instead of eating a peach with me?" he asked, walking to the bar and filling two snifters with brandy.

"He had a prior commitment and I couldn't wait to tell you my good news." She paused. "Antoine gave me silver snowflake earrings from Cartier, and I was disappointed they weren't an engagement ring. I realized if I want him to propose, I need to give him a hint." She fiddled with her bracelet. "Tomorrow night we're taking a cruise on the Seine. It will be bitterly cold, so we'll sit in a dark corner and watch the lights on the Pont Alexandre III. I'll say I've never seen anything so beautiful, I wish I could pick up and move." She sipped the brandy. "He'll laugh that I can't be serious, and I'll reply I've never been more

serious about anything. Paris is like diamonds; a girl could never refuse either.

"He'll take that as his cue and get down on his knee and ask me to marry him. He'll say he wanted to give me his grandmother's emerald ring but it's in a safe-deposit box, so would I accept a token?" She paused. "Then he'll take off his pinkie ring and slip it on my finger."

"He wears a pinkie ring?" Alec frowned.

"It's gold with a red coat of arms." Isabel nodded. "We'll have a civil ceremony at the Hôtel de Ville. After the ceremony it will start raining and Antoine will murmur that's good luck. The wedding luncheon will be at the George Cinq and we'll take a short honeymoon to Venice."

"Don't you want your family to be here?" Alec cut in. "Your parents just spent months planning your wedding to Neil. I don't think they'd appreciate receiving a postcard with your new name and address."

"You're right, but I know they want me to be happy." She bit her lip. "We'll have a reception at Antoine's château in August! My mother can help plan it and we'll have so much fun picking out the menu and choosing the flowers."

Alec refilled her brandy snifter and she bumped his arm and brandy spilled down the front of her dress. He blotted it with a napkin and she felt his hand press against the chiffon.

"I'm terribly sorry, I've ruined your evening gown," he gasped. "I'll pay to get it cleaned."

"It's nothing. I'll send it to the hotel cleaners and they'll get it out." She looked down at the gold stain. "But I should go take it off."

She glanced at the coffee table and saw a sketch of Gus kneeling in front of a young woman in a red satin dress. Gus wore pantaloons and a gold cape and held a purple velvet cushion.

The woman had dark hair and diamond earrings and was wearing a jeweled slipper.

"I like this one." She picked it up. "Is it Gus and Cinderella after the ball?"

"*Cinderella* is one of Grimm's best fairy tales," Alec grumbled, pointing to the drawing. "But my story is completely different. Cinderella is a blonde, and she's a brunette."

ISABEL ENTERED HER suite and unzipped her Balenciaga gown. It wasn't Alec's fault he'd spilled brandy on the dress and it was nice of him to offer to pay to remove the stain.

She folded it over a chair and thought she'd send it to the hotel cleaner in the morning. She had so many things to think about: she had to pick out the perfect outfit to wear tomorrow night and brush up on French history. And should she update her résumé if she was going to look for a job in Paris?

She selected a cotton robe and noticed the red satin gown she'd worn to the Red Cross charity ball. It looked so familiar, perhaps she saw a woman wearing it at the Palais Garnier.

She climbed into bed and remembered where she had seen it; it was the dress that was in Alec's illustration. She pulled the sheets over her shoulders and fell asleep.

chapter thirteen

❧

Alec fiddled with his colored pencil and studied the sketch of Gus wearing a red cape and carrying a wicker basket. Gus stood next to a bed and looked worriedly at the wolf under the covers. Alec tossed the pencil on the desk and strode to the window.

He had stayed up all night drawing Gus and two little pigs waiting for the wolf to blow down their thatched cottage, and Gus striding through the forest on his way to Grandma's house. He wondered why there were so many wolves in fairy tales and poured another shot of brandy. He finally switched to coffee and fell asleep clutching his notepad.

Now it was midmorning and clouds hung over the Place de la Concorde. He really should take off his suit and shower, but first he was determined to finish one illustration.

Usually ideas came so quickly, he kept a notepad in his pocket. He could be buying honey at the outdoor market in Montmartre and suddenly want to draw Gus fighting off a swarm of angry bees at a bee farm in Tanzania.

But ever since he and Isabel returned from Versailles, his mind was blank. At first he thought it was because he was sick,

and all he needed was a bowl of soup and some aspirin. But now his fever was down and he still couldn't think of a drawing that didn't include a handsome prince or wicked witch.

The last time he had been blocked was a few weeks after he proposed to Celine. He got two wisdom teeth extracted and accepted her invitation to recuperate on her sofa. It was still the honeymoon period of their relationship, when he didn't mind that her coffee cups had lipstick stains and she allowed him to dry his undershirts on the clothesline in her garden.

"GETTING ONE'S WISDOM teeth extracted is like agreeing to a lobotomy," Alec groaned, holding a frozen bag of peas against his cheek. "You go into the dentist's office with a jaunty step and eating a bag of toffees and come out feeling like a zombie and with cheeks the size of pillows."

"You can barely see the swelling," Celine said. It was Saturday and she was curled up in an armchair with a bowl of café au lait and a copy of *Don Quixote* in Spanish. "I don't know why you're complaining. The dentist gave you a bottle of painkillers and I stocked the fridge with fresh orange juice and ice cream."

"If I take the painkillers, I feel like I'm in a car wash," he muttered. "I have a deadline and I haven't been able to draw anything except Gus lying in bed with a cold compress."

"It can't be that difficult." She flipped the page. "It is a children's book."

"Just because I'm not writing a six-hundred-page tome about chasing windmills doesn't mean it's not important." Alec bristled, glancing at the cover of her book. "And who reads an original text of *Don Quixote*? I'd rather get my remaining two wisdom teeth out."

"I have to read it for work." Celine smoothed her hair.

"We have a Spanish diplomat speaking before the General Conference."

"And I have to fill this sketch pad or I'll be eating frozen peas for dinner for a month." He grimaced. "Children expect Gus to cross a rushing river with crocodiles snapping at his paws or dangle from the tail of an airplane above shark-infested waters. I can't draw him sitting in his doghouse with a cup of tea and his remote."

"It's a warm afternoon, I'm going to walk in the Bois de Boulogne." She stood up and peeled off a sweater.

Alec waited until she left and then moved around the living room. His cheek throbbed, but it felt good to stretch his legs. He picked up Celine's sweater and chuckled. Her books were lined up in alphabetical order and her lipsticks were arranged by color, but she shed her clothes like a harem dancer.

He inhaled her scent on the fabric and sighed. They hadn't made love since he returned from the dentist and he longed to kiss her. Suddenly he froze. That's why he was blocked! Every time he tried to picture Gus ambushing a stagecoach, he saw Celine's ripe breasts and luscious thighs. All his fantasies involved the woman standing in front of him.

He glanced in the mirror and thought he couldn't navigate the metro or call a taxi looking like a squirrel. He gathered his notebook and pencils and opened the French doors to the garden. He would get in a couple of hours work away from her porcelain teacup and silver hairbrush and the photo of her waterskiing in Ibiza.

Celine's garden was filled with rosebushes and bougainvillea and azaleas. He pictured his own fifth-floor flat with the shriveled tomato in the window box and thought it would be quite nice to live here when they were married.

He drew Gus on a tropical island reclining under a palm tree. Gus held a frothy drink in one paw and nibbled a slice of

coconut. But then the natives appeared and announced they were going to sacrifice a maiden at sunset. Gus dropped the daiquiri and grabbed his spear and followed them to the base of the volcano.

How could Gus save the maiden without getting them both thrown into the molten lava? He felt a raindrop on the back of his neck and rain splattered his sketchbook. He gathered his pencil box and hurried into the living room.

He settled on the sofa and hunched over the notepad. He had to finish; he couldn't be distracted by Celine's hair ribbon on the love seat or her sandal wedged under the rug. The front door opened and Celine entered the foyer.

"I was in the middle of the Bois de Boulogne when it started raining," she said, shaking water out of her hair.

"What are you doing?" he asked, watching her shrug off her jacket.

"I'm sopping wet," she explained. "I'm going to take a hot shower."

"You can't get undressed here," he protested, his forehead covered in sweat. "Go into the bedroom."

"I can do whatever I want," she replied. "It is my apartment."

He tried to concentrate on his sketch, but it was no use. Her slacks outlined her thighs and her wet blouse clung to her breasts. God, he missed touching them! But his jaw ached if he made any sudden movements and he could as easily make love as climb into the mouth of the volcano.

She crossed the living room and opened the door to the bedroom. He watched her unzip her slacks and slip off her panties. She unsnapped her bra and he knew he was finished.

He looked down at his sketch pad, and all he could see was Celine's full mouth and the birthmark on her thigh. The water ran in the shower and the desert island evaporated like a mirage.

He didn't know what was worst: the pain in his jaw, Gus's failure to save the sacrificial maiden, or the fact that the most beautiful woman in Paris was naked and soaking wet and he could do nothing about it.

He grabbed the bag of frozen peas and sank back onto the sofa.

ALEC GLANCED AT the fruit basket Isabel had left on the coffee table and his heart raced. He was blocked because he was falling in love with Isabel! She had never looked so lovely as last night. The diamond earrings made her dark eyes sparkle and her lips shimmered with red lipstick. When she talked about the opera and supper at Café de la Paix, he could listen to her forever.

How had this happened and what could he do about it? Isabel was hoping she'd be engaged by this evening. And if he didn't finish this set of illustrations, he'd never pay off his charge cards.

There was a knock at the door and he answered it.

"Did you sleep in that suit?" Mathieu asked, entering the suite. "You look like one of the homeless people on the Pont Marie."

"It's an old trick I use to unblock my creativity." Alec waved his hand. "I was awake all night trying to come up with an original story line, and all I have is Gus entering a cottage made of candy canes. If Gus was thinking clearly, he would realize you can't devour gumdrops without paying a price." He crumpled the paper. "Of course the cottage is owned by a wicked witch."

"I don't understand." Mathieu folded his raincoat over a chair.

"The minute you let someone into your heart, they ruin your thought processes," Alec groaned. "Love is more destruc-

tive than drinking a bottle of Absolut and eating a box of Henri Le Roux chocolates."

"Has Celine come back?" Mathieu glanced around the living room.

"Of course not." Alec shook his head. "Last night Isabel appeared in an emerald ball gown and diamond earrings. Her eyes were coated with mascara and she looked like an ingénue." He paused. "She has a business degree, but she trusts her future to a fortune-teller. She's like a child exploring Paris, but she knows more about French history than most Parisians." His eyes flickered. "And when she laughs you try to remember what you said because you never want her to stop."

"This is great news," Mathieu said. "Your problems are solved."

"How can it be good news? Tonight she's taking a dinner cruise on the Seine and hoping Antoine will propose." He ran his hands through his hair. "The next time I see her, she'll practically be Comtesse de Villoy."

"Tell her you're a viscount and that you're in love with her," Mathieu insisted. "You'll get your inheritance soon. Go to Van Cleef and Arpels and ask for Henri. He'll let you buy a diamond ring on credit."

"I can't tell her I'm a viscount!" he spluttered. "She'd be furious I didn't mention it sooner. And if I did, I'd never know if she was in love with me or thought she should marry a French aristocrat."

"But you are a viscount and you are in love with her." Mathieu poured a glass of sparkling water. "You'd be telling the truth."

"Love is hard enough without knowing how the other person feels," Alec argued. "What if I came down with a terrible disease and she had to take care of me? I couldn't expect her to

feed me consommé and change my bed linens unless she was in love with me."

"You're thirty-one and healthy as a horse," Mathieu said. "You have decades to look forward to."

"You don't understand, I fell in love with Celine and thought she felt the same," Alec said slowly. "We were going to live in her flat on the Rue Saint-Honoré and have a chubby baby. Eventually we'd want more children, so we'd move to a bigger apartment in the seventh arrondissement or buy a house near my mother," he mused. "In the month of August, the children would stay at Celine's parents' and we'd make love in the kitchen and marvel how we can still be hungry for each other.

"But she ran off with the first guy who batted his blue eyes at her and left me with an arrow through my heart and a hole in my bank account." He loosened his collar. "I'd rather walk the plank than fall in love again. But if I have no choice, it has to be with someone who is willing to take out my false teeth and push me in a wheelchair."

"You have a curious view of marriage." Mathieu grinned. "I'm happy if Helene makes crepes on Sundays."

"But I would do the same," he insisted. "Every morning I would bring her café au lait in bed and in the evening I'd stop at the market and pick up pork and haricots verts. We'd drink a bold Syrah and talk about the bank and my illustrations. Later we'd move to the study and nibble chocolate profiteroles and discuss art and music." He paused. "Our lips would touch and we wouldn't want to be anywhere else."

"Getting married sounds like a bad idea," Mathieu laughed. "You'll both get fat."

"The only people getting married are Isabel and Antoine," Alec sighed.

"I have something to give you." Mathieu reached into his

pocket. "Bettina sent me, in my capacity as your attorney, a letter for your mother."

"What does it say?" Alec felt like he had been punched in the stomach.

"Legally Claudia should vacate 40 Rue de Passy on January fourth. But since it is the holidays, Bettina will allow her to remain an additional two weeks." He unfolded the paper. "She is welcome to take the desk in the den, but the furniture in the grand salon and dining room must stay in the house."

"How kind," Alec snapped. "I'm surprised she didn't include a farewell *bûche de Noël* and bottle of Château Pétrus."

"The contents of the wine cellar belong to the estate." Mathieu looked up. "And your father's cigar collection and Edith Piaf albums."

"I hope Édouard smokes all the cigars and gets bloody lung cancer," Alec grunted. "You're an attorney, isn't there something you can do?"

"Bettina is within her rights, you're the only one who can stop her."

"I'm not Gus who can stop a speeding bullet with his paw," Alec sighed.

"You could marry Isabel by January third," Mathieu suggested. "Then 40 Rue de Passy would be yours."

"Even if I am in love with Isabel, I haven't asked her on a date," Alec spluttered. "I can hardly ask her to meet me in the judge's chambers of the Hôtel de Ville." He paused. "Oh, and please wear white, preferably with a veil." His voice softened. "She would look lovely in a knee-length dress, she has slender calves."

"You're in Paris! Falling in love is as common as cheese soufflé," Mathieu said, handing Alec the envelope. "I have to go, Helene and I are picking out a baby carriage. Please give Claudia the letter."

"I'll go see my mother today." Alec nodded.

"You might want to change your suit." Mathieu walked to the door. "You look like a street performer at the Christmas markets."

Alec took off his tie and wished he and Isabel had never visited the Christmas markets. Then she wouldn't have met the fortune-teller and believed she had to marry a French aristocrat.

Maybe Mathieu was right. All he needed was a few days to make her fall in love with him. Antoine might take her to Tour d'Argent and *Rigoletto,* but he could show her the cheese shops on the Rue Mouffetard and the wine bars along the Canal Saint-Martin and the view of the Boulevard Haussmann from Promenade Plantee.

"This isn't over yet," Alec murmured. He glanced at the sketch of Gus climbing to the top of a bean stalk and thought Isabel had to fall in love with him. His publisher wouldn't be happy if he kept drawing fairy tales.

"DARLING, IT'S LOVELY to see you," his mother said, opening the front door. "Join me in the kitchen, I'm having breakfast."

Alec followed her into the wide kitchen and thought it was always his favorite room. French doors led to the garden and copper pots hung from the ceiling. A round table filled the breakfast nook and there was a ceramic vase of daisies.

"I'm surprised to see you," Claudia said, pouring two cups of coffee. "I thought . . ."

"That because Celine left, I'd stick my head in the oven," Alec replied.

"I didn't mean that exactly." She added cream and took a small sip. "You never think the pain will go away, but one day you'll be sitting at Café Verlet across from a print of Renoir's *Luncheon of the Boating Party.* You'll comment to the waiter

it's your favorite painting and he'll look at you strangely because you've been coming in for brioche with Échiré butter for six months and it's been there the whole time." She paused. "Then you'll stroll along Rue du Faubourg Saint-Honoré and the store windows will be filled with paisley dresses and strapless sandals. You'll laugh that fashion gets further ahead every year, until you see women in scarves and boots and realize it's almost January and you missed a whole season."

"It's only been a year since he died," Alec said softly. "It will get better."

She wiped her eyes and looked at Alec. "I'm hosting a dinner party in a few weeks. One of your father's oldest friends is retiring, and he and his wife are moving to Avignon. Would you like to come, maybe you could bring someone?"

Alec sipped his coffee and thought he couldn't tell her about Isabel. If he hinted he'd met someone, she might get her hopes up she could stay in her home.

The whole way in the metro, he examined his feelings for Isabel. As much as he adored his mother, he couldn't get married to save the house. But if he forgot about Bettina and his mother and 40 Rue de la Passy, he still couldn't stop thinking about Isabel's dark eyes and wide smile.

"I don't think . . . ," Alec began.

How could he tell his mother that the Louis XIV chairs and Oriental rugs were no longer hers?

"Bettina," Claudia gasped. "How could I forget? I just thought . . ."

"That she'd develop compassion and realize this house fits you like a second skin?" he snapped. "That you could as soon move as I could become an international soccer star?"

"You were a fast runner." Claudia smiled. "You never gave yourself a chance."

"I had lunch with her yesterday," Alec continued. "I thought

I could talk to her, but I never got a chance. She's like Judas Iscariot picking out the menu for the Last Supper."

"She never got over her mother leaving," Claudia mused. "Who could blame her? I had a husband and beautiful home and baby boy with round cheeks and fists."

"Where will you go?" Alec asked.

"I'll rent a studio apartment near the Jardin des Plantes." She fiddled with her cup. "Your father wasn't the easiest man. I made him a soft-boiled egg every morning, and the yolk was always too runny or too firm. He spent hours in his study with the door closed and he could smoke a whole cigar after dinner without saying a word.

"But he was always here: his briefcase rested in the foyer and his overcoat hung in the closet and his magazines collected in the library." Her eyes glistened. "Where will he be if I move?

"Enough about me," she said suddenly. "Have you heard from Celine?"

"Of course not. I'm sure she's lying on the beach in the swimsuit we bought in Cannes. She wanted to buy the maillot and I convinced her to get the bikini," he sighed. "I didn't realize I was buying Patrick an early Christmas present."

"You are good-looking and talented, even if you are my own son," Claudia said and smiled. "You'll fall in love again and this time it will be right."

"Love is worse than the Paris metro system," Alec grumbled, finishing his coffee. "It's nothing but bumps and jolts and you always exit with a stomachache."

"It's all we have." Claudia shrugged. "We'd be lost without it."

ALEC CLIMBED THE steps of the metro into the Place des Abbesses and sighed. Usually he loved the square in the middle of Montmartre with its carousel and outdoor cafés. All of Mont-

martre was like an antidote to Paris's wide boulevards and grand department stores. The alleys were paved with cobblestones and laundry hung from windows and the air smelled of butter and garlic.

But the Christmas chalets were still set up and Alec was tired of the stalls filled with bright ornaments and oversweet candies. Hadn't people drunk enough cups of mulled wine and eaten plenty of cheeses and sausages? And when would the vendors stop wishing everyone a *joyeux Noël* and happy new year?

In January his mother would be practically homeless and Isabel would go back to America, or even worse, she would marry Antoine. He pictured her inviting him to elegant dinner parties at Antoine's flat off the Rue de Rivoli and his stomach turned.

He glanced at the famous wall covered with "I love yous" and remembered when he and Celine had scribbled their names in the cement. If only someone had told him you could never be happy and in love at the same time—it was like an ostrich expecting to fly.

Hadn't these young people read enough Stendhal to know love ended in despair? His mother loved his father for thirty years, but instead of being allowed to drink café au lait in her own kitchen, she had to move to a studio apartment.

And what hope did he have? Celine trampled his heart, and now he met Isabel and was perched at the edge of the same dizzying rabbit hole. He would give anything to stop himself from sliding inside.

He saw a street vendor arguing with a young woman in a beige sweater and navy slacks. He walked closer and realized it was Isabel.

"What are you doing here?" he said as he approached her.

"Alec! What a wonderful surprise." She beamed. "I was trying to buy a painting and somehow I offended him."

Alec spoke to the vendor in rapid French and the vendor waved his hands. Alec reached into his pocket and handed him a wad of euros. He grabbed the painting and took Isabel's elbow.

"One minute we were having a pleasant conversation," she explained. "The next he acted like I committed a crime."

"You called him by the familiar '*tu*' instead of the formal '*vous*.' His girlfriend heard you and thought you had a relationship."

"That's ridiculous!" Isabel protested. "I never saw him before in my life."

"Then you should have addressed him correctly," Alec replied.

"Or the French language shouldn't have so many pronouns," she retorted. "What did you tell him?"

"I gave him an extra ten euros and told him to buy his girlfriend a bottle of perfume." Alec grinned.

"It is a lovely painting," she said and smiled. "It's the entrance to the Place des Abbesses metro station. It's the most famous metro station in Paris and was in the movie *Amélie*."

"What are you doing here?" he asked. "I thought you were preparing for your dinner cruise on the Seine."

"I already found the perfect dress and read about the French aristocracy at the court of the Sun King. I decided to do some sightseeing." She paused and her eyes sparkled. "You can join me!"

"Join you?" Alec asked.

"I don't want to lose my way at the Bastille and get left in a dungeon, or say the wrong thing to a shopkeeper and have him call the gendarmes," she explained. "It would be more fun to explore Paris with a Parisian."

Alec remembered Mathieu saying the way to win Isabel was to show her Paris.

"I suppose I have some time." He slipped his hands in his pockets. "We can see the main chapel of the Sacré-Coeur and visit the last three remaining windmills in Paris."

"That sounds wonderful, but I know what I want to do next," she replied. "I've been looking forward to it since I arrived in Paris."

"What?" he asked, hoping she didn't want to browse in the boutiques on the Rue Lepic. His wallet was almost empty and he didn't want to spend the afternoon surrounded by salesgirls with arched eyebrows and pursed lips.

"We're going to explore the Catacombs!"

Alec had only visited the burial grounds under Paris once. He was terrified by the dark tunnels and walls of bones. But Isabel already knew he was afraid of heights; he couldn't admit he was claustrophobic, too.

"The Catacombs," he repeated and sighed. "What a marvelous idea, why didn't I suggest it?"

"AT THE END of the eighteenth century the cemeteries were overflowing, so they began transporting bones to the Catacombs." Isabel stood at the entrance of the tunnel. "Over six million Parisians are buried here, including Robespierre, and during World War II the French resistance used it to hide from the Germans. The entrance is inscribed with the words: 'Halt: You are in the realm of death!' "

"The Romantics had quite the sense of humor," Alec muttered.

They had descended the 183 steps in silence. Alec kept his hands in his pockets so Isabel wouldn't see his white knuckles. Then he reminded himself it was pitch-black and they couldn't see five feet in front of them.

"Apparently it has been an attraction for centuries," she

continued. "*Comtes* and duchesses visited the Catacombs for amusement."

"The French aristocracy hasn't always been known for their common sense. Or their heads wouldn't have ended up in a cart in the Place Vendôme," he mused. "I'd rather sit in front of a fire with a glass of cognac and a book of Baudelaire's poems."

"When I was a girl I read all the Nancy Drew books." Isabel examined the thick walls. "My favorites were where she got locked in the cellar or trapped in an abandoned well. I couldn't wait to see how she got out."

"We could save ourselves the trouble and leave now." He wiped his forehead. "Once we walk farther, we can't turn around."

"And miss seeing the wall of bones or deformed skeletons?" Isabel asked. "I wouldn't dream of it."

Alec walked beside her and tried to stop his heart from racing. Suddenly the earth shifted and Isabel gasped. She wrapped her arms around Alec's neck and her cheek was warm against his skin. God, he wanted to kiss her!

"Was that an earthquake?" she asked.

Alec peered into the dark and saw something scurry across the dirt. He looked closer and laughed.

"I think it was a mouse."

THEY FINISHED THE tour and climbed the steps out of the tunnel. Alec had never been so happy to see blue sky and white clouds.

"I'm sorry, I was sure it was an earthquake," Isabel apologized. "Did I scare you?"

"Of course not, there was nothing to be afraid of." He shrugged. "How about if I choose where we go next."

"What did you have in mind?" she asked.

He turned to her and smiled. "Somewhere green."

They took the metro back to Montmartre, and Alec bought mushroom tartlets and cheddar gougères and hard-boiled eggs. There were fruit tarts and a jar of whipped cream.

"How did you know I'm starving?" she asked when he handed her an egg. "I was so busy learning the dates of the Renaissance I didn't eat breakfast, and then I was so eager to see Paris I forgot to grab a sandwich."

"We're going to have a picnic." He took her hand. "And I'm going to show you the most beautiful garden in Paris.

"Renoir's garden is part of the Musée de Montmartre," he said, entering an iron gate. "He painted *The Swing* and *Dance at Le Moulin de la Galette* under that willow tree. Sometimes I would sneak out of the lycée with my sketchbook." He paused. "Gus fought his first sword fight while I was sitting on this bench."

"It's like being in the countryside in the middle of Paris." Isabel gazed at thick hedges and a pond filled with water lilies. There were rows of lilacs and a stone wall covered in ivy.

If only he could tell her how he felt, he might have a chance. But if he admitted he was a viscount, she'd be furious he hadn't told her sooner, and he'd never know if she was really in love with him. And if he didn't tell her, she would believe the fortune-teller intended her to marry Antoine.

He spread the contents of the paper sack on a bench, and they ate bread and cheese and fruit. Alec couldn't remember being so happy and miserable at the same time. It was like eating the most delicious birthday cake and knowing that tomorrow your birthday would be over, and you wouldn't feel special again.

"I couldn't stop worrying about Neil. I wondered if he remembered where we kept the thick socks and if he knew the milk in the fridge had expired. Finally I called him and he said

he was going skiing with friends. I was so relieved, I worried he might be holed up in the condominium watching television and eating leftover tuna salad." Her eyes flickered. "I did make the right decision. If I was in love with him, I'd wish he was with me in Paris instead of wondering how he was going to keep warm."

"I'm sure you know what you're doing." Alec nodded.

"I can't stop thinking that Antoine might propose." She sighed and ate a vegetable tart. "It will be like a scene in one of those impossibly romantic French movies. We'll be sitting at a table on the barge, gliding past the Cathedral of Notre Dame. It will be so intimate with the stone spires lit up like the tallest Christmas tree. A violin will play and we'll nibble coq au vin." She paused. "Antoine will sip his wine and I'll say many people don't believe in love at first sight, but it makes perfect sense because really love is impossible to explain. It's like a sudden rain shower from an almost blue sky. You don't expect it and there's nothing you can do about it." She gazed at the rosebushes. "But look at all the wonderful things it brings, you wouldn't want it to go away.

"Then I'll say the best thing about love is the way it makes you feel about yourself." She sprinkled salt on a hard-boiled egg. "You wake up every morning and you're exactly who you want to be. Because you're in love with the most wonderful man and he's in love with you."

Alec tried to swallow a piece of cheese, but it got stuck in his throat. He opened a bottle of Coca-Cola and drank it quickly.

"What do you think?" She brushed crumbs from her slacks.

"What do I think about what?" he asked.

"Do you think Antoine will propose?"

He gulped the soft drink and wiped his mouth. He looked

at Isabel and nodded. "Of course, he'll propose. He'd be a fool not to."

THEY LEFT RENOIR'S garden and visited Saint-Pierre de Montmartre and the Salvador Dalí museum. Finally they took the metro back to the Hôtel de Crillon and crossed the marble lobby to the elevator.

Alec was silent the whole way, trying to think of what to say. It had been a perfect afternoon; even the gray skies gave way to blue skies and high clouds. And he was sure there was a connection; they were two spark plugs waiting to ignite.

"Thank you for showing me Paris," Isabel said when the elevator reached the fifth floor. "I had a wonderful time. I'm going to take a bath, I can't be late for the cruise."

"Isabel . . . ," Alec began. All he had to do was say he was falling in love with her, and to give him a chance. But he couldn't do that without telling her the whole truth, and that would ruin everything.

"Yes?" She turned around.

"Make sure you dress warmly, it's cold on the Seine at night," he said finally. "And good luck, it will all work out."

"I don't need luck. I'm in Paris at Christmas and a handsome *comte* is going to propose," she said and her eyes were bright. "What more could I want?"

ALEC WALKED TO the bar in the suite and poured a glass of scotch. It was too early for a drink, but what did it matter. All he had to look forward to was imagining Isabel eating smoked salmon and drinking French champagne on a barge.

He couldn't give up now; he had to win her over. But then

he thought about how she was going to get Antoine to propose. Isabel was like a guided missile; nothing would make her change direction.

He glanced at a sketch of Gus wearing an eye patch and holding a bow and arrow. He tried to remember what he was going to draw next, but his mind was blank. He crumpled the paper and drained his glass.

chapter fourteen

❧

Isabel stood at her closet and gazed at the pink tulle gown. She found it at Le Bon Marché and it was perfect for the cruise on the Seine. It was early evening and she was meeting Antoine in two hours. She slipped on a cashmere sweater and wondered why she suddenly felt chilled.

Ever since she returned from Montmartre, she had felt slightly strange. She wanted to read a paperback book, but she had left it on the metro. All the magazines in the suite were in French and she didn't feel like battling pronouns. And when she went to pour a cup of hot cocoa, the silver pot was empty.

Now she glanced at the brochure on the Catacombs and pictured throwing her arms around Alec's neck. He took her hand and led her into Renoir's garden. They sat on the bench eating berries and whipped cream, and she never wanted to be anywhere else.

Suddenly she caught her breath. She couldn't be falling in love with Alec! But she remembered him finding her glass bracelet at Versailles and appeasing the artist in the Place des Abbesses. He always seemed to appear when she needed him, and there

was something about him that made her feel secure. Like when you were sitting inside during a snowstorm and didn't have to worry about catching cold.

She thought about the first time she saw Rory at Saks. His blond hair curled around his ears and his eyes were the color of emeralds. And Neil was so handsome in his Ralph Lauren suits. He was well educated and confident and was going straight to the top.

She had been certain Rory was the love of her life, and their romance fizzled like an expired aspirin. And Neil gave up his stock options and 401(k) plan without asking her opinion. If she was wrong about Alec, she would be back where she started.

Everything that had happened since she arrived in Paris was magical. The woman at Le Printemps who picked out the satin ball gown and the man at Shakespeare and Company who found the book on French aristocracy and the store in the Marais where she discovered the Hermès bag for her mother. She would be breaking the spell if she ignored the fortune-teller's predictions.

Antoine was handsome and charming, and when she was with him she almost felt French. Tonight he would propose and her whole life would be like a sparkly Christmas ornament. There would be elegant dinner dances and summers on the French Riviera.

She knew the fortune-teller was right; it was like watching Google stock surge and knowing she had predicted it all along. But why did she keep thinking about Alec when she should be choosing a lipstick?

And Alec was still getting over Celine. Even if he developed feelings for her, he might not want to get married for years. How could she give up becoming Comtesse de Villoy with a château and two towheaded children for someone who was allergic to love? The fortune-teller said she was going to fall in

love and marry a French aristocrat, and that's what she was going to do.

The fortune-teller! Maybe she had meant something else. She had to see her and make certain she was following her instructions. She wouldn't ask anything specific, like was she sure she was going to marry a French aristocrat and not a man whose mother was British and father was French and who drew illustrations of a cocker spaniel named Gus.

She would just ask her to repeat her prediction to be certain she had heard her correctly. It had been noisy, with taxis honking and bells ringing and children demanding nougat.

She wrapped her scarf around her neck and wondered why she hadn't thought of it sooner.

"I will do whatever the fortune-teller says," she said, opening the door and hurrying to the elevator.

ISABEL STROLLED ALONG the Champs-Élysées and admired the twinkling lights. There was the wooden chalet where Alec had bought a bag of gumdrops and the stall selling glass ornaments. She searched for the fortune-teller and her stomach rose to her throat.

Why did she think the fortune-teller would still be here? She was a gypsy; she could be at the Christmas markets at the Place du Trocadéro or have moved on to Vincennes.

A thick fog settled over the Place de la Concorde, and she wrapped her arms around her chest. She bought a cup of hot apple cider and bag of Pont Neuf fries and sat on a wooden bench.

She had a business degree from Wharton and was a respected financial analyst; she couldn't panic because a woman in a patterned scarf and felt coat had disappeared. But if she couldn't find her, how would she know whether she was supposed to marry Antoine?

The fries with béarnaise sauce looked delicious, but now she couldn't eat a bite. Tonight was the most important night of her life and she didn't want to get it wrong.

A little girl sat on the next bench clutching a doll. She had dark hair and wore a corduroy smock.

"*Voudriez-vous mes frites?*" Isabel asked.

"Yes, please," the girl said in accented English. "You are a very pretty American."

"How did you know I'm American?" Isabel asked, joining her on the bench.

The girl popped a French fry in her mouth and shrugged. "Because your accent is terrible."

"When I studied in Paris, I was almost fluent, but now I am a little rusty," Isabel laughed. "Where did you learn English?"

"My mother says it's important to be able to talk to tourists," the girl explained. "Especially Americans, they always have extra chocolate drops."

"We tend to buy more than we need," Isabel said and smiled. "That's a pretty doll."

"My mother said if my brother and I were good, Santa Claus would bring us presents," she replied. "I didn't believe her—Santa Claus has never visited us before. But on Christmas night he left this doll and a racing car for my brother!"

"You are very lucky." Isabel paused. "Is your mother here? You're too young to be alone."

"My mother is working. She reads people's palms and they give her money."

"What did you say?" Isabel gasped.

She remembered the fortune-teller saying she couldn't afford Christmas presents for her children.

"She reads people's palms," the girl repeated. "She sent me to buy dinner. I had a bag of warm chestnuts and a candied apple."

"I would love her to read my palm." Isabel's face broke into a smile. "Could you show me where she is?"

They crossed the Place de la Concorde and Isabel saw a dark-haired woman wearing a felt coat and velvet slippers.

"I'm glad I found you, I thought you disappeared." She approached her. "I met a little girl and we struck up a conversation." She stopped and her eyes sparkled. "She said her mother was a fortune-teller and I knew it was you."

"I'm sorry, I meet so many people." The woman shrugged.

"You said I would receive a gift and almost get killed." Isabel reached into her pocket and took out a twenty-euro note. "You made one more prediction and I have to make sure I heard you correctly. It's going to decide my whole future, it's the most important thing in the world."

"Ah, yes, the pretty American." She put the note in her pocket.

"I knew you wouldn't forget." Isabel beamed. "You said I was going to fall in love with a French aristocrat and get married at an elegant château."

"Let me see your hand," the woman took her palm. "You have been busy. I see new clothes and dinners at intimate bistros."

"Paris at Christmas is everything I dreamed of," Isabel sighed. "The department stores are decorated like a six-tier wedding cake, and I could spend all day eating escargot at an outdoor café."

"There is more," the fortune-teller interrupted. "You met a man and you are falling in love."

"Antoine is a *comte* and we met at the Red Cross charity ball. Tonight we're taking a dinner cruise on the Seine and I think he's going to propose." She paused and her eyes were huge. "But what if I'm in love with the wrong man?"

The fortune-teller turned over her hand. "There will be obstacles in the path and a sudden change in direction."

"There will?" Isabel asked.

"But in the end you will marry the French aristocrat." She dropped Isabel's palm. "I see a mansion and three beautiful children."

"You see, I met someone else, but he's not an aristocrat at all. He lives in a fifth-floor walk-up in the Marais and draws illustrations for children's books." She bit her lip. "So it was very important I see you again. Everything else you predicted came true and I know you are right about the man I'm going to marry."

"If you follow my instructions you will have a life filled with happiness," the woman replied. "For another twenty euros I can tell you the sexes of your children."

"I'd like it to be a surprise," Isabel said and laughed. "Though I never imagined I'd have three!"

ISABEL SAT AT her dressing table and had never been so excited. She imagined all the monuments they would see from the boat: Napoleon's tomb and the Île de la Cité and Pont Alexandre III lit up with gold and silver lights. She couldn't wait to eat lamb semolina and cooked cherries with pistachio ice cream for dessert.

Antoine had sent a bouquet of pink roses with a card saying he was eager to see her. She debated showing them to Alec and changed her mind. She'd tell him all about the cruise when she returned to the Hôtel de Crillon.

She was so glad she had visited the fortune-teller. Antoine might be part of the French aristocracy, but Isabel had grown up on the Main Line with some of America's oldest families. They both attended debutante balls and loved fine wines.

His boarding school friends seemed so sophisticated and spent their time flitting between ski resorts, but she had stud-

ied at the Sorbonne and skied in Vermont. She'd brush up on her French and buy a few chic sweaters and pairs of boots.

She remembered the picnic in Renoir's garden with Alec, and something caught in her throat. It had been nothing. She was nervous about Antoine, and Alec was there at the right time. Alec thought of her as a friend anyway; he had no interest in love.

She rubbed her lips with red lipstick and spritzed her wrists with floral perfume. She grabbed her satin clutch and closed the door behind her.

ISABEL STOOD AT the base of the Eiffel Tower and gazed up at blue and gold lights. The postcards didn't do it justice. It really was spectacular, with its wide arches and iron latticework reaching up to the sky.

It was Isabel's idea to meet under the Eiffel Tower instead of in the Crillon's lobby. She wanted Antoine to catch sight of her standing on the grass bank in her pink tulle dress and silver stilettos.

But she had been waiting for twenty minutes and the damp air settled on her shoulders. She should have worn a sensible coat, but she couldn't bear hiding the luminous fabric under thick wool. And anyway, she wouldn't be cold when they sat at a candlelit table eating tarte flambés and sipping Veuve Clicquot.

She remembered reading in an article that nothing kept you as warm as the way you felt in a gorgeous dress. The writer had never been to Paris in December. Her lips were turning blue, and she couldn't stop shivering.

Now she understood why Parisians disliked tourists; they made the streets so congested. It took thirty minutes to drive from the Crillon to the Champ de Mar. When she paid the taxi

driver, he muttered that Americans were lazy and she could have walked there faster.

Isabel slipped the tip she was going to give him back in her purse, and almost blurted out that if all the tourists walked he wouldn't have employment.

Perhaps Antoine had left a message or sent a text that he had been delayed. She opened her purse and realized she'd left her phone in the hotel suite.

She fleetingly wondered if he had decided not to come, but that was impossible. He sent her roses and said he couldn't wait to see her! She had to go back to the Crillon and retrieve her phone; there must be a simple explanation.

But she couldn't navigate the metro in her stilettos and the line at the taxi stand stretched around the Eiffel Tower. She started down the Rue Saint-Dominique and thought she'd give anything for a bowl of hot soup and a baguette.

She peered into a café and saw a familiar-looking man. He wore a red sweater and she realized it was Alec.

"What are you doing here?" he asked, opening the door.

"I've been waiting under the Eiffel Tower for thirty minutes," she began. "But I must have got it wrong because Antoine didn't show up. I left my phone at the Crillon and I have to go back and get it. It's impossible to get a taxi, so I decided to walk."

"You're going to walk two kilometers in those shoes?" Alec raised his eyebrow.

"I'll be fine," Isabel said doubtfully. "I don't have a choice, I can't keep Antoine waiting."

"He's the one keeping you waiting. And you won't do him any good if you get pneumonia," Alec replied. "Join me for a bite and we'll go back to the hotel together. I know the owner of the restaurant, he can call a taxi."

Isabel peered inside and inhaled garlic and oregano.

"I could have a quick bowl of soup." She hesitated. "I haven't eaten since our picnic."

"You can't just have a bowl of soup." Alec steered her to the table. "We're at Les Cocottes, they make the best casseroles in Paris."

"I didn't realize I was so hungry," Isabel said when Alec ordered a salad with poached eggs and bacon. There was a casserole of rabbit and chanterelle mushrooms. "But what if I mixed things up entirely and Antoine is waiting at the Crillon?"

"You're the most precise person I know." Alec dipped a baguette into tomato bisque. "Maybe he came down with the flu or had an emergency. You can't flit around Paris wearing something out of *A Midsummer Night's Dream*."

"I love this dress, and I'm sure Antoine would have lent me his jacket." Isabel ate baby peas and carrots. "What are you doing here? I thought you avoided trendy restaurants that charge twenty euros for a bowl of leeks."

"Les Cocottes is a Paris institution," Alex explained. "All the main courses come in iron pots and the chocolate torte is delicious. Besides, I needed to clear my head."

"Are you still having trouble getting inspiration?" Isabel asked.

"Not exactly. I left Gus in a diamond mine in South Africa. The walls caved in and he's trying to save the other miners before they all run out of oxygen."

"I shouldn't have suggested visiting the Catacombs," she laughed.

"I enjoyed it and it cured my fear of heights. I realized I'd rather fall from a five-story building than be buried under thirty kilos of dirt." He looked at Isabel. "Aren't you afraid of anything?"

"What's the point?" She shrugged. "Fear only holds you back, life is about moving forward."

"It saves you from dying," Alec pointed out. "God invented it so we wouldn't sail into a typhoon or swim with sharks."

"I've never gone skydiving and I don't like thunder and lightning." Her eyes clouded over. "But the only thing I'm afraid of is not falling in love and being alone forever."

"Isabel . . . ," Alec began.

"I don't know why I said that," she interrupted. "Of course I'm not going to be alone, I'm going to marry Antoine. I visited the fortune-teller this afternoon; I needed a tune-up. She knew everything I've been doing in Paris. She said I bought new clothes and dined at wonderful restaurants."

"Every tourist leaves Paris with a suitcase of new clothes and you can't walk half a block without discovering a café," Alec spluttered.

"I searched the Place de la Concorde and couldn't find her. I was quite upset, and then I met a little girl and it turned out to be her daughter," Isabel explained. "Magical things keep happening and it's because of the fortune-teller. She said I'd have a wonderful life as long as I follow her instructions."

"The only magical thing that happened is she convinced you to pay her twenty more euros," Alec grumbled.

"She didn't ask for money, I wanted to give it her," Isabel corrected. "Aren't you afraid you won't find someone? I know Celine broke your heart and you have your illustrations, but Gus can't be good at conversation. Don't you want someone to share baby photos and first dances and high school graduations with?"

"No one looks at photo albums, they click through images on their phones." Alec shrugged. "And if I had a son or daughter, I'd tell them to skip school dances. Being in an overheated room makes your skin break out and the fruit punch gives you diabetes."

"But don't you see, it's not enough to spend all day in an office and travel once a year to Morocco or Crete. You have to

have someone to share it with or you're like a hamster on a treadmill. You're not building anything, you're just running in circles."

"I don't mind being alone. I can spend hours drawing and there's nothing I enjoy more than sitting on my fire escape with a brandy and watching the sun set over the rooftops." He put down his fork. "What's worse is finding the person you can't live without and discovering they belong to someone else."

"But you have to try again," Isabel said and looked at Alec. "If you don't have love, you don't have anything at all."

ALEC SUGGESTED SHARING a chocolate torte for dessert, but Isabel said she had to get back to the Crillon. They sat cramped in the backseat of the taxi and she felt slightly off. Like when you step off an airplane after an international flight and the ground still feels shaky.

They took the elevator to the fifth floor and Isabel fumbled with her key.

"Thank you for seeing me home." She turned around. "I'm sure Antoine left a message on my phone. Maybe he decided it's too cold and made a restaurant reservation at the George Cinq." Her face lit up in a smile. "That's the wonderful thing about Paris, everywhere you go is romantic. He could propose at the Grand Palais or Les Invalides. Wherever it happens, I'll never forget it."

"Isabel." He touched her shoulder. "What I said at the restaurant, I wasn't talking about Celine."

"Of course you were," she replied. "It must have been dreadful when Celine ran off with another man less than two weeks before the wedding. Neil and I didn't agree on anything, but he didn't cancel the wedding. Though when I called him, he didn't sound too upset." She paused. "If I hadn't decided to

stay at the Hôtel de Crillon, I wouldn't have met Antoine. Now I'm going to be a *comtesse* with a château and three beautiful children!"

He ran his hands through his hair. "I was talking about you."

Isabel dropped her purse and bent down to pick it up. She smoothed her skirt and looked at Alec. "I don't understand."

"When Celine left, I swore I'd never fall in love again," he began. "I couldn't stand the pain, it was like sticking needles in my back. But then you threw a shoe on my balcony and everything changed. You're beautiful and smart and your optimism makes the world a better place." He stopped and looked at her. "I think I'm falling in love with you."

"That's impossible, you don't believe in love at first sight." She shook her head. "You're probably still getting over a fever. Once I had the flu and thought I wanted to become an astronaut." She paused. "You mustn't fall in love with me. I'm in love with Antoine."

"How do you know you're in love with Antoine?" he asked.

"He's good-looking and charming and his family dates back to the fourteenth century," she continued. "He might not work with numbers, but someone has to entertain the clients, or they'll take their money somewhere else." She fiddled with her bracelet. "The fortune-teller said I was going to marry him, and she's been right about everything."

Alec leaned forward and kissed her. His mouth was warm and for a moment she kissed him back.

"I have to go," she gasped, pulling away. "The casserole was delicious and you saved me from getting frostbite." She opened the door. "I'm sure I'll see you tomorrow."

ISABEL PACED AROUND the hotel suite and caught her breath. Antoine hadn't left a message and his phone went straight to

voice mail. She remembered when the dry cleaner lost her phone number and Antoine called every five-star hotel in Paris. He'd call any minute and it would all be straightened out.

She walked to the balcony and thought about Alec. He'd rush over in the morning and apologize. It had been the red wine and casserole and the twinkling lights of the Eiffel Tower. Of course he wasn't in love with her; that was ridiculous.

The fortune-teller said there would be obstacles; she didn't mean to kiss him. It was like when you ate a bite of nougat and couldn't help wanting to finish the whole piece.

For the first time since she'd arrived in Paris, tears spilled down her cheeks. She closed the silk curtains and walked to the closet. All she had to do was follow the fortune-teller's instructions and everything would be perfect.

chapter fifteen

❦

Alec pulled back the curtains and gazed at the blue sky and high white clouds. It was midmorning and the Place de la Concorde was filled with men and women wearing bright scarves and patterned sweaters.

He couldn't believe he'd followed Isabel to the Eiffel Tower last night without telling her. He was like Gus unable to resist a juicy T-bone steak. But he was glad he did. The casserole at Les Cocottes was delicious and the taxi ride back to the Crillon was magical. Isabel had sat so close that he could inhale the scent of her floral perfume.

But now he wished it was pouring rain or even snowing so he could curl up on the brocade sofa with a stack of magazines. He only had two more nights at the Crillon; he was entitled to enjoy the heated marble floors and Egyptian cotton sheets.

But in three weeks Bettina would evict his mother from 40 Rue de Passy. He pictured the grand salon with his father's ivory cigar box and bottles of cognac and knew he had to find a way to stop her.

He picked up a sketch of Gus perched on a flying carpet.

Gus wore a purple velvet hat over his floppy ears and clutched a genie's bottle. If only he could stuff the fortune-teller into the bottle. Or maybe Gus could cast a spell so Isabel never met her.

He poured a cup of café au lait and thought he really had to stop drinking coffee. It was putting him on edge, and that wouldn't solve anything. He added sugar and pictured Isabel in her pink tulle gown. God, she was beautiful, like an angel on top of the Christmas tree.

Kissing her had been even better than he had imagined. And she kissed him back! For one moment he allowed himself to be happy. Then she hurried into her suite and something hard pressed against his chest.

This is why he was promising himself to never fall in love again; it was as uncomfortable as sitting in a public sauna. He was sure Isabel had feelings for him, but she was determined to listen to the fortune-teller. She was as likely to change course as he was to fly on a magic carpet.

He was tempted to go down to the Christmas markets and talk to the fortune-teller himself. How could she make Isabel believe she was going to marry a French aristocrat and live in a château?

But that was what was wonderful about Isabel. She had a childlike trust that made him want to wrap his arms around her. He pictured her dark eyes and never had wanted anyone more.

There was a knock at the door and he answered it.

"You look worse than I do, and I got up at five AM to find Helene seaweed mustard." Mathieu entered the suite. "I found lemon mustard and horseradish mustard, but not a single boulangerie carries seaweed mustard."

"You might try Japan," Alec mumbled. "This is why love is impossible. You are a successful attorney who can afford a wardrobe of Paul Smith suits, and you look like you slept in your

clothes. We should save ourselves the trouble and join a monastery."

"Isabel?" Mathieu asked, surveying the empty coffee cup.

"She was supposed to meet Antoine under the Eiffel Tower, but he didn't show up. I was sitting in Les Cocottes and she walked by wearing a tulle gown and diamond necklace. We ate tomato bisque and cassoulet and it was the best meal of my life."

"She sounds overdressed for rabbit stew." Mathieu perched on an armchair. "What happened next?"

"We took a taxi back to the Crillon." He rubbed his brow. "I couldn't stop myself, I told her I was falling in love with her. I kissed her and she kissed me back. And then . . ."

"You didn't?" Mathieu glanced through the bedroom door at the four-poster bed.

"Of course not! I wouldn't dream of it until we know each better," Alec spluttered. "She thanked me for the casserole and said she'd be sure to see me tomorrow."

"You should open a bottle of Dom Pérignon!" Mathieu congratulated him. "Ask the Hôtel de Crillon to pack a picnic and rent a hot air balloon. There's nothing more romantic than nibbling chocolate-covered strawberries high above the Pont des Arts."

"Even if Isabel has feelings for me, she won't do anything about them," Alec explained. "She visited the fortune-teller again and the woman told Isabel she's going to marry a French aristocrat and have three beautiful children. I wouldn't be surprised if Isabel was at Cartier picking out silver rattles."

"But *you* are a French aristocrat," Mathieu reminded him. "Now is the time to tell her. Claudia can stay at 40 Rue de Passy, all your problems will be solved."

"Isabel would never speak to me again if she knew I lied."

Alec shook his head. "And I still wouldn't know if she said yes because she loved me or because of my title. It's useless, Antoine is going to propose and I'll be invited to the wedding." He tore open a packet of peanuts. "Maybe I can regift the Limoges soup tureens Celine's aunt gave us as a wedding gift."

"You must tell Isabel sometime," Mathieu insisted. "There's only one thing you can do. You have to ask Isabel to marry you before Antoine proposes."

"Ask Isabel to marry me after one kiss?"

"Romeo was willing to give his life for Juliet." Mathieu looked at Alec. "Do you love her?"

Alec sank onto the sofa and wished the word "love" could be stricken from the dictionary. But could he imagine a world without Isabel's sparkling eyes and bright smile? He pictured her saying good-bye and his heart turned over.

"Yes, I love her," he whispered.

"If you think Antoine is going to propose, you have to act fast," Mathieu began. "You are staying at the most exclusive hotel in Paris. Litter the floor with rose petals and order room service sautéed scallops and mimosas. You can propose on the balcony overlooking the Champs-Élysées."

"You should have a second job as a wedding planner," Alec muttered.

When had he ever risked anything? Even proposing to Celine wasn't a risk because he had been certain she would say no. She had to repeat herself before he realized she was agreeing to marry him.

But he couldn't make Gus fly World War I airplanes forever if he wasn't willing to take a chance. At some point he had to take control of his own life or the children who read about Gus the Cocker Spaniel would realize he was a fraud.

He wiped his brow and nodded. "I'll do it."

"Now you need a ring." Mathieu beamed. "Your grand-mother's sapphire-and-diamond ring is perfect. Do you have it, or did you give it back to your mother?"

Alec rubbed his brow. "I think Celine took it to Australia."

"You let your ex-fiancée leave the country with a family heirloom?"

"You know how careless Celine is about jewelry." Alec shrugged. "She probably forgot she was wearing it. I'm sure she'll send it back, Patrick probably gave her a diamond the size of a cricket ball."

"My guy at Van Cleef and Arpels is on vacation until Janu-ary." Mathieu hesitated. "Run down to Chopard's and ask the salesgirl to pick out something."

"My bank account is almost empty and my credit card couldn't afford a silver dessertspoon."

"The Crillon's gift shop must have an emerald-cut diamond on a platinum band," Mathieu suggested. "You can charge it to the suite."

"Celine's father can't pay for Isabel's engagement ring!" Alec spluttered.

"She owes it to you for pain and suffering," Mathieu in-sisted. "You can't propose without a ring. Isabel won't think you're serious if you whisper 'Will you marry me?' over chocolate soufflé."

"I know the perfect ring." Alec jumped up. "You stay here and make sure Isabel doesn't leave her suite."

"She's not here, I ran into her in the lobby," Mathieu said. "We had a nice conversation. She was on her way to Galeries Lafayette to buy a ball gown. She's attending the Imperial Ball at the Grand Hotel; it's quite the event. Even Helene couldn't get an invitation."

"Why didn't you tell me?" Alec demanded. "Antoine must have invited her. I'm sure he's going to propose."

"What are you going to do?" Mathieu asked.

Alec grabbed his jacket and opened the door. "I'm going to stop her."

ALEC CROSSED THE Boulevard Haussmann and opened the double glass doors of Galeries Lafayette. Ivory columns reached the ceiling and the counters were littered with gold and silver boxes.

When he was a child, his mother brought him every year to see the giant upside-down Christmas tree with its jeweled ornaments. It was like a pharaoh's tomb transported to a Paris department store.

He remembered riding the escalator to the basement and selecting his favorite Alain Ducasse chocolate. It was impossible to choose between hazelnut nougat and orange marzipan. He thought he was the luckiest boy in the world until his mother asked what flavor Bettina would like and he was reminded of his sister.

Now he took the escalator to the fourth floor and felt like Clark Kent becoming Superman. He was going to find Isabel and ask her to marry him. He pictured telling his mother she could stay in her house and his heart swelled. That would be the icing on the wedding cake.

He searched the aisles and his heart raced. What if Isabel had already picked out a gown and was back at the Crillon?

God, Paris really had the most amazing women. You needed a seven-figure bank account and private island to just talk to any of the shoppers with their blond chignons and diamond teardrop earrings.

"Alec, what on earth are you doing here?" a female voice asked.

He turned around and saw Isabel holding a silver silk dress.

"How nice to see you." Alec smiled. "Galeries Lafayette is my mother's favorite department store. I came to buy her a present."

"Isn't it magnificent?" Isabel gazed up at the blue mosaic dome and stained glass windows. "It opened in the late 1800s and was the most luxurious department store in Paris. The grand staircase was modeled after the Palais Garnier and the Duchess of Windsor was a regular customer."

"I don't want to buy anything elaborate," Alec said, loosening his collar.

He never shopped at Galeries Lafayette—what if he couldn't afford a bottle of cologne? He should have waited for Isabel outside and asked her to visit the Christmas markets.

"The first anniversary of my father's death is coming up," he explained. "My mother has had a difficult time and I wanted to give her something special."

"It should be something that reminds her of her husband but doesn't make her miss him," she suggested. "Sort of like when you watch *Titanic* so many times, you don't cry at the sad parts."

"Every Sunday my mother served brunch with French onion soup and veal sweetbreads and legumes from the garden. My father was gone all morning and she was always afraid he'd be late. But every week he appeared with a dessert from the bakery at Galeries Lafayette: a tarte tatin or crepes or chocolate *religieuse*."

"That's what you should get her," Isabel exclaimed. "It's impossible to be unhappy when you are eating meringue and chestnut cream."

"There are so many pastries to choose from." Alec rubbed his brow. "Maybe you can help me."

"You want me to help?" she asked.

"The central heating in the suite made my sinuses act up

and I can't taste a thing," he implored. "I don't want to buy crème brûlée if it's too rich or a lemon tart if it's bitter."

"I suppose I have a little time. I didn't tell you what happened," she said and her eyes sparkled. "When I woke up this morning, there were two dozen yellow roses and a note from Antoine. He took a client to Provins and there was a spillage and the road was blocked for hours. His phone ran out of battery and he didn't get home until midnight."

"Surely he could have used the phone at a gas station," Alec said and stopped. He wasn't going to try to win Isabel by belittling Antoine, like a politician running a smear campaign.

"He didn't know my number," Isabel laughed. "These days we plug a phone number into our phone and don't memorize it." She paused. "But he called and said he was terribly sorry. He's taking me to the Imperial Ball at the Grand Hotel, I have to find the perfect ball gown."

"The dress you're holding is exquisite," Alec suggested. "Ask the salesgirl to wrap it up and we'll take the escalator to the bakery. The scent of fresh baked bread and chocolate is intoxicating."

"I could use a café au lait and croissant," Isabel sighed. "I've been shopping for hours."

"About last night—" he began.

"You don't need to say anything," she interrupted. "It's Paris at Christmas, it's impossible not to talk about love." She looked at Alec. "I know you're going to be happy for me when I marry Antoine, and we'll always be good friends."

Alec opened his mouth, but he was hardly going to propose surrounded by salesgirls in shiny jumpsuits and red lipstick. He would wait until they strolled down a cobblestone alley or sat at an outdoor café.

"I'll wait here." Alec smiled. "And don't let the salesgirl overcharge you."

THEY TOOK THE escalator to the basement and entered the bakery. Alec glanced at the trays of pistachio macarons and raspberry clafoutis and was suddenly nostalgic.

Christmas was a wonderful time when you were a child. All you had to worry about was whether the train set was under the tree and how to eat multiple cream puffs without getting a stomachache.

"I don't know how Frenchwomen stay so slim," Isabel mused. "Everything looks delicious: the French butter cookies and gâteau Basque and cherry *bûche de Noël.*"

"Frenchwomen don't have a heart, they probably don't have a stomach either," Alec mumbled.

"I thought you were over Celine." Isabel raised her eyebrow.

Alec wanted to say he was thinking about his sister. But this wasn't the time to tell Isabel that Bettina would only be happy when his mother was sleeping in a dining alcove and sharing walls with boisterous students.

"People say the British aren't demonstrative, but the French can be worse," Alec said, changing the subject. "My father spent so much time in his study, I thought he forgot he had a family. But he would return from a business trip with a new dress for my mother and a doll for Bettina and the book I wanted." Alec paused and his eyes were moist. "He died on his sixty-fifth birthday parasailing in Majorca."

"My parents have been married for thirty years and they still spend hours discussing books and music," Isabel said. "Every Sunday night my father cooks dinner and they always travel together."

"The problem with marriage is there are no happy endings," Alec said. "My mother was twenty when they met, and now she lost the only man she loved."

"Think of everything she has," Isabel replied, sampling a cognac truffle. "A son and a house full of wonderful memories."

Alec thought of 40 Rue de Passy and grabbed a raspberry charlotte wrapped in clear cellophane.

"This is perfect, the pastry is light and the raspberry cream is delicious."

THEY WALKED ONTO the Boulevard Haussmann and Isabel looked up at the sky.

"It's such a beautiful day, I'm going to feed the ducks in the Bois de Boulogne."

"Come with me to my mother's house on the Rue de Passy," Alec suggested. "You must see the sixteenth arrondissement, it's one of the most beautiful sections of the city."

Suddenly he couldn't think of anything more important than Isabel meeting his mother.

"The guidebook says it's full of leafy streets and private driveways." Isabel smiled. "The architecture is stunning, and Gwen Stefani and Bono have homes there."

"I can't promise you'll see them." Alec took her arm. "But the gardens and parks are breathtaking."

They walked up the gravel drive of 40 Rue de Passy and Alec wondered what he was thinking. He should never have invited Isabel to visit his mother.

What if Claudia mentioned that Bettina was going to evict her or Isabel discovered he was a viscount? But his mother would never discuss family matters with a stranger, and she was as likely to mention their title as swim the English Channel.

"Oh, what a gorgeous garden," Isabel said as they approached the porch. "It's like a Cézanne painting."

"The house is a little tired, but the grounds are beautiful." Alec felt a warmth spread through his chest. "Bettina and I used

to play hide-and-seek for hours, until I realized she had no interest in finding me."

"Alec!" Claudia opened the front door. "What a lovely surprise, I was about to visit my cabbages."

"This is Isabel," Alec introduced them. "We brought you a present."

"It's a pleasure to meet you." Claudia took the cellophane package and smiled. "I'll inspect the vegetables later, let's all eat cake."

"How did you meet?" Claudia asked when they sat in the grand salon. The coffee table was set with a silver coffeepot and porcelain demitasses.

The sun streamed through the French doors, and Alec thought how much he loved the Oriental rugs and faded velvet wallpaper. How dare Bettina think she could refinish floors and knock out walls and replace the furniture!

"I was locked out of my suite and threw my shoe at Alec's window. If he hadn't rescued me, I would have spent my first night in Paris on the balcony. I was supposed to be here on my honeymoon, but the wedding was canceled." She sipped her coffee. "It's a bit of an epidemic, I wonder how many engaged couples never make it to the altar."

"Isabel is a financial analyst," Alec told his mother. "She works for one of the biggest banks in America."

"In my day, not all women were so accomplished. Alain thought my job was to have his martini waiting and hang up his overcoat." Claudia paused. "I loved being a wife and mother, but now I wish I had a career."

"When I was a child I'd rather practice my multiplication tables than read bedtime stories," Isabel began. "And there's nothing more exciting than analyzing spreadsheets and feeling like you discovered a map to buried treasure.

"But you can't hang a photo of a stock trade over the fire-

place or sit down to Sunday brunch with clients from Hong Kong." She looked at Claudia. "What could be better than being married to the man you love and having a beautiful home and two children?"

"You're right," Claudia said and sipped her coffee. "I was very happy."

"ISABEL IS CHARMING, I approve," Claudia said, rinsing cups in the sink.

Isabel had gone to explore the vegetable garden, and Alec offered to help his mother in the kitchen. He remembered sitting next to Isabel on the brocade sofa and something shifted inside him. God, she was lovely! Her hair was glossy and her eyes sparkled and she smelled of expensive lotions.

When he was with her, he felt confident and alive. He pictured Gus in a blue cape, flying over the Eiffel Tower. A girl was stranded on the ledge and Gus swooped down and saved her. He set her down in the Place Vendôme and the crowd cheered.

"Approve of what?" Alec pulled his mind away from Gus. Even though he'd wanted his mother to meet Isabel, he couldn't admit he was in love with her. If Isabel turned down his proposal, his mother would be devastated.

"You're madly in love with each other," Claudia explained. "It was as clear as the revolving glass doors at Le Bon Marché."

"We barely know each other and I'm still paying off Celine's wedding ring," Alec spluttered. "I'm hardly looking for love."

"I came to Paris to sit in smoky cafés and dance in discotheques and kiss cute boys under thousand-year-old arches. Instead I fell in love with a cantankerous Frenchman who was ten years my senior."

"That was different," Alec insisted. "Isabel has a good job and family in Philadelphia. Just because she admired your

Renoir and enjoyed the raspberry charlotte doesn't mean she's ready to move to Paris."

"When I met your father, my favorite food was Yorkshire pudding and I thought French was an impossible language." Claudia stacked silverware on the counter.

"If you think I can marry Isabel and save the house, I don't—" Alec began.

"This has nothing to do with me," Claudia interrupted. "You're the only thing I have left, and I want you to be happy. Love can be difficult and painful, but really nothing else matters."

"I had enough pain with Celine to last decades," Alec said, suddenly flustered.

Why did he think things would work out with Isabel? He should go back to his flat in the Marais and be content with Gus and the tomato plant in the window box. But he pictured Isabel's wide smile and knew he had to try. He didn't want to live without her.

"Let's go out to the garden, I was just picking snow peas." Claudia took Alec's arm. "And thank you for bringing Isabel, it's wonderful to meet my future daughter-in-law."

"WHAT A SPECTACULAR boulevard," Isabel said. "It's like Fifth Avenue but with even bigger houses and so much history."

Isabel wanted to stroll down Avenue Foch and Alec agreed. It really was beautiful with its chestnut trees and creamy stone mansions and elegant boutiques. The Arc de Triomphe stood on one end and the Porte Dauphine was on the other, and Alec felt a sense of pride.

"Your mother's story is so romantic." Isabel stopped in front of a window filled with bonbons. "She was a young au pair living in a foreign country. She fell in love with an older man

whose wife deserted him and left him with their three-year-old daughter," she continued. "It couldn't have been easy, children that age think their parents were created just for them. It's like something out of a Jane Austen novel."

"More like a Stephen King novel," Alec mumbled.

Now was the time to tell Isabel about his family. But what if Isabel thought he wanted to marry her to stop Bettina from evicting his mother? Being in love was like the Phantom Manor at Disneyland Paris. Everywhere you turned there were trapdoors and quicksand.

"But true love conquers everything," Isabel mused. "Antoine sends a dozen roses every day! It won't be easy being away from my family, but you can't expect to find love next door." Her eyes were bright. "If your mother stayed in England, you would never have been born."

"My mother is quite Parisian. She might still have a British accent and like her tea with lemon and honey, but she adores French fashion and macarons." He paused. "And she loves 40 Rue de Passy. It's like living in the country in the middle of Paris."

"It reminds me of my parents' home in Ardmore." Isabel nodded. "I had no idea that you—"

"Grew up in a large house?" Alec cut in. "You thought because I live in a fifth-floor walk-up and illustrate children's books, I was raised in a three-room flat in the twentieth arrondissement."

"Not exactly." Isabel flushed.

"My father was successful, but I have to live on my own salary," Alec explained. "My sister might be content living on the allowance my father provided her and having Édouard take her to dinner at Le Meurice. But I couldn't look myself in the mirror if I didn't pay rent and buy my own groceries."

"That's what I said to Rory!" Isabel exclaimed. "His family has piles of money, so he just wanted to have fun. But none of this would have been built if the great architects were satisfied with what already existed." She waved at the elegant mansions and tall apartment buildings. "And what if Thomas Edison thought gaslight was perfectly adequate or Henry Ford was happy riding horses? We all have to make a contribution, there's nothing more important."

Alec looked at Isabel and wanted to kiss her. She was so enchanting, like a young girl collecting shells at the beach. But she might get cold feet and he'd miss his chance.

"I have to go back to the Crillon and get ready for tonight." Isabel glanced at her watch. "Antoine is meeting me in the hotel lobby at seven thirty."

"You have plenty of time," Alec said. "We haven't explored the Place du Trocadéro or visited the galleries on the Rue de Rivoli."

"I loved meeting your mother, but I have to take a bath and do my hair and makeup," Isabel said and smiled. "You can't prepare for an Imperial Ball by zipping up a dress and rubbing on lipstick."

Alec had intended on proposing on the balcony of his suite. But what if they arrived at the Crillon and Isabel insisted on going straight to her room? He pictured the room service bottle of Veuve Clicquot and platter of duck foie gras and sighed. Love was so expensive; he couldn't wait until they were married and could stick to a budget.

But if he dropped to his knees on the pavement, she probably wouldn't hear him over the honking cars and chattering tourists. Instead of realizing he was asking her to marry him, she might think he'd lost his wallet.

He took her hand and led her down a narrow passageway.

"Where are we going?" she asked.

"We must visit the Marché de Passy," he explained. "It has the best organic fruits and vegetables in the city."

Alec glanced at the baskets of tomatoes and trays of asparagus, and his shoulders sagged. Could he really ask Isabel to marry him surrounded by leeks and artichokes? But at least it was quiet and the smell of cooked sausage was quite pleasant.

He bought a packet of olives and bag of chestnuts. He took Isabel's hand and led her to a bench.

"You have to try one." He handed her the bag of chestnuts. "There's nothing more Parisian than warm chestnuts wrapped in newspaper."

Isabel put her hand in the newspaper and gasped. She drew out a black velvet box and looked at Alec.

"Ever since you tossed your Ferragamo on the balcony, my life has changed." He took the box and held it in his palm. "You've made me see the world in a new light, and when I'm with you, I don't want the day to end. I love you and want to spend the rest of our lives together." He opened the jewelry box. "Isabel Lawson, will you marry me?"

"You can't propose!" Isabel exclaimed. "I'm going to marry Antoine."

"I know you've made mistakes and think you have to listen to the fortune-teller," Alec implored. "But you're beautiful and smart and this time you're making the right decision. I will spend every day making you happy." He paused. "You make me believe I can do anything and it's the best feeling in the world."

"We don't know anything about each other, we've only had one kiss."

Alec leaned forward and kissed her. Her lips were warm and she tasted like raspberry and cream.

"Now we've had two," he said, suddenly feeling cocky. "If you want, we can have more."

"The kisses are lovely, but I've put everything into choosing the right husband." Isabel twisted her hands. "The fortune-teller said I was going to fall in love and marry a French aristocrat, and I met Antoine the next day. I can't ignore the magical things that have happened since I arrived in Paris." She paused. "If I listen to the fortune-teller, everything will be perfect."

"You'll get a good job and with our combined incomes we'll rent a garden flat in Saint-Germain-des-Prés. We'll buy a little car and visit the cathedral in Rheims on the weekend." He paused. "Then we'll come home and eat chocolate soufflé in bed." He took Isabel's hand. "Everything is perfect. You just have to give us a chance."

"I do have feelings for you . . ." She hesitated. "I promised Antoine I would go to the Imperial Ball and I can't go back on my word." She looked at Alec. "Can I give you my answer tomorrow?"

Alec rubbed his brow and wished he'd learned how to pray. Could he ask God for the most important thing in the world, the first time he needed help?

"Yes," he breathed. "You can give me your answer tomorrow."

ALEC TOLD ISABEL he had to run some errands and would see her tomorrow. He sat at Café Carette and ordered café au lait and brioche. God, that kiss! It was like a movie where the couple kisses in the final frame and the screen erupts into fireworks.

He pictured Isabel attending the Imperial Ball with Antoine and his chest tightened. It didn't matter if Antoine presented her with the Hope diamond; he was certain she loved him. All he had to do was make it through tonight, and tomorrow she would say yes.

He felt in his pocket and realized he still had the jewelry

box. He forgot to give her the ring! He couldn't run after her now—she was preparing for the Imperial Ball.

Why didn't she ask to see the ring? Maybe she wasn't in love with him; she just wanted to let him down slowly. Being in love wasn't like the Phantom Manor at Disneyland Paris; it was more like Space Mountain. One minute you were looking at the stars, the next you dropped so fast your stomach stayed in your mouth.

He pushed aside the café au lait and signaled the waiter. What he needed was a large scotch.

chapter sixteen

꙳

Isabel sat at the dressing table and picked up her mahogany hairbrush. She admired the folds of the silver silk dress and wished she could concentrate on choosing a necklace and earrings.

She tried pushing Alec out of her mind, but you couldn't ignore a marriage proposal. It was like watching *To Kill a Mockingbird* on Netflix and trying to forget you knew how the trial ended.

How could Alec expect her to say yes when they had just met? She wanted Antoine to propose, but that was different. The fortune-teller said she was going to marry a French aristocrat. Antoine was like a preapproved credit card you received in the mail.

Usually she could solve a problem by analyzing the facts. But they kept rearranging themselves like objects in a Harry Potter movie. Alec was warm and good-looking, and when she was with him, she felt like she was watching a documentary where you see a flower bloom in slow motion.

But she had been certain Rory was the love of her life and

Neil would provide her with a stable future. She couldn't ignore her track record; it was like betting on a horse that lost every Kentucky Derby.

And Antoine was so thoughtful! Every woman wanted to receive a dozen roses and dine at Michelin-star restaurants.

She remembered Alec kneeling on the cement in the covered market and had to smile. Of all the places he could have proposed in Paris, she couldn't think of anything less romantic.

But when he kissed her, she wanted it to last forever. Even if she was in love with him, was that enough? Could she ignore all the signs because of a flutter in her chest?

Alec's mother was lovely and the house on Rue de Passy was gorgeous. But it didn't matter if Alec grew up with English rose gardens and a Renoir on the wall; he still wasn't a French aristocrat. The fortune-teller's prediction had been specific; it would be like ignoring the fine print on a contract.

She fastened a gold necklace around her neck and gasped. How could she not have looked at the ring? And now it was back in his pocket. Not that it would have influenced her decision, but it would have been nice to know if he bought a one-carat diamond from Cartier or an antique ruby from an estate sale.

She wasn't even sure what kind of engagement ring she would like. That's why she had to listen to the fortune-teller; love and marriage were so confusing. She couldn't make the decision by herself.

She must marry Antoine; she couldn't take a chance. She pictured a stone house with a gabled roof. They would have a black Labrador, and on Sundays Antoine would make raspberry crepes.

Tomorrow she would tell Alec it was a mistake. She shouldn't have said she'd think about it—it was out of the question. He was very kind and she valued their friendship.

She stood at the window and thought the Champs-Élysées was beautiful in every light, and she never tired of seeing the Petit Palais. And soon it would all be hers! She and Antoine would attend balls and give dinner parties. Maybe she'd meet a few expatriates and trade James Patterson books and Ralph Lauren catalogs.

She fastened her hair with a diamond clip and slipped on stilettos. She grabbed her purse and hurried to the elevator.

Isabel stood in the Crillon's lobby and gazed at crystal vases filled with orchids. A harpsichord stood in one corner, and silk sofas were scattered over Persian rugs.

Antoine entered the glass revolving doors wearing a white dinner jacket and black bow tie. His blond hair was slicked back and his cheeks glistened with aftershave.

"Isabel, you look beautiful." He kissed her on the cheek. "I feel terrible about last night, I should never have taken a client to Provins during the holidays. The roads are so congested, the sheep move faster."

"It's quite all right." Isabel smiled. "I had a pleasant evening and went to bed early."

"We'll make up for it tonight, the Imperial Ball is attended by all of Parisian society." He reached into his pocket and drew out a flat velvet box. "I'm so glad you could come, I wanted to give you something special."

Isabel snapped it open and discovered a diamond-and-ruby tiara. She looked at Antoine and gasped.

"It's the de Villoy tiara, it was given to an ancestor by Napoleon. It's been worn by *comtesses* to Imperial Balls for decades." Antoine picked it up. "My parents couldn't attend this year, so I thought you could wear it."

"You want me to wear a priceless family heirloom?" Isabel stammered.

"When I saw you at the Red Cross charity ball, I thought

you were the most beautiful woman in the world." He kissed her. "I hope we attend many balls together."

Isabel placed the tiara on her head and caught her reflection in the mirror. Her eyes sparkled and her lips shimmered and her skin was like peaches.

"It's the most beautiful thing I've ever seen." She turned to Antoine. There was a sudden twinge in her chest and she ignored it. "I can't wait to dance and drink French champagne."

ISABEL NIBBLED SALMON tartare and gazed around the ballroom. The walls were covered in rich tapestries, and glittering chandeliers dangled from the ceiling.

Everything about the evening was wonderful: The twelve-tier raspberry fondant cake and sixteen-piece orchestra. The platters of guinea fowl and stuffed partridge.

Antoine went to get a plate of mushroom crepes, and Isabel stood at the bar. She saw a woman with a blond chignon and emerald earrings.

"Isabel, it's lovely to see you." Jacqueline approached her. "What a fabulous gown, did you buy it in Paris?"

"I found it this afternoon at Galeries Lafayette." Isabel nodded. "I didn't know I would be attending so many balls or I would have packed more than one cocktail dress." She paused. "Of course, one doesn't need an excuse to visit Paris's department stores. I could spend all day in the shoe department of Le Bon Marché."

Isabel bit her lip. Jacqueline probably had a personal shopper who delivered Lanvin dresses and Chanel purses to her apartment. She would never fit in with Antoine's friends if she behaved like a tourist who exited the metro and discovered herself in the Place Vendôme.

"The January sales are terrific," Jacqueline confided. "Last

year I scooped up Marc Jacob slacks and Courrèges sweaters." She fiddled with her earrings. "We'll go together, I have a friend who can get us into Le Printemps before the doors open."

"I'd love to, but I don't know if I'll be here in January." Isabel hesitated. "I fly back to Philadelphia in two days."

"Antoine mentioned you might join us in Chamonix," Jacqueline said. "I ran into him at the market, and you're all he talked about."

"I am?" Isabel asked.

"He's quite taken with you," Jacqueline continued. "I'm pleased. Our circle is very tight; we've known each other since nursery school. It will be nice to include an American who can teach us about F. Scott Fitzgerald and the Kardashians."

"I studied *The Great Gatsby* in high school, but I don't get many popular magazines," Isabel laughed. "Though when I attended the Sorbonne, I read *Paris Match* to practice my French."

"*Paris Match* is worse than *Hello!* Of course, the people who are worth mentioning aren't in it at all," she mused. "For that you have to attend the private salons on the Rue du Faubourg Saint-Honoré."

"It's the same in America," Isabel agreed. "The Kelloggs and du Ponts may as well not exist, but that's where the power is."

"Antoine said you would fit in," Jacqueline said and smiled. "Give me your number. We'll have tea at Le Meurice and you can tell me what happened on the last season of *Homeland*."

"Do you watch it?" Isabel asked curiously.

"We wouldn't miss it." She nodded. "But French television is two seasons behind."

Jacqueline drifted away, and Isabel felt a shiver of excitement. Antoine had lent her the de Villoy tiara and wanted her to go to Chamonix!

She remembered Alec asking her to marry him and flinched.

Alec would understand—look what happened with Celine. They were madly in love and it ended badly. You couldn't figure out love by yourself; it was like trying to win at blackjack. The only people who had a chance were the ones who controlled the cards.

Alec would find someone and they'd all be friends. She felt something squeezing her chest. Perhaps her gown was too tight and she should adjust it.

"There you are." Antoine put his arm around her. "Come with me, I want to show you something."

They walked down a marble hallway and entered a paneled room with tall bookshelves. It had a large globe and a Louis XVI desk. There was a leather Bible and cabinet filled with Fabergé eggs.

Antoine poured two glasses of brandy and handed one to Isabel.

"Is that a first edition copy of the *Decameron*?" Isabel gasped, gazing at a leather book in a glass case.

"The Grand Hotel has one of the finest antiquarian book collections in Europe." He pulled a book from the shelves. "This one is about witchcraft trials in France during the Middle Ages. Almost half the witches sent to trial were men." He sipped his brandy. "In 1560 my ancestor François de Villoy was accused of putting a spell on a young woman and convincing her to marry him. The girl's father pressed charges because nine months after they married, his daughter died in childbirth."

"What happened to François?" Isabel asked.

"I'm afraid he was burned at the stake." He paused. "Of course it wasn't witchcraft at all, it was love at first sight."

Isabel gulped the brandy and felt a tightness in her chest.

"I've waited thirty years for the right woman," Antoine began. "The moment I saw you standing at the coat check in the Petit Palais, something stirred inside me."

Antoine reached into his pocket and the glass tipped and brandy spilled over his slacks.

"If you will excuse me—" Antoine watched the gold stain spread over silk. "I'll be right back."

Antoine strode out of the library and Isabel let out her breath. If Antoine hadn't spilled brandy, he would have pulled out an engagement ring. Why was her heart racing like a hummingbird poised for flight?

She had been waiting for this moment since she met Antoine at the Red Cross charity ball. She could already picture the emerald-cut diamond and lace wedding dress and Chanel suit she would wear on the train to Venice.

But was it a sign that he bumped his glass for no reason? She suddenly remembered the old man at Shakespeare and Company saying if she found true love, she had to hold onto it. If she truly wanted to marry Antoine, she would have given him a handkerchief and begged him to finish his sentence.

She remembered throwing her Ferragamo on Alec's balcony. She saw his dark wavy hair and slender cheekbones. He had a habit of rubbing his brow, and when he held her hand she felt secure.

It didn't matter what the fortune-teller said; she was in love with Alec. It was as simple as the addition tables she learned in kindergarten.

Why hadn't she seen it before? It was like when you had to try a banana split, even though you didn't like nuts. It looked delicious until you ate a spoonful of pecans and whipped cream and couldn't eat another bite.

Antoine was handsome and charming, and his family had been in France for centuries, but she wasn't in love with him. What was the point of any of it if her skin didn't tingle and she couldn't bear being apart?

She was contradicting everything she had said, but that was

the thing about love. It didn't have any identifiable properties and you couldn't study it under a microscope.

She rushed down the hallway, feeling like Marie Antoinette escaping the rabble. She reached the lobby and collided with a woman wearing a silver evening gown.

"I'm sorry. I was in a hurry and didn't see you," Isabel said, picking up the woman's purse. "I hope I didn't ruin your dress."

"I'm all in one piece." The woman inspected her hem and glanced at Isabel. "You're the American girl I met at the Red Cross charity ball."

"You're Alec's sister, what a lovely surprise." Isabel beamed. "You must be on your way to the ball. The band plays a wonderful version of 'La Vie en Rose' and the spinach crepes are delicious. Make sure you try the pistachio macarons, they melt in your mouth."

"Why are you leaving and what are you wearing on your head?" Bettina asked.

Isabel touched her hair and gasped. She was still wearing the de Villoy tiara! But she couldn't return it to Antoine now; she would have to explain everything. She would send it by courier as soon as she reached the Crillon.

"I came with Comte Antoine de Villoy," Isabel began. "We were in the Grand Hotel's library examining their antiquarian books. He spilled brandy on his slacks, and I suddenly remembered something terribly important."

"You're at the Imperial Ball with a French *comte*," Bettina mused. "Alec was right, I was sure he was lying."

"What are you talking about?" Isabel asked.

"I had lunch with Alec at the Crillon a couple of days ago," Bettina continued. "I thought he was going to ask you to marry him so I couldn't evict Claudia. He assured me I was wrong, you were in love with a French *comte*."

Isabel's heart pounded and she couldn't breathe.

"Could you repeat that?" she whispered.

"French law is so complicated. The one-year anniversary of my father's death is next week, and Alec and I will own two-thirds of 40 Rue de Passy. Claudia can't stay there, it was meant for his children." She paused. "It will need a lot of work. The roof will cost a fortune and we haven't looked under the floor-boards."

"What does that have to do with Alec getting married?" Isabel wondered.

"My father put in his will that the first child who marries can live in the house," she explained. "Alec would never ask his mother to leave, they have always been close.

"I thought that was why he was marrying Celine, though he denied it and I believe him. He really was in love with her, like a stray puppy scooped up by a generous benefactor.

"Then I saw you together at the Red Cross charity ball and was sure Alec was determined to get you to the altar."

Isabel's cheeks were pale and she felt like she might faint.

"It was nice to see you, but I really have to go," Isabel said, walking toward the revolving doors.

"What about Antoine?" Bettina called after her.

Isabel's lips trembled. "Tell him I had a lovely time, but there's something very important I have to do."

ISABEL RACED DOWN the steps onto the Place Vendôme. A taxi pulled up and she climbed inside.

She thought of when she left Rory in San Francisco and went through three boxes of tissues on the plane to Philadelphia. She pictured sitting in her childhood bedroom after she can-celed the wedding and Neil calling and saying she should go to Paris alone.

But this pain was so deep she couldn't breathe. Her heart

pounded and something hard pressed on her chest. She gazed out the window at the Christmas lights on the Champs-Élysées and blinked away tears. First she had to see Alec; then she would let herself fall apart.

"ISABEL, WHAT A lovely surprise," Alec said when she knocked on the door. He wore a red sweater and tan slacks. "I was eating duck foie gras. Would you like some, there's plenty left. It cost ninety euros, so I don't want it to go to waste."

"No, thank you." Isabel entered the suite. "I just came from the Imperial Ball and I'm not the slightest bit hungry."

"Of course, the ball." He nodded. "Your dress is stunning, but what are you wearing on your head?"

Isabel felt her hair and wondered how Queen Elizabeth or the Duchess of Cambridge went anywhere, if people kept commenting on their tiaras.

"Antoine lent me the de Villoy tiara. We danced and drank champagne and ate lobster canapés." She paused. "Then he took me into the Grand Hotel's private library."

"Did he try to seduce you?" Alec demanded.

"He was about to ask me to marry him," she replied. "But then he spilled brandy on his slacks and went to clean it up and I realized I'd been wrong all along. I couldn't act on the fortune-teller's prediction as if it was privileged information in a stock trade. The only way to decipher love is to listen to the voice inside you. I've been falling in love with you since we met, and no matter how I analyze the situation, you come up as the answer. I rushed out of the library to tell you and collided with your sister."

"My sister!" Alec exclaimed.

"Bettina recognized me right away, apparently she had lunch with you at the Crillon. She was certain you were going to ask

me to marry you so she wouldn't be able to evict your mother. You insisted I was in love with a French aristocrat, but she thought you were lying." Isabel voice faltered. "Why didn't you tell me about your mother, and how could you propose if you weren't in love with me?"

Alec walked to the bar and poured a glass of scotch. He downed it quickly and looked at Isabel. "The French are stoic and the English are even worse, we don't air our family squabbles like the inside pages of the *Daily Mirror*.

"I doubt my father ever saw my mother without her cheeks powdered and her lips rouged, appearances are important even in private. What would you think of me if you saw my sister behaving like she was on an episode of *Desperate Housewives?*"

"If you get married by January third, can you stop Bettina from evicting your mother?" Isabel asked.

"Well, yes, but that has nothing to do with us," Alec implored. "I never wanted to fall in love, it's like walking around with the flu. You break into a sweat and lose your appetite.

"After Celine left, I swore I'd rather take a cyanide pill than go through it again." He paused. "But you entered my life with your brown eyes and seductive smile like a Bouguereau painting." He looked at Isabel. "God, if only I could have stopped myself! I've read Stendhal's *The Red and the Black* and Tolstoy's *Anna Karenina,* great love always ends badly."

"How can I believe you when you lied to me about one of the most important things in your life?" Isabel asked.

"I didn't lie," Alec corrected. "I didn't tell you the whole truth."

"You can't keep secrets in a relationship. What if you fall in love with a beautiful redhead and don't tell me because you don't want to hurt my feelings? There's nothing more important than honesty, it's the basis for everything."

"I can't stop thinking about you. I drew Gus in a field pluck-

ing daisy petals and chanting, 'She loves me, she loves me not.' "
He pointed to his sketchbook. "I've never felt this way about
anyone, you have to give me another chance."

Isabel glanced at the sketch of Gus wearing a caftan and
making daisy chains and wavered. She so wanted to be in love
and live happily ever after. But how could she trust Alec if he
lied from the beginning, and how could she risk getting her
heart broken?

"Send Gus to a tropical island with some hula dancers, I'm
sure he'll recover." She walked to the door. "I'm leaving in two
days, and it's best if we don't see each other again."

She thought she heard Alec call her name and was about to
turn around. Then she turned the handle and closed the door
behind her.

Isabel entered her suite and considered running back to the
Grand Hotel and telling Antoine she'd had to take an impor-
tant phone call. Now she couldn't wait to eat profiteroles and
drink amaretto and listen to the band play "Le Mer."

She slipped off her earrings and knew she couldn't do it. She
closed her eyes and the image of a playroom scattered with
colored blocks and a kitchen filled with juice boxes disappeared
and was replaced by a bedroom with a single nightstand. She
imagined a galley kitchen with a coffeepot she never used and
an oven that was used only for heating up single-serving lasagna.

The Christmas tree in the Place de la Concorde glittered and
the lights on the Champs-Élysées sparkled and it looked like a
postcard. She was in Paris at Christmas, and she would never
be happy again.

chapter seventeen

❧

Alec ate a handful of Brazil nuts and washed them down with scotch. He felt like a rock star on an all-night bender. Except he couldn't afford to trash the hotel suite and there weren't any groupies waiting under his balcony, waving bras and panties.

He glanced at the sketch of Gus wearing a kimono and committing hari-kari. There was a drawing of Gus treading hot coals with a blindfold over his floppy ears. Alec picked up a pencil and studied the sketch of Gus jumping out of a fighter jet. He erased his parachute and threw the sketch pad on the coffee table.

No matter how many disastrous situations he put Gus in, he couldn't get rid of his pain.

When Isabel entered his suite, he had been sure she was going to admit she was in love with him. He wished he hadn't sent back the bottle of champagne and eaten most of the duck foie gras. But then he saw her flashing eyes and glittering tiara and knew it was over.

Why didn't he tell her the truth from the beginning, and how could he have ruined the only thing that mattered?

There was a knock on the door and he answered it.

"Helene had a dream that you jumped into shark-infested waters in Mexico," Mathieu said, entering the suite. "Pregnant women are so superstitious, she insisted I come here and make sure you didn't drown in the bathtub."

"I'm fine." Alec finished his scotch and ate another handful of nuts. "I was having breakfast."

Mathieu picked up a sketch of Gus falling off a ladder into a wasp nest and frowned. "I miss the drawings of Gus strolling along the Pont Neuf with a cute poodle."

"I asked Isabel to marry me yesterday," Alec began. "She said she had feelings for me, but she promised Antoine she would attend the Imperial Ball. So she would let me know tomorrow.

"Antoine took Isabel into the Grand Hotel's private library and he was about to propose." He refilled his glass. "Isabel realized she was in love with me and ran out of the room. Right into Bettina."

"What happened?" Mathieu gasped.

"When has Bettina ever missed a chance to cause havoc with my life?" Alec groaned. "She told Isabel she thought I was going to ask Isabel to marry me so she couldn't evict Claudia from 40 Rue de Passy.

"Isabel burst into the suite wearing an exquisite silk gown and priceless tiara and demanded to know if the only reason I asked her to marry me was to stop Bettina." He sank onto the sofa. "It was like a period drama my mother watches on the BBC."

"Did you explain that you're really a viscount and were afraid to tell her? You'd never know if she was in love with you or wanted to marry a French aristocrat."

"She was furious, it wasn't the time to discuss my family genealogy."

"You have to tell her," Mathieu urged. "She might forgive you."

"I insisted my feelings for her have nothing to do with Claudia and Bettina," he sighed. "She said even if it was true it didn't matter. Honesty is more important than anything. Then she said she never wanted to see me again and stormed out."

"I begged you to tell the truth," Mathieu muttered.

"You're an attorney," Alec spluttered. "You don't even know the correct definition."

"You can't lie to women," Mathieu continued. "If you tell her you didn't get the roast beef she was craving because the butcher closed, she'll sniff out the truth like a German shepherd." He paused. "And never make the mistake of saying she doesn't look pregnant from behind when she's standing in front of a three-way mirror."

Alec started to laugh and stopped. He would give anything to buy Isabel bonbons when she was pregnant and admire her rounded stomach. God, what had he done! He had given up a lifetime of happiness because he forgot a simple rule: if you love someone, you have to trust her.

"It's too late now." Alec sank onto the sofa. "She's leaving tomorrow."

"Do you remember when we were nineteen and got stuck on the metro with some young thugs?" Mathieu asked. "They started hassling us for a packet of cigarettes and you told them you were a black belt in karate."

"I didn't have a choice, we were locked inside," Alec laughed. "They believed me. When the doors finally opened, we ran as fast as we could."

"Sometimes you just have to believe in yourself. If you love Isabel, you need to fight for her." He walked to the door. "I have to help Helene buy some new bras, her breasts are the size of ripe melons."

Alec walked to the desk and glanced at a sketch of Gus tied to the train tracks. He picked up his pencil and drew Gus untying the rope. Gus jumped up and stopped the speeding train with his paw.

He remembered receiving a letter from a boy in Montreal who said he fended off bullies at school because he read *Gus and the International Drug Ring* and told the other boys he was actually CIA. There was the note from a little girl in Madrid who was sure her cancer was in remission because she read *Gus and the Hospital Stay* and knew miracles were possible. He still cried every time he read it and had sent a copy to the pope.

He couldn't disappoint children all over the world by letting Gus be eaten by cannibals. Somehow he had to convince Isabel that he had lied for the right reasons and it would never happen again. But first he had to do something he should have done a long time ago.

He glanced in the mirror and thought he really had to stop wearing this sweater. Christmas was over, and red made his skin look washed out. He pulled it over his head and put on a white button-down shirt and twill slacks. He grabbed his leather jacket and walked to the door.

"ALEC, WHAT A surprise," Bettina said when he rang the doorbell of her apartment. "I was taking down the Christmas ornaments. Now that your wedding is canceled, Édouard and I are leaving for Mustique."

Alec entered Bettina's living room and wondered how she kept it so pristine. You could dust the glass coffee table for fingerprints and find nothing.

"I was in the neighborhood and thought I'd stop by." Alec wished he could ask for a scotch and soda. But it was too early

for a drink, and if he showed any sign of weakness, Bettina would pounce like a lioness on an unsuspecting rabbit.

"I ran into Isabel at the Imperial Ball last night. She was wearing a Chanel gown and diamond-and-ruby tiara." Bettina sat on the white silk sofa. "I was mistaken, I don't know how I imagined you together. She's quite beautiful and apparently she's a successful analyst."

Alec remembered when he was five years old and Bettina took him to show-and-tell and introduced him as her younger brother. He was very proud until he heard the other children whispering that Bettina was right, he had unusually large ears.

After school, his mother found him in her dressing room, examining his ears in the mirror. She gave him a bowl of chocolate mousse and assured him his ears were normal.

He couldn't let Bettina get under his skin. He had to behave like an adult.

"I have a proposition," Alec said. "You can have my portion of our father's assets in exchange for allowing Claudia to remain at 40 Rue de Passy."

"What did you say?" Bettina asked.

Alec had rehearsed the speech on the metro, but now he felt like something was stuck in his throat.

"I'll sign over my share of Alain's stocks and other monies as long as Claudia can stay in the house for the rest of her life."

"Sometimes when people go through a dramatic breakup, it affects their rational thinking," Bettina replied. "I can have a technician in Édouard's neurology department do an MRI or CAT scan."

"There's nothing wrong with me, but there is something wrong with evicting a woman who spent her whole life making her family happy," Alec spluttered. "Do you think you would have got braces if it was up to our father? He wouldn't have noticed if you had teeth like a donkey. And who let you bor-

row her makeup and wrote a note that you had the flu so you wouldn't fail a chemistry exam?"

"That was the only test I was not prepared for," Bettina retorted. "And I stopped wearing Claudia's makeup when I was fourteen. She bought her lipstick at the chemist."

"I refuse to have my mother thrown on the pavement like a Christmas tree on New Year's," he fumed. "Mathieu will draw up the agreement."

"Édouard and I could buy a six-room apartment on the Avenue Montaigne," she mused. "But how will you pay for upkeep on the house? The plumbing is from the Middle Ages and the back porch is sagging."

Alec treated publishing like a gentleman's profession and didn't talk about money. The point of illustrating children's books was to bring joy to thousands of children, not to own an Audi and spend three weeks in Monte Carlo. But surely Gus was selling well enough to ask for a raise.

He would ask his agent to pursue more merchandising opportunities. He pictured Gus on the side of a lunch box and at the bottom of a cereal bowl, and his chest puffed out.

"I'm an internationally best-selling children's book illustrator, I can afford to replace a few planks of wood," he said hotly.

"I'll discuss it with my attorney and bring you my terms." Bettina looked at Alec. "You are a quick learner and have a strong basis in the classics. You should take continuing education classes, you never know what you could achieve."

"Thank you for the advice." Alec walked to the door. "I'm very busy."

"Celine and Isabel were both in love with you, you must have something." She followed him to the foyer. "If you get some assertiveness training and invest in a new wardrobe, you might keep the next woman."

"How do you know Isabel was in love with me?" Alec turned around.

"I could see it in her eyes when she said your name."

Alec strolled along the Rue du Faubourg Saint-Honoré and felt like Fred Astaire in *Funny Face*. He wanted to dance under the Arc du Triomphe and fly kites in the Bois de Boulogne. He looked in a boutique window, and the salesgirl winked as if he was a movie star.

Why hadn't he done that weeks ago? He suddenly flashed on his meager bank account and overextended charge cards and his chest tightened. He'd create a whole new character and write a second line of books. He wouldn't let Bettina belittle him again.

He stopped in front of Maison du Chocolat and glanced at the pyramid of pastel macarons. There were trays of flavored ganaches and glazed chestnuts.

He might not be able to afford dinner at L'Arpège or Cartier earrings, but he could still buy Isabel presents. He would fill a *boîte maison* with hazelnut truffles and pralines.

He couldn't give up now. Mathieu said he had to fight for Isabel, and he was going to start with chocolate profiteroles with a raspberry filling. He glanced at his reflection in the window and straightened his shoulders. He entered the store and approached the counter.

ALEC CROSSED THE Crillon's marble lobby and pressed the button on the elevator. His arms were full with a box of chocolates and a bouquet of tulips and a hardbound book on Monet's gardens at Giverny.

He had to convince Isabel to give them a chance. Love could be cruel and make you want to put a noose around your neck. But without it every day was as bleak as Paris in January.

The elevator stopped at the fifth floor and he fumbled for his key. He would grab a bottle of Bordeaux from the suite's minibar and knock on Isabel's door.

He opened the door and inhaled the scent of jasmine perfume. A woman sat on the sofa, sipping a café au lait and eating a brioche. She had blond hair and wore diamond teardrop earrings and a white pantsuit.

Alec dropped the box of chocolates and gasped. What was Celine doing in Paris, and why was she in his hotel suite?

chapter eighteen

꧁

Isabel opened her guidebook and gazed at the tall spires of the Cathedral of Notre Dame. It had twelve-foot brass doors and stone buttresses and stained glass windows. The guidebook said construction began in 1163 under Louis VII. They had to build a new road to bring building materials to the site on the Île de la Cité.

All morning she explored the Musée d'Orsay and Centre Pompidou and the Panthéon. She climbed to the top of the Eiffel Tower and rode a bicycle in the Luxembourg Gardens. She paddled a rowboat in the Bois de Boulogne, clutching the guidebook as if it was a life raft.

This was what she should have been doing in Paris all along instead of looking for love and getting her heart broken. Her eyes welled with tears and she brushed them away. She couldn't cry in the middle of a guided tour.

She sent Antoine the tiara with a note asking if they could meet to talk. He had taken her to the ball and dinner and the opera. She didn't want to leave him a Dear John letter.

She pictured bumping into Bettina in the lobby of the Grand

Hotel and her stomach rose to her throat. Did Alec really propose to stop his mother from being evicted? And even if he hadn't, how could she trust him?

Everywhere she turned reminded her of Alec. They had gone shopping in the Marais and visited Victor Hugo's house. They explored the Catacombs and had a picnic in Renoir's garden. She remembered sharing cassoulet at Les Cocottes and then Alec saying he was falling in love with her.

How could she keep getting love wrong, and why did she keep trying? She was going back to Philadelphia and throwing herself into her work. Maybe she'd get a rescue dog and volunteer at a soup kitchen on the weekends.

Couples strolled along the Pont Neuf, and she wondered how it looked so easy. Could she be the only one who was unlucky in love, or did she simply not know when she found it?

But she had been in love with Alec. If she hadn't, her heart wouldn't pound and she wouldn't feel like she had when she was five years old and her favorite teddy bear unraveled in the dryer.

She heard footsteps and turned around. She saw a tall man wearing an overcoat and carrying a paper sack.

"Isabel, wait," he called after her.

"You're Mathieu, Alec's friend. We met at the Red Cross charity ball." She paused and her eyes were wide. "What are you doing on the Pont Neuf? Did you follow me?"

"Not exactly," Mathieu explained. "I saw you on the Pont Alexandre III. I tried to catch up, but you walk so fast. I had to stop and catch my breath."

"This is my last day in Paris and there's so much to see," Isabel explained, sitting on a stone bench. "I want to visit Sainte-Chapelle and buy watercolors in the Latin Quarter." She flipped the page of the guidebook. "Did you know the organ in the Cathedral of Notre Dame has seven thousand one hundred forty-three pipes?"

"You can't leave tomorrow." Mathieu opened the paper sack and took out two croissants. He handed one to Isabel and sat beside her.

"I have to get back to work," she explained. "A fortune-teller said I was going to get a promotion and have a glass office with a large desk." She stopped and her eyes were bright. "The fortune-teller might not be right about everything, but she was right about me receiving a gift and almost being run over. So I'm sure she's right about that."

"You can't leave because you have to give Alec another chance." Mathieu looked at Isabel. "He's in love with you."

"Thank you for the croissant, but I have to go." She jumped up. "It was nice to see you, and say hello to your wife. Alec told me she was having a baby."

"I'll walk with you." Mathieu followed her. "Just give me half an hour and I'll explain everything."

"Alec said you were an attorney, so I'm sure you're used to standing in front of a jury and making them believe your client isn't guilty. But Alec didn't tell me the truth, so he can't be in love with me at all." Her eyes flashed. "The most important thing about love is being honest."

"He should have told you about Bettina and his mother, but he also didn't tell you something else," Mathieu said. "He's really a viscount."

"What did you say?" she gasped.

"His father's name was Alain de Gagnon. His family is a *noblesse anciennes*. It's one of the oldest titles in France and was given to his ancestor in the thirteenth century."

"Alec's last name is Braxton." Isabel frowned. "I saw it on the cover *of Gus and the Sea Monster*."

"His British publisher thought Alec de Gagnon sounded too French," Mathieu said. "Braxton is his mother's maiden name."

"Why didn't he tell me?" she wondered. "The fortune-teller

said I was going to marry a French aristocrat, that would have solved everything."

"He started falling in love with you. And he was afraid he'd never know if you truly loved him or simply wanted to marry a French aristocrat." Mathieu paused. "Celine hurt him quite badly. He was afraid of love, it was like a spoiled soufflé."

"I would never have said yes unless I loved him. I used the fortune-teller as a guide because I'm hopeless at choosing men," she fumed. "I've had two failed engagements and couldn't risk another mistake. I had to look for outside guidance. It's like when you lose almost all your money in the stock market and turn over what's left to a financial planner."

Isabel gazed at the Seine and wondered whether she was being accurate. Had she been attracted to Antoine, or did she make herself fall in love with him because that's what the fortune-teller suggested? If she had known Alec was a viscount, would she have tumbled into a relationship without first discovering her feelings?

"I know what you're doing. I saw it on an episode of *The Good Wife*." Her eyes were wide. "You're changing the angle of the case so your client looks less guilty. Perhaps I let the fortune-teller's prediction color my actions. But that doesn't change the fact that Alec lied to me.

"What if he wanted to get married to stop Claudia from being evicted, and never loved me at all?"

Mathieu pulled his iPhone out of his pocket and handed it to Isabel.

"What's this?" she asked.

"I'm a corporate attorney, so I've never been in front of a jury," he began. "But I do have a habit of recording my conversations. I recorded a few chats with Alec. You might like to hear them."

Isabel's hands shook and she handed the phone back to Mathieu.

"You better press play," she whispered.

Mathieu clicked the button, and Isabel heard Alec say he never wanted to fall in love again; it was worse than being thrown into a vat of molten lava. Isabel looked beautiful in her red Oscar de la Renta ball gown, and she had the loveliest brown eyes and wide smile.

Mathieu fast-forwarded, and Alec admitted he was falling in love with her. Mathieu urged him to tell her he was a viscount and Alec explained he would never know if she just wanted to marry a French aristocrat. Love was almost impossible, and marriage was even worse. He had to know she really loved him.

Mathieu said if Alec proposed to Isabel, Claudia could stay in the house and it would solve everything. Alec replied that he loved his mother but he could never marry just so that Bettina wouldn't evict her.

Mathieu clicked the stop button, and Isabel's eyes filled with tears. He did love her! It was as obvious as the Christmas lights in the Place de la Concorde.

"Alec should have told you the truth, but he didn't mean to hurt you," Mathieu said. "You have to give him another chance."

"When you fall in love with someone, you trust them with your whole future." Isabel paused. "How do I know Alec will always love me if he keeps secrets?"

"When we were nineteen, other boys scribbled graffiti on the Pont Marie and tossed beer caps into the Seine. Alec picked up litter and helped old people navigate the cobblestones.

"He visits the children's hospital once a month, and insists his publisher donate books to orphanages in Italy and Greece.

"When Helene found out she was pregnant, Alec was the first person we called. Helene wanted to be certain he'd be the godfather." He stopped and smiled. "Marriage can be more taxing than sitting in a conference room of opposing high-powered

attorneys. But I couldn't recommend anyone better than Alec for the job."

Isabel remembered the fortune-teller saying she would change directions but end up marrying a French aristocrat. This was what was supposed to happen all along! Antoine was a detour to make sure she was really in love with Alec.

She ate the last bite of croissant and wondered what would have happened if Mathieu hadn't followed her from the Pont Alexandre III. But he had, and now she was certain she was doing the right thing. It was like the strange woman in Le Printemps and the old man in Shakespeare and Company and Alec discovering her bracelet in the vegetable garden at Versailles.

She leaned over and kissed Mathieu on the cheek.

"What was that for?" he asked.

"You made me the happiest girl in the world." She jumped up. "Thank you, I have to go."

"I'll walk with you," Mathieu suggested.

Isabel's eyes sparkled and she laughed. "I don't think so, I'm in a hurry."

ISABEL CLIMBED THE steps of the Hôtel de Crillon and entered the marble lobby. Her arms were full of packages, and she wore new leather pumps.

She had stopped at Le Bon Marché and bought Chanel perfume and pink lipstick. She and Alec had never gone on a proper date and she wanted to look pretty. She passed the men's boutique and selected a navy cashmere sweater and leather belt. The end-of-the-year sales had started and she wanted to buy Alec a Christmas present.

They could stroll along the Canal Saint-Martin and have

dinner at an outdoor café. She pictured climbing to the top of Sacré-Coeur and gazing at the Paris skyline. Alec would wrap his arms around her and kiss her.

She pressed the button of the elevator and couldn't wait to tell Alec about bumping into Mathieu. She would apologize for not believing him that their relationship had nothing to do with 40 Rue de Passy, and say she understood why he didn't tell her he was a viscount. They could get married right away and have a reception in the spring.

The elevator doors opened and she saw a woman standing in front of Alec's suite. She had blond hair and wore a white pantsuit. She took a key out of her purse and inserted it in the lock. The door opened and she stepped inside.

There was only one person who could have the key to Alec's honeymoon suite. What was Celine doing in Paris, and how could anyone be so beautiful? Isabel gasped, and the packages scattered all over the marble floor.

chapter nineteen

⁓

Alec poured a glass of scotch and turned to Celine. She looked exactly as she had when she left. Her hair was knotted in a loose chignon and her cheeks were lightly powdered and she wore thick mascara. But there was something different. He downed the scotch and tried to put his finger on it.

"What on earth are you doing here?" he demanded. "You're supposed to be in Australia."

She brushed brioche crumbs from her slacks and put her demitasse on the porcelain saucer. "It's an impossible country. They eat black spread on white bread for breakfast, and I couldn't find L'Occitane Crème Précieuse at any department store. They wouldn't let me take my jar on the plane and my skin dried out."

"It's called marmite, and it's quite delicious once you get used to it," he snapped. "And I'm sure they have some kind of decent face lotion at David Jones. You didn't have to come back to Paris. What about Patrick—did you leave him at the arrivals terminal?"

"Of course not. We spent two nights in his flat in St. Kilda."

She inspected her fingernails. "All his furniture was on the floor. I felt like I was on a yoga retreat.

"It never would have worked out," she continued. "Apparently he's not a championship cricket player, he's in the bush leagues. And his French was terrible; he didn't understand the concept of personal pronouns. He kept calling a table 'he.' "

"It seems to be a common problem," he said and thought of Isabel. "You can't just show up and order afternoon tea. I'm busy."

"My father is paying for the suite." She eyed the box of chocolates and bouquet of tulips. "When did you start shopping at Maison du Chocolat? Their truffles cost as much as gold bouillon."

"That's none of your business," Alec spluttered. "We canceled the ceremony at Cathédrale Notre-Dame and the reception at the George Cinq and the Aston Martin that would have driven us to the airport. You can't pretend nothing happened."

"I was only gone for ten days." She shrugged. "We'll have a destination wedding; I'm dying to get on the slopes. We'll get married in St. Moritz and stay at the Palace Hotel."

"We're not getting married anywhere," Alec exclaimed.

As soon as the words were out of his mouth, he felt better. He remembered when he was a child and did terribly on a math test. He kept the paper in his pocket and had a stomachache by the time his mother found it. But he didn't care what Celine said; he just wanted her to leave.

He refilled his scotch glass and realized that was what was different. Celine could have violet eyes and a turned-up nose, but he wasn't in love with her.

"What do you mean we're not getting married?" Celine demanded.

Alec wanted to say he was going to marry Isabel, but then

he remembered she had walked out of the suite and said she never wanted to see him again.

"You left with your passport and my favorite pair of slippers," Alec said hotly. "Did you really expect me to be here waiting for you?"

"My feet get cold on the plane." She looked at Alec. "And I didn't expect you to wait for me. I expected you to follow me."

"What did you say?" Alec stammered.

"You turned me over to Patrick like a dog breeder giving away a puppy." She ate another bite of brioche. "You should have seen your face when you appeared at the café in the Place Vendôme. You gave up in the first round."

"Was I supposed to draw a pistol like John Wayne in an American Western?" Alec demanded. "And did you see his muscles under that white shirt? David Beckham couldn't compete."

"If you loved me you would have booked the first flight to Melbourne," Celine insisted, "instead of moping in the hotel suite like a wounded animal."

"I had a wonderful week exploring Paris," he replied. "I visited the Catacombs and Montmartre and Versailles."

"You visited the Catacombs?" Celine looked up. "You're terrified of closed spaces."

"Maybe I'm not, I just needed my eyes opened," he snapped. "Relationships might require work, but they're not supposed to be an ongoing battle with one person claiming to be the victor and the other waving a white flag." He paused. "If you love someone, you spend every day making them happy."

Celine stood up and stretched. Even her high breasts and long legs left him cold. She was like a cat that had been declawed.

"I have terrible jet lag." She walked toward the bedroom. "I'm going to bed, we'll discuss this tomorrow."

"You can't sleep here," Alec insisted.

"What do you mean I can't sleep here?" Celine untied her chignon. "My father paid for twelve nights in the honeymoon suite with a private butler and continental breakfast."

"There's only one bed and I'm tired of sleeping on your sofa. There are other suites at the Crillon, I'll tell the valet to move your bag and I'll pay for the room."

He wished his shrinking bank account matched his new bravado, but he wasn't going to let Celine push him out of the suite. He needed one more night to win back Isabel.

"I've had enough overripe peaches and bottles of Evian." She picked up her suitcase and walked to the door. "I'll go to my apartment."

"Celine, wait," Alec called.

"Yes?" She turned around.

God, she was beautiful with her pink mouth and slender cheekbones. He felt like Odysseus staring down the sirens.

He suddenly pictured Isabel's bright smile, and a warmth spread through his chest.

"You forgot to return my grandmother's diamond ring."

ALEC PACED AROUND the suite like a prizefighter who had scored an unexpected victory. His heart raced and his brow was covered with sweat.

He wished he could replay Celine placing the sapphire-and-diamond ring on the coffee table. He had never seen her linger over a piece of jewelry before.

He thought of what she said about giving up too easily, and an uneasy pit formed in his stomach. Perhaps he should have insisted Patrick didn't join them for dinner. But Celine and Patrick were like a blond Angelina Jolie and Brad Pitt. You had to know when to retreat; it was a basic rule of survival.

Should he have followed her to Melbourne? Twenty-four

hours on an international flight gave him a backache, and the blanket never stayed in one place.

He remembered the way men looked at her in the street and knew he would have been setting himself up for a life of torture. He had taken the quickest escape route, like a pilot jettisoning himself from a burning plane.

Or perhaps she was right; he didn't know how to fight for the woman he loved.

But he wasn't going to lose Isabel. He picked up the bouquet of tulips and hardbound book on Monet's gardens at Giverny. He ran his hands through his hair and sighed. Celine had taken the gold box of chocolate profiteroles.

chapter twenty

❧

Isabel sat on a yellow silk armchair in the Crillon's lobby and gazed at the intricate tapestries and wide marble staircase. The blue velvet wallpaper was flecked with gold, and crystal vases were filled with white roses. She glanced up at the mosaic ceiling and felt like she was inside a box of gourmet chocolates.

After she saw Celine enter Alec's suite, she gathered her packages and stepped back into the elevator. She couldn't risk walking down the hallway and having Alec open the door.

She had been so sure Mathieu was right and Alec was in love with her. But now Alec and Celine were back together and Isabel was leaving tomorrow. She wasn't going to think about Alec. It was like trying to read when you had a terrible headache.

She gazed at women wearing Chanel suits and men in cashmere overcoats and thought all the other guests looked so sophisticated and happy. In two days it would be New Year's Eve and they were enjoying the end of their vacation.

A bellboy in a gold uniform offered her a plate of petits fours and she suddenly needed to be alone. She scooped up her par-

cels and walked down the marble hallway. She entered a pan-
eled library with a Louis XVI desk and walnut cabinets filled
with Fabergé eggs. Her phone buzzed and she pressed accept.

"Isabel!" Her mother's voice came over the line. "I'm so
glad I caught you."

"Is everything all right?" Isabel asked, suddenly wishing she
were nibbling fruitcake in the kitchen in Ardmore.

"You sounded a little off the other day and I know you can
be quite stubborn," her mother explained. "I wondered if any-
thing is wrong."

Isabel glanced at the jewel-encrusted eggs and thought she
could pretend nothing happened and board the plane. Her par-
ents would greet her at the Philadelphia airport and they'd talk
about her new work projects and going to St. Bart's in April.
But she pictured Alec's dark eyes and white smile and her heart
shifted in her chest.

"I met a fortune-teller who said I'd fall in love and marry a
French aristocrat. The next night I met a count at the Red Cross
charity ball and was sure he was the one. We had dinner at Tour
d'Argent and attended the opera and I hoped he was going to
ask me to marry him.

"But when he was about to propose, I realized I was in love
with Alec all along. He's a children's book illustrator who
turned out to be a viscount, though he never told me.

"I thought he'd lied to me, so I said I never wanted to see
him again. But then his friend followed me on the Pont Alex-
andre III and explained Alec was madly in love with me, and I
had to give him another chance.

"I hurried back to the Crillon to tell Alec I was in love with
him." She paused. "The elevator doors opened and I saw a beau-
tiful blonde enter his suite. I'm sure it was his ex-fiancée and
now they're back together.

"I'm coming home tomorrow, and everything is ruined."

Her lips trembled. "I was really in love this time, it's like nothing I felt before."

"Isn't it a little sudden?" her mother wondered. "You've barely been in Paris a week."

"Remember when you said that eventually I would meet the right person and I replied next time I fell in love it would be forever?" Isabel fiddled with her necklace. "I know Alec is the one. I'm as certain as I am that Apple stock will always be a good investment. He's warm and sincere, and when we're together, I don't want to be anywhere else."

"Then you have to tell him you're in love with him," her mother urged.

"It's too late," Isabel sighed. "I'm sure he's back with Celine."

"He may have moved on," her mother suggested. "He might not want her back at all."

"I never thought of that." Isabel faltered. "It's possible, though she did look gorgeous in that white jumpsuit."

"Do you really have a choice?" her mother asked. "If you want something, you have to fight for it."

Isabel pictured the pink and blue lights of the Eiffel Tower and couples holding hands on the Pont Neuf. She saw Alec in his red sweater, clutching a colored pencil and studying a sketch of Gus riding an elephant.

"I have nothing to lose and he did say he was in love with me." She jumped up. "That doesn't change because a willowy blonde appears, reeking of Chanel No 5."

"Call me and tell me what happens," her mother said. "And Isabel, I know this time you're going to make the right decision."

ISABEL STOOD AT the dressing table and zipped up a beige wool dress. Her hair was held back with a gold clip and she wore pink lipstick. She fastened the glass bracelet around her wrist

and thought Alec had to say he loved her; she couldn't live without him.

She heard a sound on the balcony and stepped outside. It was early evening and a thick fog had settled on the Place de la Concorde. Colored lights glittered on the Christmas tree, and shoppers strolled along the Champs-Élysées.

"God, there you are!" Alec exclaimed. "I thought you'd never come outside."

Isabel glanced at the adjoining balcony and saw Alec holding one shoe. He wore a white button-up shirt and twill slacks.

"That's a beautiful dress," he said, rubbing his hands. "Are you going to dinner with Antoine?"

"I sent Antoine back the tiara. I'm going to have lunch with him tomorrow. I could never send him a Dear John letter after everything he did, but it's over." She hesitated. "What are you doing out here, and why did you throw a shoe on my balcony?"

"I need to talk to you and locked myself out," he explained. "The Crillon has to do something about the locks on the French doors. I'm surprised more guests don't get stuck outside in their underwear."

"Why didn't you just knock on my door?" Isabel asked.

"It's a long story and I'm shivering," he said. "Could you call housekeeping and ask them to let me in?"

ISABEL GLANCED AROUND the living room of Alec's suite and saw a silver tray set with porcelain demitasses. A bouquet of tulips stood on the glass table and she wondered if Celine was in the bedroom. Alec and Celine were back together and he didn't know how to tell her without hurting her feelings.

"I thought Celine might be in the hallway and I was afraid she'd see me," he explained. "She has a pretty good arm and I didn't want to end up with a stiletto mark on my forehead.

"I decided the easiest way was to climb onto your balcony," he continued. "But when I walked outside, I realized I may not be afraid of heights anymore but I'm not stupid. The railing is too narrow and there's a five-story drop. Then the French doors closed and I was stuck outside."

"Celine is still here?" Isabel gasped.

"She showed up in the suite this afternoon." He poured a glass of scotch. "Things didn't work out in Australia. She's not fond of the cuisine and the climate dried her skin."

"Why did she come back to the Crillon?" Isabel wondered, her heart pounding in her chest.

"She wanted to get back together." He sipped the scotch. "Apparently Patrick isn't quite the cricket hero and his French pronunciation is terrible. She said I let her go too easily. If I loved her, I should have fought for her.

"I realized she was right. If you love someone, you don't give up at the first hurdle. Even if you keep falling down and your knees are scraped and your clothes are muddy, you make it to the finish line." He paused. "That's when I knew I couldn't let you go. I had to convince you to give us another chance."

"You did?" Isabel whispered.

The air left her lungs and she was almost dizzy. She glanced around the room and thought she hadn't noticed the gold drapes and Lalique statue before.

"I should have told you about my mother and Bettina, but it had nothing to do with us. I could never get married to save Claudia from being evicted." He took her hand. "And there's something else I didn't tell you. I'm really a viscount. My father hated using his title, especially after Bettina's mother ran off with a farmer." He paused. "Perhaps if she left with a *comte* or a *duc* he would have felt differently.

"I started falling in love with you, and you were so intent

on marrying a French aristocrat," he finished. "If I told you the truth, I'd never know if you really loved me."

"Mathieu followed me from the Pont Alexandre III and told me the whole story." Isabel nodded. "He said you never meant to hurt me and I had to give you another chance. We both made mistakes. You shouldn't have kept secrets, and I shouldn't have based my future on the fortune-teller's predictions.

"I came back to the Crillon and my mother called. She was worried about me," she continued. "I told her about the fortune-teller and Antoine and realizing I was in love you. Then I explained I saw Celine enter your suite and I was sure it was too late." She looked up. "She said if I loved you, I had to fight for you.

"It seems everyone wants to give advice, not just the fortune-teller," she mused. "But you can't listen to other people when it comes to love. It's not like asking the guy at the hardware store to pick out paint or the salesgirl at Saks for the right stockings." She took a deep breath. "The only person you can listen to is yourself."

He put his arm around her and kissed her. She kissed him back and tasted scotch and salted nuts.

"I love you," he whispered.

"I love you too," she said and smiled. "And it has nothing to do with the fortune-teller or helping your mother stay in 40 Rue de Passy."

Alec reached into his pocket and pulled out a black velvet box.

"I may not have generations of wealth like Rory or an MBA like Neil, but I promise to provide a good home for us and our children." He paused. "I have big plans for Gus, he's going to get new branding.

"Celine gave me back my grandmother's ring, but I thought I'd have it reset," he continued. "In the meantime I wanted to give you a ring with special meaning."

He opened the box and took out a pink-and-blue glass ring.

"I visited the magician at the Christmas market and asked if he had a ring to match the bracelet." He paused. "He gave me this and said it has magical properties."

"What kind of magical properties?" Isabel asked.

"When you put it on, you are guaranteed a life full of love and happiness and two children and a standard poodle."

"Wouldn't Gus be jealous if we got a poodle?" she laughed.

"You're right, we'll get a cocker spaniel." He looked at Isabel. "Isabel Lawson, will you marry me?"

"Yes," she whispered.

Alec slipped the glass ring on her finger and kissed her.

chapter twenty-one

❦

Isabel stood on the balcony of her suite and thought there was nowhere more beautiful than Paris on New Year's Eve. The silver and gold lights in the Place de la Concorde twinkled, and the cars that pulled up at the Hôtel de Crillon were all creamy Rolls-Royces and midnight blue Bentleys.

Women stepped onto the pavement wearing sequined evening gowns and carrying jeweled clutches. The men wore custom tuxedos with silk bow ties and tasseled shoes.

She walked back inside and thought so much had happened in the two days since Alec had proposed. They drove to 40 Rue de Passy and told Claudia the good news and called Isabel's parents and shared their excitement. Isabel even insisted they tell Bettina. What better time to mend their relationship than during the magical time of the holidays.

She thought of everything they had done together and a warmth spread through her chest. They waited in line at La Poilâne for *pain au chocolat* and café au lait. They spent a whole afternoon at Shakespeare and Company, and Alec introduced her to the books he loved as a child: *The Secret Garden* and *A*

Bear Called Paddington and *The Adventures of Tintin*. Afterward they saw a romantic comedy in French with English subtitles and held hands in the dark.

Now she glanced at her gown in the mirror and thought it really was perfect. The silver bodice hugged her chest and the chiffon skirt fell just below the knee. And the pumps she discovered at Le Printemps were like a prop from a Disney movie: satin with a jeweled heel and gold bow.

She remembered the price tag and felt slightly guilty. But it was a special occasion and everyone would be here to celebrate. Her parents had arrived at Orly Airport a few hours ago and Mathieu and Helene were coming and Isabel was going to meet Alec's publisher. She draped a pink pashmina around her shoulders and grabbed her quilted evening bag.

"I would have been ready half an hour ago, but I couldn't tie my tie," Alec said when he opened the door. He looked handsome in a white dinner jacket and beige slacks. "It's impossible to tie a bow tie without looking in the mirror. Then it always ends up looking backwards."

"You should have knocked on my door." Isabel reached up and adjusted his collar. "I would have tied it for you."

"We could have just stayed in the same suite," he sighed. "I haven't been able to concentrate on a thing all afternoon. I keep drawing Gus tangled up in a white sheet like Casper the ghost. All I want to do is stay in bed with you. Do you think we can tell our guests to come back tomorrow?"

"We can't stay in the same honeymoon suite until we're on our honeymoon," Isabel laughed. "I don't think the Crillon will be happy if we cancel a five-course dinner for fifteen people in the private dining room."

"We could get married and share a suite tonight," Alec suggested. "Think of all the money we'd save. Having two honeymoon suites is exorbitant."

"Winter weddings are bad luck, they never seem to happen." Isabel perched on a love seat. "Spring is the perfect time to get married in Paris. We'll take photos in the Bois de Boulogne and have the wedding luncheon in your mother's garden. My mother has already started thinking about the colors. She suggested the bridesmaids wear pale green and the centerpieces be pink and yellow roses."

"Our mothers will get along wonderfully. They'll probably spend the evening exchanging gardening tips." He slipped his wallet into his pocket. "Did we really have to invite Bettina and Édouard? It's like Little Red Riding Hood asking the big bad wolf to come over for *boeuf bourguignon* and potatoes au gratin."

"It's our engagement dinner, we want all our family there." Isabel fiddled with her sapphire earrings.

"Just make sure no one leaves her alone with the soup." Alec bristled. "You never know what she'll slip in it when no one's looking."

"You read too many detective novels." Isabel smiled. "I'm sure Bettina will be happy for us. You are her brother and you're engaged to the woman you love."

"You haven't spent any time with her. But it is New Year's Eve. I'll make sure the waiters keep her champagne flute filled with Dom Pérignon." He kissed her. "I don't care who we invited, all I want is to be with you."

Isabel felt the warmth of his mouth and a tingle ran down her spine. They had made love for hours, and it had taken all her willpower to insist Alec return to his suite. But they had so much to look forward to: preparing for the wedding, finding an apartment, planning their honeymoon. She wanted to savor every moment, like opening one present at a time on Christmas morning.

"We better go downstairs now"—she smoothed her hair— "or we'll never leave the suite at all."

"You know I'd happily attend dinner parties every night and wear impossible bow ties and even go dancing if it means being together." Alec took her hand.

Isabel reached up and kissed him. "Why would we dance all night when we have other things to do?"

THE LOUIS XVI salon in the Hôtel de Crillon was so beautiful it took Isabel's breath away. Red damask walls were covered with rich tapestries, and parquet floors were scattered with Oriental rugs, and gold candelabras flickered on the polished sideboard. Crystal chandeliers dangled from the ceiling, and a huge ornate mirror hung above the marble fireplace.

The long mahogany table was covered in a red-and-gold tablecloth and set with Limoges china and Baccarat wineglasses. Royal blue vases were filled with red roses, and there were framed paintings by Matisse and Chagall. Pinpoint lighting illuminated bronze statues, and French doors opened onto a walled patio.

"Darling, I can't tell you how wonderful it is to see you." Isabel's mother approached them. Adele wore a black cocktail dress and diamond earrings. Her ash-blond hair was swept into a bun and she wore red lipstick. "There was a snowstorm in Philadelphia and I was afraid we wouldn't get out. But we're here now and our suite is gorgeous. It has a piano and private balcony and heated bathroom floors. Your father thinks we should install them in Ardmore, his feet get cold after he takes a bath."

"I'm so glad you came." Isabel hugged her. "It was such short notice, I didn't know if you had other New Year's Eve plans."

"Miss your engagement dinner and New Year's Eve at the Hôtel de Crillon?" Adele raised her eyebrow. "We couldn't

gather our passports fast enough. Where is Alec? I can't wait to meet him."

Isabel turned around and saw Alec talking to her father. They both held plates of foie gras and crystal champagne flutes.

"We were getting acquainted." Her father joined them. He wore a black dinner jacket and gold cuff links. "I was telling Alec how your mother almost left me in the suite because I couldn't put on my cuff links. You have to be a contortionist to do it with one hand."

"I offered to help, but John can be quite stubborn," Adele laughed. "And I wanted to get down here and meet my future son-in-law."

"We're so glad you came." Alec offered his hand. "I'm sure traveling on New Year's Eve is a challenge."

"The flight was a little bumpy and it took ages to get through customs." Adele glanced at Isabel's sparkling brown eyes. "But we'd fly all night to see Isabel looking so happy."

"I hope the menu makes up for it." Alec ran his hands through his hair. "I thought a soup course and fish or poultry would be sufficient. But the chef convinced us our guests needed buckwheat pancakes and Dublin bay prawns with warm mayonnaise and some kind of black pudding." He squeezed Isabel's hand. "We're only going to do this once. I told him to serve whatever he wants."

Isabel looked up and saw Claudia admiring a gilt frame. "You stay here and talk to my parents," she whispered to Alec. "I want to say hello to your mother."

"It's lovely to see you," Isabel said to Claudia. "Is that a Dior gown? It's stunning."

Claudia kissed Isabel on the cheek. Her dress was pale blue chiffon, and she wore an emerald necklace and silver pumps.

"It was the first dress I ever bought at the Dior store. I thought Alain would have a heart attack when he saw the price

tag," she said and smiled. "I hid it in my closet and every day I thought I'd return it. One evening I came home and Alain was waiting in the salon with a box wrapped in tissue paper.

"It was my birthday and he bought me a present. I tore it open and discovered the same dress! He said the minute he saw the dress at Dior, he knew it was perfect." Her eyes filled with tears. "I never told him about the other dress, I returned it the next morning."

"I'm glad you had so many happy years together," Isabel said softly. "I love your son very much."

"I know you do and he loves you." Claudia reached into her purse and took out a velvet jewelry case. "I have something for you."

Isabel opened the black case and discovered a strand of pearls with an antique clasp.

"I know Alec is getting my mother's diamond-and-sapphire ring reset, but I wanted you to have this necklace," Claudia explained. "Alain and I put it aside years ago for the woman Alec was going to marry."

"Why didn't Alec give it to Celine?" Isabel wondered.

"I didn't tell him about it." Claudia paused. "Let's just say I wanted to make sure the engagement would last."

Isabel looked up and saw a couple standing in the doorway. The woman had a smooth pageboy and wore a red dress and long white gloves. Her lips were coated with shimmering red lipstick and she carried a satin clutch.

"I think I better go and see Alec," Isabel murmured.

"Don't worry about Alec and Bettina." Claudia followed Isabel's gaze. "They're adults, they'll work it out."

"Bettina and Édouard," Isabel greeted them, "I'm so glad you came, we were afraid you had other plans."

"One of Édouard's patients is an Arabian prince and is hosting a private party at the George Cinq," Bettina began.

"Ten pounds of osetra caviar and sautéed escargot and a performance by Sting at midnight. But I told Édouard we had to come to the Crillon, nothing is more important than family."

"Are you sure you weren't worried we were really getting married?" Alec said, joining them. Isabel noticed his tie was slightly crooked and his cheeks were flushed. "After all it is before January fourth."

"It did cross my mind," Bettina admitted. "Isabel seems very intelligent, it would be the smart thing to do."

"Isabel wants to have a spring wedding and I agree." Alec put his arm around her. "You can grab a glass of Dom Pérignon to go if you like. We won't stop you from hobnobbing with royalty."

"I think we'll stay. I've never been able to eat escargot. It reminds me of the snails you collected in the garden when we were children." Bettina took off her silk gloves. "We have our own announcement. Édouard and I are engaged."

"That's wonderful, what a gorgeous ring," Isabel gasped, admiring the emerald-cut diamond on a platinum band. "When is the wedding?"

"We don't have a date yet, Édouard wants a long engagement." Bettina hesitated. "I quite agree, it will take months to pick out my dress. I already set up showings in Milan and New York."

"We are happy for you." Alec shook Édouard's hand. "We'll have to open a bottle of Château Lafite Rothschild from our father's cellar to celebrate."

A couple walked over to them, and Isabel recognized Mathieu's light brown hair and angular nose. His wife wore a black dress over her rounded stomach and a diamond bracelet.

"This is a scene that would warm the heart of any estate attorney," Mathieu said. "Marriages and births do bring families together."

"We weren't sure if you could make it." Alec clapped Mathieu on the shoulder. "It's an impossible night to get a taxi and I didn't think Helene would take the metro in her condition."

"We wouldn't miss it," Mathieu laughed. "Next year we'll be spending New Year's Eve surrounded by baby bottles and those jumpy things you attach to the doorway." He sipped his champagne. "I tried to install it yesterday and almost brought down the plaster ceiling."

Isabel saw the maître d' motioning to her and smiled. "I think we should be seated. Chef Jean-Paul is very particular. He won't be pleased if we let his spinach gnocchi get cold."

The guests sat on embroidered high-backed chairs and waiters served green asparagus soup topped with sour cream. There were platters of milk-fed lamb and risotto with chanterelle mushrooms. Isabel ate breast of duckling with black currants and thought she had never tasted anything so delicious.

"It's proper etiquette for the groom to make a toast at the engagement dinner," Alec said when the main courses had been replaced by sponge cake and chocolate tarts and slices of Emmental cheese. Demitasses held Turkish coffee, and there were silver bowls of licorice ice cream.

"The last time I spoke at a dinner party, I embarrassed everyone by thanking an imaginary dog. I swore I'd never put myself in the same position, but then I met Isabel. Somehow it's not as frightening to stand up here tonight." He glanced at Claudia. "Though I might still be afraid of a few things, like parasailing on a Spanish island. I don't want to leave the people I love a moment too soon.

"Many of you know Isabel, but those who don't are in for a treat. She's the most beautiful and genuine woman I ever met and I can't believe she said yes." He paused. "Now I'm going to do the intelligent thing and turn the evening over to my fiancée. She can express our gratitude better than I can."

Isabel stood up and brushed a tear from her eye. She glanced at the candles flickering in the gold candelabra and took a deep breath.

"A short time ago I sat in my mother's kitchen and said I thought I'd never find the man to marry. She replied this wasn't the nineteenth century and I'm not Jane Austen. You only get married if you discover the person you can't live without." She looked at Alec. "When I met Alec, I finally understood what she meant. He's warm and kind and I'm the luckiest girl in the world." She paused. "We can't thank you enough for coming. Being happy is wonderful, but sharing your happiness with the people you love is the best thing in life." She fiddled with her earrings. "And I have to thank Gus. He may be imaginary, but he's brought joy and hope to children all over the world." Her face broke into a smile. "I can't wait to read his next adventure."

Alec kissed her and everyone clapped. Isabel heard a clock chime midnight and inhaled the scent of French perfume and dark chocolate. She gazed out the window at a light snow falling on the Place de la Concorde and wondered how anyone could be so happy. She kissed him back and knew she was exactly where she belonged.

Acknowledgments

Thank you to Melissa Flashman, my agent, and Lauren Jablonski, my editor, for being the best two people I could hope to work with. Thank you to my publicist, Staci Burt, for tirelessly getting my books into the world. And thank you to the whole team at St. Martin's Press: Karen Masnica and Laura Clark in marketing, Danielle Fiorella for her wonderful cover, and always to Jennifer Enderlin and Jennifer Weis.

This book is a little magical, so I want to thank the people who add magic to my life, my family: my husband, Thomas; my children, Alex, Andrew, Heather, Madeleine, and Thomas; and my daughter-in-law, Lisa.

1. Isabel calls off her wedding to Neil three days before the ceremony because they can't agree on anything. Do you think she is doing the right thing or should she have tried to work things out?

2. Isabel is pragmatic in her career, but entrusts her romantic future to a fortune-teller. Have you ever done something that seems to be the opposite of who you are? If so, how did it turn out?

3. Alec doesn't tell Isabel about his mother's situation because he doesn't want to air the family's dirty laundry. Do you agree with his decision or should he have confided in Isabel?

4. What are your thoughts on Bettina? Does she deserve sympathy because her mother abandoned her or is her behavior unforgivable?

5. Isabel has been dreaming of going to Paris on her honeymoon since she was a girl. What is your dream honeymoon destination and why?

6. Paris is almost another character in the novel. Can you imagine the story being set anywhere else? If so, where?

7. Isabel meets Rory when she is very young and is instantly attracted to him. Do you think that colored her actions and have you ever had a relationship based on physical attraction?

8. Alec is somewhat insecure even though he is good-looking and charming. What do you think is the cause? Bettina or his unique career or something else?

9. Alec and Celine had a fraught relationship. Do you think they would have gotten married if Celine hadn't left in the beginning?

10. Describe the role that fate plays in the story. Do you believe that "things happen for a reason"?

St. Martin' Griffin